STOCKHOLM SYNDROME

Melissa Yi

The Hope Sze novels, in chronological order

Code Blues

Notorious D.O.C.

Terminally Ill

Stockholm Syndrome

Shorter works featuring Hope Sze, in chronological order

No Air

Cain and Abel

Trouble and Strife

Butcher's Hook

Family Medicine

Student Body

Blood Diamonds

More mystery & romance novels by Melissa Yi

The Italian School for Assassins

The Goa Yoga School of Slayers

Wolf Ice

High School Hit List

The List

Dancing Through the Chaos

STOCKHOLM SYNDROME

Melissa Yi

First edition

Join Melissa's mailing list at www.melissayuaninnes.com

Cover designed with Zeljka Kojic

For more information, please address Olo Books.

Published by Olo Books
http://olobooks.com/

In association with Windtree Press
http://windtreepress.com/

Dedicated to Séverine, Bernadette, and Emmanuel:
three literate baby-delivering machines.

Chapter 1

Birth smells.

I'm not saying it stinks—well, to some people, it does. I remember the classmate who finished our med school OB/gyn rotation without ever delivering an infant. He delivered half of the head, and then the look on his face was so horrid that the obstetrician delivered the rest of the baby.

I've got a stronger stomach than that classmate, but when I stepped into the delivery room at Montreal's St. Joseph's Hospital, it only smelled like sweat and a little blood. The odours would grow more intense once the amniotic fluid broke and the afterbirth emerged, but for now, I didn't hold my breath.

My eyes adjusted to the darkness. The nurse had turned the lights off, except for a small fluorescent lamp beside the bed. The baby's heartbeat chugged along on the fetal monitor. Whump, whump, whump at 162 beats per minute.

Most of obstetrics is nice and normal. Even our C-sections tend toward planned events instead of crash OR's. They screen out congenital abnormalities at our small, Canadian community centre.

"This is the only happy area of the hospital!" an obstetrician told me on my first day. "Everybody's smiling!"

The black woman labouring in the bed wasn't smiling. She was sweating. Which made sense. "That's why they call it labour," the nurse often says, while the woman recovers from the latest contraction. That's normal, too.

So I was pretty surprised when my obstetrics rotation transformed into a bone-chilling bloodbath.

But that evening of November fourteenth, I didn't suspect anything except the fact that I might not get to eat the lentil casserole I'd stashed in the residents' lounge for supper. I smiled at my newest patient, Ms. Beauzile. The nurse had cranked the back of the bed up so that the patient was half-sitting, squinting at me from her pillows, with her legs bent at the hips and knees, and her thighs spread over a foot apart. Can't say I'm looking forward to the indignity, should I ever get the chance to procreate. Especially if I had to labour solo, like this lady.

According to the electronic whiteboard posted in the nursing station, Ms. Beauzile was 28 years old, or only a year older than me. This was her first baby, and she was at six centimetres, or sixty percent en route to pushing out this passenger. She also had a low-grade fever of 38.1 Celsius, but the med student had noted that they weren't giving her antibiotics, because she had a runny nose and they figured it was a cold. Good call.

"Madame Beauzile, I'm Dr. Hope Sze. I'm the resident doctor on call for obstetrics." I glanced at the top right hand corner to find the stamp with her first name. It was one I'd never heard before, and sounded Russian to me: Manouchka.

Now was not the time to inquire about how she got such an unusual name. Not when she clutched the white plastic bed rails, dragging herself forward with both arms, heaving herself to 90 degrees, and started to huff.

The nurse grabbed her hand. "Yes, Manouchka! That's it!"

I took a step forward and said, "Yes! Keep going!" I felt silly, since I was crashing their two-person party and didn't really know how to encourage her.

But after half a minute, the patient sighed and settled back down in the bed. The dim, yellow light reflected the sweat on her deep brown forehead. The baby's heart rate, which had only slowed down to 139, climbed back up again. The mini-contraction was over.

"Next time," said the nurse, studiously ignoring me. OB nurses generally hate medical students and residents. You have to prove yourself. They'd rather you left them alone while they coach the patient through labour and handle, well, just about everything else.

This Asian nurse was shorter than me, which always gets me excited, since I'm only five foot two and a quarter. (The quarter makes people laugh, but it adds up to 158 centimetres instead of 157, and I've got to treasure every millimetre.) Her hair was a short bob, not unlike the cut I'd sported over the summer, until I decided to grow my hair down to my shoulders. Like me, she wore glasses. When I'm on call, I'm all about the glasses. Not only do they dry out my eyes less than contact lenses, but they're also a built-in eye shield from bodily fluids.

However, the nurse was probably twenty years older than me, wearing fashionista-frightening purple scrubs covered in owls, and scowled like she'd rather push my face into a newly-delivered placenta than shake my hand. Too bad. Sometimes, I'll meet another Asian and we'll nod at each other in recognition, but not this time.

The speaker built into the wall at the head of the bed crackled with static. "Do you have a visitor in there?"

The nurse pressed the red button mounted on the wall. "No, it's just the resident." She had a way of biting off her words that sounded maybe Filipina.

"The junior obstetrics resident, Dr. Sze," I called out. I tell people to pronounce it like the letter C.

The nurse snorted. Her flowery name tag, clipped to her already-blinding purple scrub top, said JUNE, but she seemed more like a porcupine, to me.

The intercom crackled, and the unit secretary's voice quavered, "We've got a woman here saying that her friend is in one of the case rooms. Casey? Maybe she's with Dr. Beeman?"

"I can't help you," said June, letting go of the red button and turning back to Manouchka.

My pager beep-beep-beeped.

I had a feeling it was Dr. John Tucker, so I grinned even before I turned the pager so that its little plastic face could tell me who called. I shouldn't have been smiling. I should've been keeping my distance from him, since I'd officially contacted the University of Ottawa about transferring so that I could finally move back to my hometown and back to Ryan Wu, my past and present boyfriend, ideally before the end of 2012. And I usually yell at Tucker for paging me when I'm on call, when I'm already pulled in ten million directions. But he was also on call, albeit one floor up, and I could use a friend plus or minus benefits.

It wasn't Tucker.

It was 3361. My senior resident, Stan Biedelman.

I'd have to answer it back at the nursing station, since the phone in the room belonged to the patient, and I didn't want to use up my iPhone battery or my personal minutes. St. Joe's was too cheap to give every resident a hospital phone. "Excuse me, Ms. Beauzile," I said. "I'll be back."

She turned her cheek away from me, her face puffy with pregnancy. Her hair tufted against the pillow.

I hadn't even had a chance to check her cervix. I don't always, because the fewer hands travelling up the va-jay-jay to contaminate the amniotic fluid, the better.

Luckily, the delivery rooms, or case rooms, are lined up one after the other, on the right side if you're heading down the hall, and mine was directly opposite the nursing station on the left. So it was less than ten strides to the nearest beige phone sitting on the counter. I punched the four-digit extension in and introduced myself.

"There's a consult in emerg," said Stan, who's only a year ahead of me in the family medicine program. "Vag bleed at ten weeks."

That was slightly unusual. Nearly all our emergency consults are for vaginal bleeding at five to seven weeks, from women who may be miscarrying. Ten weeks is a bit late.

"It's Dr. Callendar on, so you know what that means," said Stan.

I did. It meant that he hadn't done a vaginal exam. Theoretically, the emergency staff should do a complete physical exam, but if they're lazy like Dr. C, they'll slog it off on the specialty service. Tonight, that meant me. The rash on my ankles started to itch under the cuff of my socks. I started playing with the tinsel on the desk so that I wouldn't scratch myself or say something I'd regret.

"Page me when you're done, and we can talk to her together."

"Thanks," I said. Still holding on to the phone receiver, I walked around the counter to eyeball the whiteboard mounted above the clerk's head. They keep it inside the nursing station for patient privacy. We only had three patients, including Ms. Beauzile. If I was going to deliver any babies before supper, she was my best bet. I grabbed the mouse, right-clicked her name, and added my name beside Ms. Beauzile's, so Stan or the medical student shouldn't try to swoop down and steal her.

I'd only delivered two infants as a medical student—not so many more than my queasy med school friend—but I had to liberate at least fifty this month, because St. Joseph's has an unofficial quota. For every month on OB, you're supposed to check off at least fifty newborns. If it's a less fertile month, tough. Elbow the medical students out of the way and try and get the other resident to take over the wards while you run to the case room a minimum of fifty times.

So far, I'd delivered two babies in my first two days. Not bad, but I'd have to step it up if I was going to make quota before December tenth. I remembered something else to tell Stan. "Oh, by the way, the clerk said someone was looking for you. I assume it was you, anyway. Dr. Beeman?" Sounded kind of like Biedelman. I'm used to people massacring my last name.

"If they need me, they know where to find me."

"Three-three-six-one?" I said, citing his current extension.

"Yeah. You got my cell phone, too, but don't give it out to strange men."

"Strange women okay?"

"Yeah. Just don't tell my wife."

We both laughed, and I hung up, forgetting to tell him not to steal my delivery. Oh, well. He was probably too busy eating Cheetos while I slogged away, but it didn't bother me. Much. The junior always does all the work. Or, as Jade, a second-year resident, pointed out after a particularly terrible emerg shift, "Shit rolls downhill."

The ER is kind of the mosh pit on the ground level where every man, woman, and child in Montreal ends up before we sort them out, and also where I want to work when I grow up. First, I had to get out of the labour and delivery area. I'm not sure why we call it the case room, because it's basically a series of four rooms along the hallway, across from the nursing station. Up to four women can labour at once. If you continue past the case rooms to the end of the hall and turn left, along the bottom of a U shape, you'll come out at the OR for emergency C-sections.

Instead, I forged a straight line in the opposite direction, toward the elevators. I passed a pregnant woman in a black burqa shuffling in the same direction. We often see women who wear head scarves—actually, I'm the one who gets them, because they invariably ask for a female doctor, and I often smile when I spot the trendy clothes underneath—so maybe this one would be my second delivery of the night. She was moving a little oddly, though. Not quite waddling, but kind of stiff-legged, although it was hard to tell because the fabric covered her from head to toe. The hem swept the floor, and the material hung over her hands, with only a letter slot opening for the eyes.

I turned sideways to pass the two couples waiting for triage. The women's glazed eyes flickered past me. They were already tired, even before going into labour and actively pushing. Neither of them wore that eager, first-time relish. These women and men probably already had a kid or three at home, and wanted to get this over with so that they could start a new routine.

Triage is a doleful spot at the top of the corridor, because patients are waiting for one nurse to decide if they're far enough along in labour to warrant being assigned to one of those four rooms, or if they're going to get told to walk around and come back later. We also do non-stress tests here, or NST's. Sounds horrible, but it just means a pregnant woman is strapped up to a monitor and we check the fetal heart rate for twenty minutes, to make sure it's okay.

Usually, I'd sweep straight down to the emerg, the better to catch more deliveries. Instead, I glanced over my left shoulder. My potential new patient wore the most extreme sort of burqa, with a type of fabric grille over the eye opening. I couldn't make out her expression, which freaked me out a little. Still, she was pointed toward triage, which was probably the right place for her, although it was hard to tell under all that cloth.

One lucky couple entered the triage room, leaving just the other couple in the hallway. Instead of queuing behind them, the burqa woman slowly passed them, following in my footsteps.

My eyes followed the burqa lady. My gut was trying to tell me something, although I couldn't exactly tell what.

I had to finish the emerg consult before Manouchka delivered her baby. I should have shot right downstairs, but that nagging feeling made me wheel back toward the burqa woman, and I found myself saying, "May I help you?"

The figure in black turned toward me without speaking.

The same uneasy vibe made my scalp tingle and my voice rise. I said, "Were you asking for Dr. Biedelman? He's a male physician. If you want a female physician, I can help you. I'm the junior resident on obstetrics and gynecology."

The woman in black looked me up and down, still silent.

I was trying to peer through the grille of the veil. I figured I had to be able to look in so that she could see out, yet all I could make out was a bit of pale forehead and some deep brown eyes. The eyebrows seemed a bit bushy to me, which could've been a cultural thing. Or she didn't have time to groom her eyebrows while she was in labour.

The triage nurse called out from her room, "It's okay, I already paged Dr. Biedelman for another case."

"Okay," I said. I didn't know why I was trying to save Stan more work. I was already doing the emerg consult for him.

I spun on my heel, toward the wider hallway in front of the elevators. I narrowly avoided running into a pregnant woman with bright blonde hair, a well-cut navy coat, and enough bling on her hands to blind an army. She clung to her husband's arm. He was wearing a good-looking suit and surveyed the queue in front of him, his forehead already pleated with exasperation. They looked like money. You don't see that often at St. Joe's. Not that we don't have middle class, but a lot of people are immigrants adjusting to a new country, not the Kennedys slumming it.

A set of elevator doors binged open to my right, and Stan stepped through the candy cane-stickered doors, coming toward me. He's a big guy, probably six feet tall, made a few millimetres taller by a yarmulke. I'm not good at gauging heights. For me, most adults fall into the category of "tall" and "taller." Anyway, Stan's hilarious. I prize anyone who can make me laugh when I'm on call.

I started to wave at him. He said, "If I don't answer my page, it's because I've got a woman in labour."

"Who?" I said. "The one at six centimetres, I've got my name down on her."

"Mine just came in. She's full term and fully dilated."

"I want her!" I said.

He smirked. "Not a chance. The nurse called me about her directly. She's gonna push. And you've got the emerg consult."

I clenched my hands into fists. He glanced down at them with a little smile, so I forced my hands to relax as I asked, "Stan, how many women have you delivered so far?"

"Let me see." He pulled out his phone and pretended to check. "Oh. Eleven."

"I've only got two. Let me have her, and then I'll go right down to do the emerg consult. Please."

"Forget it. I've got to get to fifty."

"But you're already over 20 percent of the way there! And we're on day three. Come on, Stan."

He waved. "Hey, enjoy Dr. Callendar. I did, when I was the junior. Now it's my turn."

Right. His turn to cherry-pick the women in labour. I steamed.

"Your turn will come. You said you had your name down on the six-centimetre one. All in good time."

With my luck, Manouchka Beauzile would deliver while I was in the emerg, at the exact moment when Stan miraculously stepped into the room. Then I could end up with zero deliveries during my night on call. I took a step toward him. "Stan."

He waved me away. "See you later, Hope. Look, the elevator's already open for you. Just ride it on down."

As if on cue, the usually molasses-slow elevator doors slipped closed. Stan chortled.

I wanted to hit him. He was so *smug*. And anyway, I usually took the stairs, at least at the beginning of the night, while I still had some juice. The stairs were around the corner, closer to the ward rooms where moms cuddled with their newborns and a few women lay on bed rest, trying not to give birth to premature twins. I started toward the stairs, but the burqa woman said, in a muffled voice, "Excuse me."

She stood before the single doorway to the case room, blocking Stan's way in toward triage and the labour rooms.

Stan hesitated. "Yes?" He gazed over her head, down the hall, clearly already ticking off number twelve in his mind.

She didn't have an accent, exactly, but she pitched her voice low. "What is the name of your patient?"

That was an odd thing to ask.

"Sorry, I can't disclose any patient names," said Stan, glancing at the triage line-up behind her.

"It's important," said the woman, crossing her arms over her shoulders, like she was cold and giving herself a hug.

"Just ask at the desk, if you're a friend or family," said Stan, starting to brush past her. I could already hear the triage nurse's voice, raised in irritation at the blonde couple trying to cut ahead in line.

"Tell me," said the burqa woman, louder now, with a strange note to her voice. The fabric billowed around her arms and chest.

"No can do," said Stan, head down and bustling toward the case room and his next delivery.

The burqa woman pulled a big, black gun out of the folds in her robe and shot him in the back.

Chapter 2

I screamed. It happened so fast. I'd never seen anyone use a gun, except my dad fooling around with a BB gun in our back yard, and now Stan dropped to his knees before he caught himself on his hands, gurgling.

Behind him, the blonde woman and her husband ducked into triage and slammed the door behind them. Suddenly, only me, Stan and the gunwoman stood in the hallway.

"Call 911!" I yelled in the general direction of the nursing station, ignoring the gunwoman. The triage nurse had probably seen or heard enough to call for help, but it never hurt to sound the alarm.

Meanwhile, I'd focus on the A, B, C's of resuscitation. Especially the airway and breathing. My eyes fixed on the bloody hole in Stan's back, just below the point of his left scapula. Probably too far from the midline to cut his spinal cord, but right in "the box" where shrapnel could pierce a heart or lung or both, depending on the trajectory.

Stan dropped on to his stomach, still breathing, so his heart probably hadn't been hit. I have zero experience with gunshot wounds, but they say that after a heart attack, if you have myocardial rupture, and the heart bursts open, the person dies in a few beats. He'd already made it past that.

I fell on my knees beside Stan, who was barely sucking air into his lungs. Did he have a pneumothorax? The hole in his chest could still kill him within minutes.

My first instinct was to turn him on his back, because that's how patients always roll into the emerg on a stretcher, face up. Also, the exit wound in front of his chest would gape more than the relatively neat hole in back.

I stopped and grabbed the stethoscope hung around the back of my neck. Even with Stan face-down, I could listen to his breath sounds.

"Don't touch him," said the burqa woman.

I looked up.

She trained her gun on my face.

My hands stilled, slowly relinquishing the navy rubber tube of my stethoscope. It wasn't that I'd forgotten her, but I had a higher calling here. I lifted both palms in the air. "Look. I'm a doctor. He's a doctor."

"I need Casey Assim," the woman said. Her voice had descended into growl territory.

It took me a second to process that. Casey. That was the name the ward clerk had buzzed us about in Manouchka's room. So Casey Assim must be a patient, a new one who hadn't made it on the whiteboard yet. The one Stan had been on his way to deliver?

Stan tried to cough. He choked instead. The breath rattled in his lungs before he boosted himself on to his hands and started crawling on his hands and knees toward the open doorway. Toward the case room. Or the closed triage door. Or the nursing station. Any way you sliced it, civilization.

He knew where to go. His brain was still clicking. He had the strength to crawl. Should I try and distract the burqa woman? Maybe try and wrestle the gun away from her?

But that was an insane Hollywood move. And also, I couldn't help noticing that Stan was deserting me while this woman held us at gunpoint.

I could distract her for the few crucial seconds while Stan got away, but I wouldn't jump her.

I heard a nurse scream from further down the hallway. She tried to stifle it, which made it sound even worse.

From my view, at least thirty feet away, I could tell that they'd sealed all four case room doors, but the nursing station was an open desk area. The counter might protect you a little, but not the open table.

Maybe the staff would run toward the OR and back out the other side of the U, toward the ward. But could the patients run that fast?

The overhead paging system blared, "Code Black, Fourth Floor. *Code Noir, quatrième étage.*"

Then someone pulled the fire alarm. The high-pitched bell made my ears cringe.

"Is Casey the person you're looking for?" I asked, raising my voice above the alarm. My arms quivered in the air. "I—"

The burqa woman looked down at Stan crawling and shot him in the back of the head.

The sound of the bullet echoed through the hallway.

His body flopped on the floor.

Blood coursed from the back of his skull.

I couldn't make a sound.

I'd met murderers before. But they'd never killed anyone in front of me.

This was like an execution. And what had Stan done? He hadn't broken patient confidentiality. He'd done the "right thing." Now he was probably dead.

I didn't want to die.

I really didn't want to die.

I gazed down the case room hall, now empty of obvious human habitat, although I knew the triage room must be packed like Sonic dance club on the night of a full moon, and at least three out of four women labouring in the case room hadn't made a break for freedom.

It was just me and the burqa murderer now.

The fire alarm shrieked overhead, a piercing scream that made my jaw ache and my arms tremble.

This couldn't be happening.

Oh, yes, it could. I'd survived enough tight situations to know that real life could surpass any nightmare.

They call me the detective doctor. But it's one thing to try and figure out any wrongdoing after the fact. It's quite another to have someone a) pull out a gun, and b) shoot your senior resident in front of you.

"How may I help you?" I said, trying to sound civil, like this was normal. Like I wasn't about to get whumped. I thought of my main man, Ryan. My first runner-up, Tucker, who made my toes curl. My little brother, Kevin. My parents. My grandmothers.

I love you. I'm sorry I never told you enough.

The burqa woman detoured to grab me from behind, her body a solid presence behind mine while she drilled the muzzle of the gun against my right temple. The muzzle was still cool after shooting Stan.

She's right-handed, I noticed with the back part of my brain. Maybe it would make a difference, maybe it wouldn't. But my shocked brain insisted on memorizing facts like this and noticing that she smelled like beer, tangy sweat, and something unpleasantly familiar.

"Get me Casey Assim," she said. "Now."

CHAPTER 3

"I can get you Casey Assim," I said, since at this point, I would have promised both my grandmothers. Not that I'd actually deliver them to this madwoman. But I'd lie up and down Main Street if it would buy me a few seconds. All was fair in love and at gunpoint.

"They just brought her in," said the killer. "She's in labour. It's her due date. I know it's her."

Faulty logic, but my shoulders jerked as my hindbrain calculated, *That's a man's voice. This is a man, not a woman. A man dressed in a burqa.*

He was crazier than I thought.

I was deader than I thought.

"Okay," I said.

"Get me to her room, or I'll kill you, too."

He wasn't that much taller than me. Maybe five foot eight, but stocky, like a wrestler, with wide shoulders and firmly planted feet. And did I mention that gun?

"No problem," I said, an expression my dad hates. He says, *There's always a problem. Why would you say there's no problem?* He had a point, especially when I was nose to nose (okay, back of head to nose) with Mr. Death.

Dad. I'm sorry. I love you.

I felt Mr. Death jerk his head toward the doorway. He knew that was the main entrance to the case room. He knew how to get there, but he wanted me to lead him, like a little Dr. Gandhi, while he kept the gun trained on my temple, the thinnest area of my skull.

He wanted me to play hostage.

Part of me thought, *No. Run.*

If only I'd run in the first place, when my subconscious brain must have recognized that the way he moved and the breadth of his shoulders didn't jibe with a pregnant woman.

Now it was too late to run. The emergency department and hospital front desk had security guards. Obstetrics had *nothing*.

I must have glanced or somehow turned left, toward the elevator, because the bastard cocked his gun, and I felt as well as heard the hammer shift.

I don't know guns, but I've seen enough TV shows to figure out what's fatal.

I froze in place like an Arctic hare dropped in downtown Tokyo.

I've actually listened to a podcast about what to do when an active shooter enters a hospital. Running is your best option.

But running with a bullet in your brain? Not possible.

Without taking my eyes off the gun, I took a step toward the doorway. Toward triage.

"That's it, bitch," Bastard whispered.

I gestured at Stan's unmoving body, which lay five feet away from us, blocking the doorway. I could *smell* Stan's blood.

I have a strong stomach, but I had to hold my breath and not-think, not-think, not-think if was going to survive even the next few minutes.

Bastard didn't answer, except to keep his gun pressed against my cranium.

I walked.

I walked with Bastard's body cemented against my back. Have you ever had an unwanted guy grind behind you on the dance floor? Like that, times a billion.

I had to glance down as I/we stepped over Stan's body, carefully picking my way to avoid his sprawled arms and the ever-widening pool of blood.

Stan's yarmulke clung to his curly hair a centimetre above the bullet hole. I scanned the green felt for dots of blood and possibly brains. Then my eyes slid south. Was it possible that I glimpsed the pale, folded surface of cerebral cortex under the film of blood dripping from the entry site?

No. Probably my imagination. I clung to the fact that his religious symbol remained intact. Maybe he and I would, too. I sent a brief prayer toward Stan and any available deity: *Please.*

People have survived gunshot wounds to the head. I've never seen it, but I remembered a neurosurgery resident explaining to me, in detail, how a high-velocity bullet could hit a non-critical area of the brain and come out the other side, necessitating surgery, ICU, and a lot of rehab, but not a one-way ticket upstairs/downstairs.

The bullet had hit Stan in the occiput, so bye-bye occipital lobe. But I thought it was higher up than brainstem, which would have spelled instant death. So it was possible, if not probable, that he might pull through. But the longer he lay on the ground, the lower his chances of any meaningful recovery.

At least by drawing the gunman away from Stan, I was allowing the emergency crew to make its way toward him.

On the other hand, it meant I was drawing the gunman toward a bunch of defenseless pregnant women.

I might have yelled for them to run, but the fire alarm was doing all the screaming for me. The sound invaded my head, made it hard to think anything except *Shut up.*

My body walked anyway, with the diaphragm of my stethoscope banging a drum beat against my chest. I held my hands up in the air, both to calm down the gunman and so that anyone looking at me would immediately compute that something was wrong. *Flee. Now.*

The case room hallway looked deserted.

It didn't feel empty, though.

First door on the right. Triage. I imagined all those exhausted pregnant women and men, plus the triage nurse, holding their breath and barring the door. I walked a little faster, hoping that Bastard wouldn't pause and knock on that door.

He didn't.

Now we'd reached the nursing station on our left. The long, white counter hung with tinsel, which the elderly ward clerk usually sat behind, answering the phone with her crystal-studded acrylic nails, and which I stood in front of to write my charts or answer my pages: empty.

Behind the counter, the communal wooden table and small alcove, where the nurses sat to chart and to watch the fetal monitors mounted to the wall, under Christmas balls dangling from the ceiling: empty.

Everyone had taken off. Or was at least out of sight, for the moment.

Bastard exhaled.

I tensed. He could easily yell, "Bring me Casey, or I'll kill this chink!"

And then, if no one answered, he'd shoot me out of spite.

The alarm screeched on. Overhead, the hospital operator intoned, "Code Black, Fourth Floor. *Code Noir, quatrième étage.*"

Bastard's left hand relaxed on my shoulder while he held the gun to my right temple.

Was he letting down his guard? I could try to break away from him now.

But which way should I run? Back toward the elevators and Stan? He'd shoot me before I got ten paces.

Around the hallway's U-shape to the OR and then the ward rooms? Much, much farther. And at least fifty feet of hallway, where I could get shot.

Under the desk, so I could hole up like a mouse before he executed me?

So many bad choices, so little time.

The only thing I didn't consider was running for a case room or triage. He'd whack me, then take potshots at anyone and everyone else in the room.

But he didn't want me. He wanted Casey Assim.

The fastest way to figure out her location was by circling behind the desk to view the whiteboard linked to the desktop computer, which faced away from the hallway to protect it from prying eyes. That information would lead him right to her room.

So many women are killed by their partners and ex-partners. Should I aid and abet a murderer, plus get caught in the crossfire?

Um, no.

"Where is she?" Bastard said. He was still so close that I could feel the shift of his head as he glanced up and down the hallway.

Hiding from you, you maniac.

The fire alarm cut off suddenly, leaving my ears ringing.

That, too, was strange. Usually, the alarm goes on forever, and everyone has to close the exam room doors until the Second Coming, or at least until the operator says, "Code Red, all clear. *Code Rouge maintenant terminé.*"

Were the police on the way?

"I don't see Casey," I said, which was true. I couldn't see any living soul. Maybe if I acted useless enough, he'd leave me alone.

Or shoot me. This was turning into a Choose Your Own Adventure where 90 percent of the endings left me unconscious and bleeding. I was not a fan.

"Go get her," he said.

How could I delay him?

Light bulb moment. I pointed to the beige phone sitting on the counter, its receiver slightly blackened and greasy from numerous hands. Less than ten minutes ago, I'd been answering Stan's page on that phone.

That phone could be my lifeline to make contact with the outside world, if he let me.

My cell phone buzzed twice in my pocket. I couldn't answer Tucker or Ryan or anyone else right now, but I wished them safe and far, far away. Tucker was just one floor above me, tending to his internal medicine patients at this exact moment. Strange to think of the fifth floor as a world away, and that I might never see him again.

"What if I called locating and asked if Casey's registered?" I asked. "They might be able to give me a room number."

I didn't have to give him the room number. Well, maybe he'd rip the phone away from me and threaten the operator to get it. But first, I might be able to speak to someone who could call the cavalry, if they hadn't already. And the more I delayed, the higher the chances that the police could storm in here.

Bastard shook his head. "I already tried that."

Right. And he'd created enough of a ruckus that the clerk had asked for Casey in Manouchka's room. They never do that. My first tip-off that something was awry.

"I'm a doctor," I said. "They might give me more information, especially since I'm calling from within the hospital."

Bastard snorted and glanced up and down the corridor. "I know she's in here some place. I should just bust down the doors and shoot everyone."

My heart thumped in my throat, but I tried to speak calmly. "You might hurt Casey by mistake."

He stopped to think about that. I could tell from the stillness in his body, even though I was facing away from him and he was still covered in a burqa.

He took a step back from me. My heart leaped, but he just repositioned the gun from my head to my T-spine, between my shoulder blades.

Still. He was giving me some space. That had to be a good sign. Also, my mother would be proud how straight I was now standing, trying to edge a few millimetres away from certain death.

"If she's registered, we can just go to the right room. That's all we need. Right?" Now I was promising him Casey's head on a platter again. I could hardly speak, my mouth was so dry.

I could hear Bastard's glower through his voice. "I don't want you calling the police."

"You can do the dialing. You can even hold the phone, if you want." The more non-gun things he used to clutter up his hands, the better.

Then I thought I heard a sound. Was it from Manouchka and June's room?

I tried to glance over my left shoulder, at their closed door opposite the nursing station, but the muzzle boring a hole in my spine reminded me not to move.

Nothing to see, anyway. June had probably hurled the door shut at the first sound of gunfire. With any luck, she'd barricaded it.

The gunman noticed my head twitch, but instead of blowing me away, he said, "Is she in there?"

"What? No. Not the woman you're looking for. It's someone else." I stared straight ahead at the wall above the nurse's table, petrified that even a quick look could sentence someone else to death.

"You're lying."

"I'm not. That's the one patient I saw before you. Her name's not Casey."

"Casey. Casey Assim. That's who I want." He grabbed my left arm and jerked me sideways, walking me the few crucial steps so I was now facing the first case room door. Obviously, all he heard was Casey's name and nothing else. He was like a missile locked on detonate. "Get her out of there. Or get me in. I don't care. She's gonna have my baby." He placed the gun at the back of my head now, which made me think of Stan.

Stan. Dead Stan.

Don't think that way. He might still make it. Come on.

At close range, I finally recognized that insistent stink emanating from Bastard's pores as marijuana. Lovely.

I forced myself to speak in a low, well-enunciated voice. "She's not there. Let me call the operator. I'll find you Casey."

He pushed the gun a little harder against my occiput. "Open. That. Door."

I stared at the edging etched into the white wood of the first case room door. If he shot me, could the bullet drive right through the wood and hit Manouchka or June too?

My hand dipped toward the metal door handle, but a sound caught my ear.

Not just any sound. A whistle.

On our right, echoing off the empty hospital corridor walls.

Someone whistling in the midst of blood and terror. It was as startling as if a bluebird had launched itself above our heads in this hospital hall of horror, singing a tale of joyful spring in mid-November.

I knew that whistle. My nails cut into my palms to stop myself from yelling. My breath rasped in my throat, and I know this sounds strange, but my nipples hardened.

I even recognized the song, "What a Day for a Daydream."

It was the stupidest, most inappropriate song for this scenario, and that would have told me the whistler's identity even if I'd been blindfolded and gagged.

It was one man I didn't want trapped with me.

I wanted to scream, *Run, Tucker.*

Chapter 4

Instead, I kept very still and prayed Bastard wouldn't notice the song.

Fat chance. I might as well wish on a star for him to shoot himself.

I heard the rustle of Bastard's clothes as he shifted behind me, just before he jabbed the gun again into the base of my skull, but it slipped an inch and caught me on the neck instead.

I bit back a cry as my neck arched involuntarily, jerking my chin toward the ceiling before Bastard swore and re-took his first position. Namely, his body stuck close enough behind me to scrape the skin off my back and the gun transferred to my right temple, with the extra-special addition of his left arm hooked around my throat, embedding my stethoscope into my breast bone.

The whistling grew louder.

Was Bastard smart enough to understand that Tucker was offering the aural equivalent of a white flag?

Probably not. He probably didn't know what aural meant. Took me a while to figure it out, too.

"Let's go," I managed to whisper through the arm lock. My hair felt like it was standing straight out from my scalp, under the pull of the world's best Van der Graaf Generator. I didn't know where to go. I just had to get us away from here.

Forget rocks and hard places. I was smushed between a closed door and a killer.

"Shut. Up," said Bastard.

Since the gun in my temple was already delivering me a Mach 1 headache, and Tucker was in imminent danger, I decided to obey.

Maybe if I were very, very quiet, Bastard could control his trigger finger. Tucker would just keep whistling his way on by.

That whistling paused, probably as Tucker encountered Stan's body, but then it picked up again, growing more intense in my right ear.

I could feel Bastard's breathing speeding up as he exhaled beer fumes on me. He didn't know what to do. He probably didn't have a Plan A, let alone B or C. I was practically pressed against the wood grain, with Tucker oncoming, yet no sign of the cavalry. Where was the fucking cavalry? I know we're in Montreal, but come *on*.

"That's my friend," I said, so that Bastard wouldn't freak out and start spraying bullets.

"I don't give a fuck who that is. It's not Casey," he said.

Fair point. I had to try again. Bastard might execute me, Tucker, or both, but I couldn't just stand here. "Yes. If you let me get at the phone—"

"Shut. Up," said Bastard, grinding the muzzle close enough to my right eyeball that I closed my eyelid, as if a thin patch of skin could protect me from potential blindness.

Tucker's whistle, as well as his steps on the beige tile floor, faded into silence. I couldn't see his body out of my peripheral vision, which was blocked by a firearm and a lunatic's arm, but from the sound, I would guess he stood about five feet to our right.

Way too close.

"I'm here to help," he said, in that baritone I'd recognize in my sleep.

Hearing Tucker's voice confirmed that one of the major loves of my life was stupid enough to run toward this maniac.

Not that I should point fingers. My own "May I help you?" retardedness had likely killed Stan and would now probably take out me and Tucker.

For the first time in my life, I wanted to faint. Just black out and let someone else take care of this mess.

Instead, I ordered, "Get out of here, T—"

The gunman slid his left hand over my mouth, silencing me, but also squashing my nose so that I could hardly breathe anything except his dirty flesh.

I choked. My body bucked.

Can't breathe. Stupid way to die.

Can't *breathe.*

I was a microsecond away from biting his hand. Just chomping down on his flesh. HIV and hepatitis be damned. I needed air.

Bastard eased up slightly, and I drew in a desperate, shallow breath, already feeling light-headed, but still hearing him say, "I'm going in. Casey's in here, having my baby. They better open it, or I'm gonna shoot this bitch."

Love you, too.

"You don't want to do that," said Tucker. "Hope's a famous doctor. She delivers babies."

Well, that was sort of true. I was infamous. I was a resident doctor. And I have delivered babies. But I was on board for promising Bastard the solar system if he'd just let me breathe.

Bastard's breath puffed while he mulled that over. His left hand drifted an inch away from my mouth, letting me gasp for oxygen while his right one stayed locked and loaded on my skull. "I gotta get to Casey."

So he wasn't a big thinker. More like the Hulk. *Smash. Get Casey. Unh.* I didn't know if his idiocy was a good or bad thing, when he could blow our brains out in a quick one-two.

"You don't need Hope at all," said Tucker. "I'm a doctor, too. I can deliver Casey's—"

Bastard tensed. I could feel it.

Tucker must have seen something, too, because he smoothly switched it to "—your baby. Why don't you let Hope go, and I'll get you in here."

Oh, God. It was the most romantic thing Tucker had ever said, and also the stupidest.

I inhaled sharply to tell them, *No. Casey's not here.*

Bastard clapped his hand on my mouth again. Not smashing my nose this time, so I could breathe, but definitely inhibiting my mouth's ability to tell him he was barging into the wrong room.

Tucker said, "It's okay. Let Hope go. I've delivered lots of babies. I'll take excellent care of yours and Casey's."

"Casey," said Bastard. Every time anyone said her name, he welded his brain to it and didn't seem to register anything else. "Casey Assim. She's having my boy. Get me in there, or I'll kill both of you."

"Then you'll have no one to deliver your baby," Tucker pointed out. "All you have to do is let go of Hope, and I'll come with you. I'm an expert at delivering big, healthy baby boys."

Tucker probably hadn't delivered any more babies than I had, but he always put on the best show.

Bastard relaxed his chokehold slightly. "I don't know who the fuck you are."

"My name is Dr. John Tucker." His voice grew louder as he approached us. I squeezed my eyes shut. I still had trouble breathing with Bastard face-palming me, but I didn't want to watch Tucker laying down his life for mine.

I forced my eyes open. I'd have to witness everything I could, if we had any chance of surviving this. 'Course, all I could see was this darn door.

Tucker was still talking. His forte. He once considered a career in psychiatry instead of family medicine, but right now he was weaving a web of words around Bastard. "I have considerable training in obstetrics and gynecology. I would be honoured to deliver your son. Just let me take Hope's place."

"No one's going nowhere until I get in to see Casey!"

"If you would allow me..." I spotted the blur of Tucker's hand at five o'clock as he took a step forward to try the door handle. He said, "Hmm. They've locked it."

"Stand back," said Bastard. He let go of my face, which was a serious relief. My eyesight was starting to pinwheel.

I sucked in some more sweet air, trying to think through my haze. Maybe he was going to bust down the door like in the movies. And occasionally, in real life. Once I got an epileptic patient who'd had a seizure in the bathroom. The door was locked with the patient's body wedged against the door. A police officer ended up breaking down the door.

Bastard dragged me backward by fastening his left arm tight around my throat and yanking me into the hallway.

I gagged, but I stumbled back with him like a dog dragged by its collar.

Dimly, I heard Tucker still offering to take my place.

Bastard shouted, “I’m warning you. Open this door, or I’m going to shoot it off. And then I’ll shoot one of these doctors, I don’t care which one.”

I held my breath. Even Tucker stopped jabbering, and that’s saying something.

Inside the room, quiet footsteps approached the door.

Chapter 5

While we waited at door number one, Bastard kept his left arm wrapped around my neck in just under a chokehold, like a scarf itching to strangle me.

He also rammed his gun muzzle into my temple again. I supposed I should be grateful it was no longer attacking my eyeball, but the metal really hurt. Before this attack, I'd never thought about how just the brute force of a circle of steel, pressed into my skin, can bruise, even before the bullet performs a craniotomy at 1700 miles per hour.

So I didn't tell him Casey wasn't home.

I kept mum.

The approaching footsteps had stopped, but I thought someone hovered inside the front door. If I could've moved my head, I would have glanced downward to look for foot shadows shifting, but I couldn't budge. I could only listen to the abnormally-loud sound of my own breathing and wonder if this was it. My last few seconds on earth, cradled by a murderer.

The door handle clicked. My heart jerked in terror, in anticipation, I didn't even know what anymore.

The door cracked open a centimetre. The inside was darker than the hallway, so I couldn't see anything except a dark shape, but June's clipped voice drifted out toward us. "Don't shoot anyone."

I wanted to say, *Please*. I wanted to say, *Don't hurt her. She's just trying to protect her patient.*

Her patient. Her patient*s*, really, since the baby was almost making its way into the world.

What a way to be born.

Bastard's body tensed. He didn't want her giving orders. But instead of yelling at her, he launched forward, using me as a battering ram to slam open the door.

Instinctively, I threw up my hands to protect my face. I guess Bastard was having trouble juggling me, the gun, and propelling both our bodies forward, because even as he yelled, "No!" to me, he dropped me.

I ended up plowing against the door with both hands, and very nearly my teeth.

I bashed into it with my forehead instead. Like a hammerhead shark without the right equipment.

A dull pain encircled the rest of my skull in a throbbing, burning headband, but I fought through it, trying to figure out what was going on.

The door was giving way.

June had braced her body against the door, but when my body weight thumped against it, she only withstood it for a second, especially when Bastard hurled his body too, using his arm to shove inward.

I remembered that June was actually a tiny woman, shorter than I was. She had no chance against our double onslaught.

She screamed.

Bastard had banged the door away from me, so I stumbled and smacked into the cool tile floor on my palms. The impact jarred me up to the shoulders, even before my knees banged down for extra impact. Greens don't provide much padding.

"Get up, bitch," said Bastard, grabbing my shoulder.

"No!" shouted June, trying to smash the door closed on both of us, and Bastard fired.

Chapter 6

It happened so fast, I didn't know what was going on. I was still on my knees in the doorway.

My ears rang. I smelled something, too, a burning smell that reminded me of fireworks.

All I knew was that Bastard had fired another bullet, and I didn't hurt anywhere. Yet.

But someone howled—June, I thought, from the high pitch.

Then June's small, shadowy body dropped to the ground, just beside the door she'd tried to guard, and I focused on her. My eyes were still adjusting to the dim light, but her face contorted in pain.

I shouted, "Tucker, get her out of here!"

Bastard snatched me by my hair. My newly-grown, long, straight black hair, which I don't usually wear in a ponytail because it's too uncomfortable after a few hours on call. He yanked it hard enough to pierce a thousand nerve endings, but that still didn't block out the sound of him hollering, "Nobody move!"

Disobeying his own words, he starting dragging me deeper inside the room. By the hair.

Pain seared through my scalp.

Pale fingers flashed at the corner of my vision. Tucker's hands, trying to grab me.

I tried to reach for him too, but Bastard kicked him and said, "I'll *kill* you if you come any closer," and I could tell he meant it.

I stumbled over something in the narrow entryway. Something soft. Not a machine—we were still to the right of the countertop holding the fetal monitor display.

My chin managed to dip in response, even though it ripped more hairs out of my scalp, and I spotted June's purple scrubs, so wildly patterned in owls that in the dark, I couldn't tell where she was bleeding.

I opened my mouth automatically to apologize. I'm Canadian. I'll say sorry in the middle of the Holocaust.

Then I realized that I'd run into her because not only had we surged forward, into the room, but June had crawled from around the door, toward us.

She was moving. She was alive. But for how much longer?

"I said, get the fuck out of my way!" Bastard yelled, and the hind part of my brain replied, *No, you said nobody move*, but I didn't dare correct him. He was not the kind of person to award me a little gold paper star for my excellent memory.

We had to get June out.

She could easily die here, with just our stethoscopes and obstetric equipment to save her. June didn't need a pelvic exam and an umbilical cord clamp. She needed a trauma surgeon.

Even if it went against every instinct to move her instead of helping her. That's what we say to ambulances sometimes: stay and play vs. scoop and run. Right now, June needed to run.

I thought I could smell her blood stronger than Stan's. Bad sign. I wanted to put pressure on her wounds, but just shifting my torso made Bastard crush down on me like he could squeeze my kidneys out of my carcass as easily as I'd squish a tube of toothpaste.

Still, I tried to lean into the room. The farther we got away from June, the more easily Tucker could move her out.

Bastard let me take one tiny step, then another.

Yes, my mind hissed, even though I was marching toward my own doom.

I heard scuffling behind us. Footsteps. The police?

Bastard sucked in his breath and whipped me around 180 degrees so that he could cover the entrance, but his hair hand wrenched my head to the left so that I couldn't assess anything except the delivery cart and the pain in my scalp.

But I could hear more quick, quiet steps. The shush of fabric rustling on the ground—June, still crawling?

Someone grunted.

I heard heavy footsteps. Someone was walking, someone bigger than June.

I blinked. Tucker?

Couldn't be anyone else.

So Tucker was leaving me. I'd ordered him to, wished him safe and far away, but my heart broke anyway. I squinched my eyes shut to try and block out the feeling. Feeling would kill me now.

The next split second, I heard sirens. Not the fire alarm, but real sirens screeching through the air and penetrating the hospital walls.

Police, ambulance, help, goddamn it, the cavalry making its way to St. Joseph's at long last.

I wanted to cry in relief, except Bastard was yelling, "Nobody fucking move!" He jerked my hair again, yanking my chin back so that I stared at the speckled acoustic tile ceiling and still couldn't make out much of anything, but I could feel him advancing toward the door, tearing my hair follicles.

"Police!" a male voice hollered from the triage side of the hallway, and I instinctively twisted toward that sound, my heart splitting with a surge of hope, even as pain blinded me.

Bastard muttered, "I'll fucking kill you first." He let my hair go, wedged his left arm back around my throat and nested the gun back against my bruised right temple, just above the earpiece of my glasses.

He danced me sideways, toward the door. He wanted to close the door, I realized. He wanted to imprison us in this tomb of a room.

I wanted to scream, "Over here!" at the police. I wanted to make sure Tucker had dragged June out to safety. But all I could do was the world's worst four-legged race, staggering while Bastard's gun threatened my brain.

Still. The police had come. Finally.

I've heard a lot of smack about police. I was scared myself, before I came to Montreal, because unarmed black men had been killed by the Sûreté du Québec, as well as everywhere else. But since the police had personally saved my skin three times before today, I was quite fond of them and now, terrifyingly grateful that they'd come.

Now I had hope. I don't use that word lightly, because of my given name and all, but for the first time, I understood why my parents had named me that.

Not that I wasn't grateful Tucker had hurled himself into the fray for me. I loved that guy. I could admit it now, with my own mortality shrieking in my face. But I didn't want him or Ryan to die for me. Ever.

I'd rather die first.

If that meant I was alone with a madman, so be it.

From the corner of my eye, I saw the door swing closed. Its latch caught, sealing off the light and air from the outside world.

Chapter 7

Bastard's muscles stiffened, still gripping me, one hand holding the gun and the other doing the neck scarf, drawing me close against his body, and I realized that he wasn't the one who'd closed the door. Not unless he'd managed to grow a third arm or leg to catch the door.

Someone else had closed it.

Someone else had cut us off from the police.

June, crawling out the door? Would she kick the door closed on her way out, as a way of shielding herself from the bullets?

Possibly, but that would also cut her patient off from the police. Not so likely.

Did Bastard have a minion on the inside?

Also unlikely, because the minion should have let him in. Not June.

Manouchka? I suppose a Superwoman in labour could have snuck out behind June, while Bastard was distracted, and make her way to safety. That was the best-case scenario. Bastard would have to be completely blind and stupid to have missed a pregnant woman working her way past him, though.

Tucker?

The word blazed through my brain. Was he still here? Had he not escaped with June? Or had he somehow managed to haul her out and sneak back in?

My neck was starting to cramp up. My eyes watered involuntarily, and I told my body, *No, save your tears. You don't have any access to water. You could die here.*

That didn't help.

Was my man still here?

Bastard said, "Nobody move."

I tried not to. I still had to breathe, though. I could feel the muscles working in my neck. The scalenes, the sternocleidomastoid muscles. In pediatrics, we check those muscles by looking at them and by touching them, to gauge their level of respiratory distress.

Bastard kept the gun pressed against my temple, deepening the bruise, but loosened his arm around my neck while he surveyed the room. His body tightened again, and he said, "What are you doing here."

"I want to deliver your baby," said Tucker, his voice resonating in the small room.

I closed my eyes, flooded with dread and relief and horror. *He didn't leave me.*

Part of me still felt like, *This can't be happening*. The other part of me replied, *I always knew the end of the world would come and that I'd be a part of it.*

I've heard that the Tibetan Book of the Dead tells you every day of your life is just preparing yourself for your death. So the three other murder cases were just prep for my Death Day, as Harry Potter would put it.

At least Tucker stayed with me on my Death Day.

"I told you to fuck off," said Bastard.

I heard Tucker shift. Maybe he nodded, but he didn't reply.

Outside, behind us, I could hear heavy footsteps and male and female voices in the hallway.

Police. Men and women with guns. Thank God, thank God, thank God.

Bastard must have heard them, too. He hollered, "If you come in here, I'll kill these fucks. I'll blow the whole place up. Don't take one step closer."

The noise stilled outside, but I imagined them silently stealing June away while the rest of them broke the door down.

Instead, a female voice said through the door, "There's no need to do that." She sounded calm.

Bastard shouted, "Don't tell me what I should and shouldn't do! I'm here for my woman and my baby, so just back the fuck off!"

The woman didn't answer right away.

I could feel Bastard's heart banging against my back, but after a few seconds of silence, he said, "No one needs to get hurt here. I'm just going to get Casey and my boy, and that's it."

"That sounds good, sir. We don't want anyone hurt," said the woman.

Couldn't she see June bleeding at her feet? Or had Tucker not pulled the nurse out before he slammed the door closed?

"Get away from the door," said Bastard. "If I can still see your feet, I'm going to execute every motherfucking one of you. Starting with this bitch doctor. I'm all set. I just have to pull the trigger."

I didn't want to move, but my throat convulsed. I swallowed, even though I had no saliva left.

I was still staring at the ceiling. Was this my last view? Acoustic tile?

I heard the police's footsteps moving away from the door. My stomach plummeted, even though I told myself, *It's okay, Hope. It's good. He was going to execute you if they busted their way in.*

(He could still execute you.)

No, no, the cavalry is here.

(The cavalry is leaving.)

They're just coming up with a better plan.

(Yeah. That's it.)

I counted the seconds. One-Mississippi, two-Mississippi. All the way up to twenty-nine. Finally, Bastard said, "All right. Now I'm stuck with both of you."

My throat spasmed again.

"What the fuck. Two docs are better than one, right?"

"Right," said Tucker. His voice didn't even tremble. He was good at talking to psychos. Maybe he should have gone into psych after all.

He still could, if we survived.

Don't think like that.

How can I not think like that? I have a gun to my head!

"Fine." Bastard started to lower his chokehold, a fraction at a time. Just that separation of his arm from my neck, my chin, my body made me feel almost light-headed with relief, although he did add, "You try anything, and this bitch gets it."

"I'm just here to deliver a baby," said Tucker, still calm, even as I was thinking, *Hey. Why should* I *have to get it? So unfair.*

Which didn't exactly make sense. I was still willing to throw my body in the path of a speeding bullet for him and/or Ryan. It just sucked that Bastard had made me his number one punching bag.

"Now. Where is she?" said Bastard.

"Good question," said Tucker. I realized that he was responding to all of Bastard's salvos, turning them into reasonable questions. I was inclined to stay silent and try to ignore his insanity, but maybe conducting a dialogue instead of a monologue would help scoop up what was left of Bastard's twisted neurons and coax him toward letting us go. Definitely, acting like a punching bag wasn't helping me at all.

Bastard encircled my left arm with his hand, bruising it to let me know he meant business.

My breath pushed out between my teeth.

I flexed my bicep, popping his grip a little, and he clamped down hard enough to make the veins bulge out in my hand and my face flush with pain.

"Don't even," said Bastard, switching the gun around to bruise my left temple and clipping my glasses while he was at it.

I tried to look at it optimistically. The right side of my head throbbed so bad, I imagined it must feel like a migraine after a bender. So now, at least, the left side of my head got an equal opportunity.

"You can take me instead," said Tucker. "I don't mind."

"Shut up and deliver my baby," said Bastard.

"Okay," said Tucker. "No problem." For the first time, his voice cracked, and I realized that it horrified him to see me like this, so literally in danger. Even though I'd fought for my life before, he'd never witnessed me like this, bent to a killer's will. It shocked him so much that he was willing to abandon a patient and shut himself up with me and a lunatic.

I couldn't think like that, or I'd get emotional. I forced myself to breathe and try to problem-solve the gun drilling a hole in my left temple.

How many bullets did Bastard have? Was there any chance he might run out?

If only I'd spent less time on the Krebs cycle and more on firearms. All I knew was that they can kill you. Stay away.

I'd read a few mystery books where you counted six bullets. But Bastard could probably reload any time, if he'd had the sense to tuck some ammo under his burqa.

Still. If he had six bullets, he'd used up three. Two on Stan, one on June.

And this was a handgun. That much, I knew. At least, it wasn't a rifle he had to carry across his body, spraying shot everywhere, and it wasn't a semi-automatic. At least, it didn't look like a paintball gun that just keeps firing and firing.

But in the meantime, he still had at least three bullets.

And where was Manouchka?

I didn't think she'd left the room. Not only was she unlikely to sneak her bulk past us, but even though it sounds weird, I *felt* like there was someone else in the room, observing us. I just didn't know where. And my ability to case the room was still severely limited.

However, without Bastard's suffocating chokehold, I felt free to let my eyeballs roam free and bend my neck ever-so-slightly. If Manouchka hadn't had the chance to run, she probably picked the second option: hide. And a birthing room only has so many hiding places. Almost none, in fact.

For a second, I thought of slaves who tried to escape on moonless nights. The darkness helped cloak them a little. Our room wasn't quite that opaque, but just one small hanging lamp glowed beside the bed.

Of course, Bastard could hit the overhead switch any second now.

And once he found Manouchka, he'd explode.

Chapter 8

I glanced around the room, searching for a place to hide. First, for Manouchka. And secondly, in case the cavalry busted into the room, spraying bullets.

If I thought of the room like a clock, against the wall, directly in front of us, at 12 o'clock, was the incubator. Small, expensive, walls made out of transparent plastic. Useless cover.

The bed covered 10 to 12 o'clock, running parallel to that wall, stuck in a half-sitting position, but with no patient in it and no one hiding underneath it. Behind us, at 8 o'clock, the fetal monitor balanced on a countertop was probably still transmitting information even though it was no longer attached to Manouchka. The black fetal monitor's belt lay on the bed, bereft. A rolling tray table sat on the left side of the bed, near the wall, its fake wood grain surface empty as well, shining under the lamp.

A ratty beige curtain pressed against the far wall, between the bed and the incubator. Curtains are now considered passé in fancier hospitals, where you get an entire suite to yourself, but St. Joe's was old school. Last century, they must have wanted the option to draw a curtain around mama in the bed.

Someone had shoved the padded visitor's chair into the corner at approximately one o'clock. Since Manouchka had been alone, they'd had no use for it.

At two o'clock, the delivery cart was still draped, but inside it lay a whole bunch of sterile stuff. Not just gloves, but the clamps for the umbilical cord, forceps to pack the vagina with gauze in case of bleeding, special forceps to pull out the baby's head in an emergency (although more often nowadays they'll use a vacuum), sutures, scissors, who knows? As far as I was concerned, a nurse would start magically pulling out items as needed. We might have to use any or all of these for Manouchka's baby. With any luck, Tucker would know the cart layout better than I did.

I did not want Bastard to get a hold of a scalpel.

I didn't dare glance beyond three o'clock, because Bastard was still gripping my left arm and pressing his gun to my left temple.

Much more pleasant to consider Tucker, probably at five o'clock, just inside in the main door's entryway, lurking in my other blind spot.

That entryway. I'd stumbled over June in this room's entrance, because it was so narrow. Why?

To make room for something else. When we were looking at apartments for university, my engineering boyfriend, Ryan, had pointed out to me that hallways don't just come out of nowhere. This wasn't like a bachelor apartment where you open the door and it's a perfect box of a room. This case room had a hallway, and therefore contained a room within a room.

A bathroom.

I'd assumed that they didn't have a bathroom because the examining rooms in the family medicine centre have no running water. Also, I'd never had to search out and use a patient bathroom on OB. But even St. Joseph's anemic budget must have stretched to adding facilities on the obstetric wing.

The entry door was on the right side of the room. Tucker's zone, at five o'clock. Which meant the bathroom must be at approximately seven o'clock. And I knew where Manouchka must be hiding now.

I closed my eyes.

If we moved forward, and Bastard was deafened by the shots, it was possible that she could sneak open her door and tiptoe out of the room.

Far more likely, though, he'd hear her and open fire. Or even decide that he needed to take a leak and get a mighty surprise.

Bastard shifted and called to Tucker, "Move it, you stupid fuck, or I'm taking you out, and your girlfriend, too."

It was the first time anyone had called me Tucker's girlfriend. And even though this was the worst imaginable scenario, with my head throbbing and a bullet threatening my brain, my heart thrummed for a second.

Girlfriend. Tucker's girlfriend.

My heart didn't care that an insane gunman spoke those words. It sang, *You Tucker. Me girlfriend.*

I clung to that. I still loved Ryan. Just thinking about him made me want to sink my nose into the perfect, brown skin between his neck and shoulder and *inhale* him, blocking out the faint ringing in my ears and the madness surrounding me.

But the fact that Tucker stood by me in the case room of death—that made me feel both elated and sick at the same time, like I imagine heroin must feel.

"No worries," said Tucker. "I'm here to help you and Casey."

Even without moving my head, I could tell he was circling around me. Instead of staying diagonally behind me, at five o'clock, he was sweeping around to seven o'clock.

Maybe he was trying to shield the patient, even though he also laboured under the delusion that it was Casey.

Or maybe Tucker was on the move because he wanted to get between me and Bastard's gun.

I sucked my breath in between my clenched teeth. *I'm here, Tucker. I'm taking the fall for us. Don't play the hero.*

But of course he'd cast himself as the white knight. Why else would he stick around?

Our friend Tori once told me that everyone thinks he or she is the hero. No one thinks, *Yo, look at me, I'm the sidekick!*

I think it goes double for doctors.

But that could get dangerous here. Too many cooks might oversalt the broth; too many heroes would dig themselves twelve feet under.

I envisioned Tucker walking toward us with his hands in the air, steering clear of June's blood smeared into the floor. Unspeakably brave.

There was no way for me to talk to Tucker, or text him. Even now, my phone buzzed angrily in my pocket, trying to feed me texts I couldn't reach. And he was coming up on my left side, the gun side, so I couldn't even face him.

How could I talk to him when I couldn't even open my mouth without Bastard trying to jam a gun into it?

I stiffened, and Tucker's footsteps stilled.

He was watching me. He was reading my body language.

That was it. One of Tucker's many quirks was that he called himself a "cunning linguist," learning everything from Farsi to Inuktitut. Why not non-verbal communication?

My heart drummed so fast, I could hardly breathe, but I only had seconds to try and "talk" to Tucker.

Bastard was still imprisoning my left arm, making a manacle out of his hand. That left my right arm free.

I snaked my right palm up so it faced the incubator. Theoretically, I was showing Bastard that I didn't have any weapons and was a helpless maiden.

But in my mind, it was an unspoken Stop sign, and I was inching it above my shoulder, trying to flash both Bastard and Tucker at the same time.

Tucker's breath rasped behind me without getting any louder, which could only mean one thing. He'd stopped dead (uh, bad choice of words).

Tucker understood me. My God. He really got the message.

Now. If only I could tell him the important part: Casey wasn't in the bathroom. It was Manouchka. But that was a lot more complicated message than "halt."

Something else pinged in my brain. When I was in high school, I picked up a tiny bit of sign language. Just the alphabet, good morning, that sort of thing. But the brilliant thing was, Casey is a name that you can do with minimal letters and hand movement.

I waggled my hand a teeny bit from side to side. Just a miniature motion, smaller than the royal wave, but I was saying NO.

And then I pressed my thumb between my index and middle finger, which is a K in sign language if you drop the last two fingers toward your palm.

I released my thumb and curved the rest of my hand, making a big letter C.

If Tucker could decode it, I was saying, *No K-C.*

No Casey.

Of course, he had to read it from behind me, which made it trickier.

I don't sweat much, but right at this moment, my armpits stung, and my Adam's apple felt lodged in my throat.

Come on, Tucker.

I did it again, with slightly bigger movements, trying to angle my hand toward Tucker.

Bastard yelled, "STOP!"

CHAPTER 9

I froze with my tongue pressed against my upper palate. My right hand trembled in the air.

"WHAT do you THINK you're DOING?" Bastard yelled.

It was like a marine sergeant bellowing in my left ear, except with a gun to my head and his hand strangling my arm so hard that I figured my veins would explode just before he fired the gun.

I smelled blood again. It seemed to rise up from the floor.

I told myself that wasn't logical. The blood should dry up and become less smelly.

But the iron tang haunted my nostrils while I opened my mouth to answer.

Tucker's voice cut in. "Looking for your son."

Bastard paused, and the pressure on my arm halved for a crucial split-second. My arm was numb, but my hand buzzed as blood surged back to it.

"My son," Bastard repeated.

"Right. Your baby, about to be born," said Tucker.

For some reason, that made me think of Jesus. It was only November fourteenth, but this Catholic hospital had broken out all the trimmings already. A pair of baby Christmas stockings hung above the little incubator in the room.

I felt dizzy. What would happen to Manouchka's baby, once Bastard realized it wasn't his? I'd heard of soldiers bayoneting infants, or grabbing babies by the ankle and bashing their tiny heads against the wall.

"My boy," said Bastard.

"Your boy," said Tucker. "Hope and I are going to make sure he comes out safely."

I noticed, even with my slightly dull brain, he wasn't saying Casey's name anymore. Maybe Tucker had received my message. Maybe he hadn't. But at least he was distracting Bastard and reminding him that we were both useful human beings with names.

"That nurse was keeping me away from Casey. I had to get rid of her," said Bastard.

"She's gone now," said Tucker. I couldn't tell from his voice if it was a double entendre and June was gone-gone, as in dead, or just kiss-your-lucky-stars-absent-from-the-case-room-of-death gone.

"It was her fault for getting in the way," said Bastard.

Right. Blame the victim, motherfucker.

Tucker repeated, "She's gone."

Bastard took a breath. I thought I felt the gun waver against my temple, drawing a circle on the loose skin and probably making me look cock-eyed. I know I shouldn't care about vanity at a time like this, but that's the curse of getting locked up with one of your soul mates: you devote precious brain cells to that sort of non-survival thing.

"Casey," said Bastard, and his voice grew softer, almost like a caress, which made me grit my teeth and try not to implode. "Why did you run away from me?"

Isn't it obvious?

Bastard said, "I just want my boy and my girl."

For a second, I was worried that he wanted to kidnap another female. It took me a second to compute that "my girl" must mean Casey.

Tucker paused, too, before he said, "Hope and I will help you."

We will?

One of the things I find most frustrating about Christianity is turning the other cheek and assuming hellfire will catch up to the wrongdoers. Buddhism does this, too, but for some reason I don't find it as annoying as the commandment to keep offering my other cheek, or eyeball, or whatever a murderer has taken a fancy to.

It dawned on me that Tucker's voice had grown a little louder. He was approaching us, and I realized that he must have stepped within arm's reach. Not only calculating from the sound of his voice and footsteps, but I could even sense the warmth of his body and the intensity of his gaze. He said, "We're doctors. We help people."

I didn't want to help Bastard. But Manouchka, Casey, and their babies? Sure. Of course.

Bastard liked the sound of helping people, because he actually pulled the gun away from my head. Not far—I could see it out of the corner of my eye, and if I turned my head a few degrees to the left, I'd run into the muzzle again—but even a millimetre away from direct contact was a vast improvement. I could breathe again.

Keep talking, Tucker.

"Go deliver my kid, then," said Bastard, but without rancor.

"Sure," said Tucker. "I'll just take Hope over for the delivery."

Oh, he was good. "The delivery" instead of naming any specific baby. But even if we hid out in the bathroom, and then presented Bastard with a black baby, I assumed he would notice.

"I'm coming with you," said Bastard.

So much for that. But points to Tucker for trying. And because he was so brave, it gave me courage. I wasn't fighting this maniac alone. Tucker was on my team.

That made me smile a little. My lower lip cracked, and I automatically slid my tongue forward to taste the blood. I could barely taste it, but it was there.

"Casey!" Bastard shouted. "Casey, come on out!"

CHAPTER 10

Of course, Casey did not appear.

"Casey!" Bastard hollered again, like she was a dog who'd race to him if he just whistled the right way.

A few drops of his spit hit my cheek. I didn't move. Didn't glance at the bathroom. But it didn't take a genius to figure out that "Casey" couldn't hide anywhere else.

Bastard's grip on my left arm loosened another millimetre, but he didn't let go, and I knew the omnipresent gun was still pointed at me, even though he'd started to whip his body around, searching for her.

"It's me!" Bastard yelled. "Come on, baby!"

Silence greeted his words, except I might have detected some footsteps in the hall. I strained my ears, wishing I were facing the door instead of the incubator and bed. Were people escaping? Or was the SWAT team ready to pounce?

"Shit!" said Bastard.

"She might feel scared," said Tucker.

The understatement of the year.

"Baby, you don't have to be scared of me. I'd never hurt you. I love you. I'm going to be the best daddy in the world!"

"Maybe she's feeling sick," I said. I thought that might be a better tack than explaining to Bastard that shooting people wasn't the best way to woo a woman, unless maybe she was Karla Homolka.

Also, it might be true. I certainly felt like barfing at the notion of Bastard slipping into a World's Greatest Dad T-shirt and raising his son just like him.

"Sick?" Bastard repeated.

"Or just in a lot of pain. She's in labour, right?" Even now, I wasn't lying. If the real Casey was in labour, it ain't no foot massage. I risked glancing at Bastard. He was still wearing the burqa with the letter slot grille, so his eyes were in shadow, but he met my gaze, and I thought his looked uncertain.

Abruptly, he released my arm and shoved me to the right. "Go help her."

I stumbled a few steps before I caught myself. For a second, I felt almost confused by the freedom of movement, the fact that he'd temporarily pulled the gun away from my head. Should I run?

I had a vision of me breaking away, dodging bullets Matrix-style, and the newspaper headlines trumpeting, BRAVE STUDENT DOCTOR ESCAPES KIDNAPPER.

This was immediately supplanted by a mental headline declaring, HOSPITAL KIDNAPPER KILLS THREE.

Better check where the gun was first. When I refocused, I realized he was now aiming it between Tucker's shoulder blades, since Tucker had crossed to the other side of him. "You say you're doctors? Prove it." Bastard's eyes flicked toward me.

Time to walk the walk. And we could, indeed, help deliver a baby. Just not his own.

I took a deep breath and said, "Let me try to find Casey. I'm going to check around the room." I added the last bit so that he wouldn't think I was fleeing and jam a bullet in my kidney.

I closed the last step toward Tucker. I needed to be next to him, needed to feel him.

Tucker took my hand in his, gripping it hard enough that I knew his nerves were bothering him too, even if he wasn't showing it to Bastard.

We hadn't held hands since we took the subway to Île Ste-Hélène, which felt like forever ago, but was just in August. I grasped his hand like I'd never held hands with anyone. The strong length of his fingers. The smoothness of his skin, although I could feel more firmness at his fingertips. Calluses, probably from playing the guitar, something he'd mentioned once or twice but I'd never heard him do.

That suddenly made me want to cry. I might never hear him play the guitar. Might never look into his eyes while he fumbled for the notes, or opened his mouth and tried to sing.

"What. You gotta hold hands to deliver a baby? What the fuck is wrong with you?" shouted Bastard.

Instead of letting go, I gripped Tucker's hand, thinking of the word *lifeline*. I used to picture a rope dangling from a helicopter that might airlift you out of Afghanistan, but it could be much simpler. Like this, getting to hold the hand of a man I loved.

Tucker squeezed back. Once, quickly, which I somehow knew meant that he was bracing himself to let go.

I was holding him with my right and dominant hand, leaving me even more defenseless.

I should let go.

I really should.

But I clung to him and said, "We'd better find our patient."

"Patient*s*!" yelled Bastard. "You gotta get my son out. Don't forget about him. Now go in the bathroom and get 'em outta there." But he aimed the muzzle away from Tucker, toward the space between us.

It felt like a blessing.

Tucker and I walked toward the bathroom, taking deliberate, unhurried steps.

Me, because I didn't want to get there and show him that we'd imprisoned the wrong woman.

And Tucker...I'm not sure, but he squared his shoulders and handed me a grin that was half fear, half stubbornness. I thought that he was trying to show Bastard that he couldn't just push us around.

Plus, maybe Tucker had gotten my signal that it wasn't Casey inside.

The lights were off in the bathroom. I would have noticed a sliver of light, just like the light slipping in to our room from the brighter hallway. Manouchka had wrapped herself in darkness, in this tiny room.

For a second, I wondered if she'd tried to arm herself and might even attack us. She'd kept amazingly quiet, for a woman in labour, but she couldn't sustain the silence forever.

I called out, "It's Dr. Sze and Dr. Tucker!"

I sounded like a bad game show host. Tucker tensed, and I realized that he would have preferred I put his name first. Oh, well. I could massage his ego later, if we survived.

Two steps from the door, Tucker joined in. "We're here to deliver your baby."

"My baby!" said Bastard. He was following us. With the gun. Hemming us toward the bathroom like he was a sheepdog and we were his wayward flock.

Baa.

Bastard said, "Casey? You doing okay, honey?"

Manouchka still didn't reply. Her name wasn't Casey. Plus, I slowly realized, what if she didn't speak English much? Did she really know what was going on here?

She knew enough to hide, even while she was in pain. But beyond that?

Bastard said, "Why won't you talk to me?" Anger had begun to thread through his voice. "Why are you hiding? Come on out, baby. I want to see you."

He was distracted now. The exit door stood less than ten feet away. I suppose Tucker and I could have run for it, abandoning Manouchka to the man with a gun.

I couldn't desert her. But I whispered, "Run."

Tucker shook his head and pointed his chin at me, then jerked his head at the door.

He wanted me to run instead. I shook my head. I could deliver the baby. I could distract Bastard while Tucker fled.

I couldn't think beyond that. It was quite possible that Bastard would soon discover that "Casey" was a black stranger and exact revenge on all of us.

Bastard ignored us, supercharged on the idea of his ex. "Honey. Don't be scared. You know I'd never hurt you."

Riiiiiight.

I half-turned toward Tucker, but enough so that Bastard could see my lips while I said, "We need to go find Casey."

Bastard was crooning now, which was horrible Too intimate, like eavesdropping on a shy couple having sex, or hauling a newborn baby off its mother's breast, or barging in on a family gathered around their loved one's deathbed. "Don't worry, baby, I love you. I was just trying to find you. You know I've never fired a gun around you, because you're scared of them. I kept 'em locked up, just like you asked me to. We were safe, right? Weren't we, Casey?"

His brain had only one gear, so in the meantime, I made sure Tucker knew. I whispered so softly that I hoped he could read my lips. "It's not Casey."

Tucker frowned at me. I guess he hadn't figured out my clever sign language earlier.

Then he understood, and his face and his body grew so still, it was terrible to witness and feel the rigidity in his grasp. He turned toward Bastard and said over his right shoulder, "There's been a mistake."

Tucker tried to let go of my hand, but I wouldn't let him. I clung harder than ever.

We get seminars in how to break bad news, since doctors are like angels of death and dying: *You have cancer. We couldn't save him. I'm sorry, we did everything we could.*

You're supposed to sit down, make eye contact, and be direct.

I couldn't sit, and Bastard wouldn't make eye contact. Still, I had to get his attention away from Manouchka, make sure he didn't fillet her.

If I could just call his name. That might snap him out of his Casey fever.

But I didn't know his name, rank, or serial number. He was just a stranger dressed up in a burqa, just some crazed man sneaking guns into St. Joseph's Hospital and shooting us.

I craned my neck so I could look over my right shoulder, too, even though a sharp pain zinged into my shoulder. I said, "I have bad news for you."

"I gave you everything I had." Bastard's voice thickened. This was the closest he'd ever come to forgetting about us. This was the time to run, if we could have lived with ourselves afterward. "I worked twelve-hour shifts for you. I gave you our baby. Why'd you run away from me?"

I bit my tongue instead of answering.

"I want you to come out now," he said, still with that weird coaxing tone that you might use on a scared stray cat. "I want to show you how good I'm going to be to you. I won't make you do anything, sweetheart. I just want to help you and our baby."

OMG. I didn't want to consider what else he might have made her do. But I had to play the messenger here. You know, the one they shoot. "Sir. We're in another patient's room."

"Can you hear me?" asked Bastard. "I'm right here. Come on out, Casey."

"She can't," I said, in my most compassionate voice. I tried to pour love into every word, the way that Buddhist monks and nuns somehow do, even when they're being electrocuted and forced to suck on each other's genitals through the electric shocks—don't ask me how I know this. It's not from experience.

Bastard's shoulders shifted. He'd heard me that time, but it was like I was an annoying fly, buzzing around his ears. He didn't want to hear me, so he wouldn't.

Tucker raised his voice. "There's been a terrible mistake." I liked how he used the passive voice, which is a big writing no-no, but very important here. He wasn't blaming Bastard. He was just saying that somehow, something had gone wrong.

Bastard said, "Shut the hell up. Both of you." But he didn't sound as angry as he had a second ago. Maybe he'd sensed that this wasn't Casey, but he was trying to convince himself.

"Her name is Manouchka," I said, quieter, but still loud enough for Bastard to hear.

He levelled the gun and bellowed, "Casey. I've got some crazy people here, and they're pissing me off. Open the door, or I'll shoot it open."

Chapter 11

Manouchka didn't answer.

I heard, or imagined I heard, her panting behind the wood.

It wasn't much of a shield, but it was something.

Wait a minute. Was it possible that Tucker and I could break for the bathroom and slam the door closed before Bastard managed to shoot us?

I grasped Tucker's hand and pointed my free index finger at the bathroom door, wondering if he'd get it.

Tucker squeezed back with a slow pressure. I wasn't sure if that was a yes or a no.

Or if Manouchka would let us in there with her.

I wasn't even sure if Manouchka spoke English.

This was a problem.

I took a deep breath and told Bastard, over my shoulder, "She speaks French."

"What?" He swung the gun toward my right ear. He was only about a foot away. My fantasy of running into the bathroom flickered and died.

I wanted to close my eyes and brace myself against the bullet's impact, but I forced myself to lock eyes with him, over my and Tucker's entwined hands, and say, "The woman in the bathroom is a francophone."

Bastard goggled at me. "Casey's not a francophone!"

"Hope." Tucker was gripping my hand harder now. He didn't want me to talk. He wanted me to hush up and let him handle it. And maybe that would have been better, since he was the tactful one, but only I had information about the woman trapped in front of us.

I pointed at the bathroom and repeated, "Her name is Manouchka." I was breaking patient confidentiality, but I thought it was more important to humanize all of us, so we weren't just random people he was snuffing out. "She's pregnant. She's having a baby too." I paused. I couldn't offer much more than that, since I'd just met her myself. Oh, wait, I could. "This is her first baby." G1P0, meaning that she'd never delivered a baby before. What a terrible way to introduce her to motherhood.

"What the FUCK?" Bastard pointed his weapon at the door, and I sucked the breath in between my teeth so hard that it sounded almost like a scream.

"Don't shoot her. She's having a baby," I said, which wasn't totally relevant—non-pregnant people deserve to live too—but you go for whatever you can. If I could wrench an angstrom of compassion out of Bastard, I'd take it.

"Casey," said Bastard, and his voice rose into danger-level territory. Mach 2. My turn to crush Tucker's fingers down to the bone. If we got assassinated right now, the only comfort was that I'd go out holding Tucker's hand. "Get out here. Now."

"Her name is Manouchka," I sounded like an iTunes song on repeat, but by giving her name, by pointing out that she was like Casey, I might tip him into hold his fire.

I couldn't hear her breathing now. She was making herself as invisible as possible, but her time had run out.

Out of the four of us, Manouchka was the only one who was entirely innocent. She just wanted to come to a hospital and have her baby. Instead, she'd had to barricade herself in the bathroom while her nurse was shot.

I licked my lips and said, my voice wavering only a little, "Manouchka."

"Come on out, Casey," said Bastard.

No sound, no movement from behind the door.

Bastard took another step toward the door. One more foot, and he'd break me and Tucker apart. I could practically feel Bastard's breath on my neck while he said, "You make me make you get out of there, and I'll make you pay for it."

Goosebumps prickled on my arms. My ankle rash itched under my socks. "She might not understand English. She speaks French."

Bastard pinned me with his eyes. He was still wearing the burqa, which made him look farcical yet threatening. I must have betrayed something in my face, because he glanced down at his own sleeves and said, "Is it this? You saw my outfit and thought I was some chick? I just bought it so I could get in to see you. It's me. Ben!"

Bastard had a name. I shuddered. I actually liked the name Ben, although not so much the name Benjamin, and definitely not Benji.

"I can take it off," said Bastard/Ben, starting to croon again, "but you've got to come out. I don't want to play hide and seek with you. I've been waiting to see you. Now, come on."

She sobbed on her next breath, and it was a sound of so much distress, even through the wood, that Bastard said, for the first time, "Casey?" with doubt eroding his voice.

"She's just trying to have a baby. Can we let her go?"

My words hung in the air.

Bastard seemed to consider them, for once. Finally, he said, "I haven't seen her face."

I figured that it was like some people say about a funeral. If they can't see their loved one's face, they can't believe he or she died. It seems unreal.

If he didn't see Manouchka, he wouldn't believe that it wasn't Casey.

It was possible that Casey and Manouchka were the same person, but I was still very worried that if she wasn't, Bastard would take us all out.

That might be the risk we had to take, though, since he didn't seem willing to say, *Oh, sure. No probs. I'll just head out now.*

I licked my lips. "We can still find the person you want."

He said, "Her face."

I said, "Can I tell her in French?"

He snorted. "Go on."

"*Il veut voir votre visage,*" I said. Vouvoyer, they call it: the most formal way of addressing someone in French. It may not be necessary (young women will just tell me, *Tu peux me tutoyer*), but I wanted her to know that I had the utmost respect for her. And if that could rub off on Bastard, so much the better.

"S'il-vous-plaît," I added, which sounded ridiculous, even to my ears. If you please. Show your face to a murderer, if it should tickle your fancy.

"Il va me tuer!" she whispered, her French rough with tears, and Bastard's head jerked to the side, hearing it.

Bastard said, "Fuck."

Tucker and I barely breathed.

Bastard walked around me, tried the locked door handle, and yelled, "FUUUUUUUUUUUUUUUUUUCK!"

He raised his gun and leveled it at the door.

Chapter 12

I screamed, "Get DOWN!" to Tucker, to Manouchka, to everyone, just as Tucker tackled me.

He knocked me sideways, so my hip and skull bashed against the tile floor while Bastard started shooting.

Tucker dropped his chest over my head, even though I wiggled and tried to throw him to one side. He clamped his hands over my ears and his legs around my waist.

In any other circumstance, I might enjoy this, but he was squashing my nose and mouth with his sternum, practically waterboarding me against his filthy hospital scrubs.

I wiggled my head from side to side, trying to shake off my Tucker earmuffs and nose crush while I tried to make out the unfamiliar sounds above us. Not gunshots, but angry, fast, repeated bangs that made the floor tremble.

Kicks? Was that possible? Was Bastard kicking the door instead of shooting?

A single, sharp crack.

Somehow, I recognized this noise. The wood had split.

Yes, he was kicking in the bathroom door.

Tucker's body locked down on me like a robot exoskeleton.

I screamed Manouchka's name from beneath Tucker's body.

Crack.

The whole room roared, a tiny echo chamber of death.

The floor shook underneath me.

I started fighting to get out from underneath Tucker, struggling to breathe, thinking, *He's trying to protect me, but he might kill me.*

I can't breathe.

I can't BREATHE.

Still, Tucker weighed me down, refusing to move.

And I realized, *Maybe he's dead. Maybe Bastard pumped him full of lead, and this is just a death grip.*

BANG.

I screamed, trying to sit up.

Wood shattered under the bludgeoning of Bastard's boots.

Meanwhile, the logical part of me thought, *Get down, you idiot. Tucker is trying to save your life*, but I couldn't relax until I registered Tucker's heart hammering against my chest and gloated, *He's still alive, he's still alive, even if he's just in hypotensive tachycardia, he's ALIVE—*

Tucker twisted above me, relieving the pressure on my nose.

I sucked stale air into my lungs and squinted at the man-shaped shadow looming above us.

The gun lowered toward my head again.

No. The hand stopped just short of jamming the metal back against my temple, but Tucker's shape blotted out the gun's exact location.

My muffled ears detected Bastard saying, "Get off of her, you stupid fuck."

Tucker's hands and feet sprang away from my body as abruptly as a triggered mousetrap.

He was leaving me.

Now I was the one grasping at Tucker. I tossed one leg over his shifting hips. I bear-hugged him, shaking my head from side to side.

Tucker's brown eyes bore into mine. He didn't blink.

But, out of the corner of my eyes, I detected Bastard's gun hand, which was now aimed at Tucker.

My gut-based longing was not as important as Tucker's immediate survival.

I forced myself to let him go. First my leg, which felt lop-sided anyway, and then my arms.

Tucker pressed his knees into the floor and now used both hands to push himself upright. Away from me.

He was healthy enough to get up. He was okay.

I realized that I must have been screaming, or crying, or something, because my face was wet and my throat ached. Or maybe that was Tucker's tears or mucous from lying on me, I couldn't tell anymore, but the ragged sound echoing in my ears was definitely breaking out of my own gullet.

I jumped to my feet, reeling a little at the change in position and the roaring in my ears.

Bastard slapped me across the face.

He hit me hard enough that for a second, I wondered if he'd dislocated my jaw. Pain blazed through my left cheek and neck.

I couldn't think anything except pain.

Then, my eyes still blurred with tears, I forced myself to open and close my jaw a few millimetres. I didn't think it was broken or displaced.

Just, ouch.

Tucker tried to lunge for me.

Bastard's hand shot forward to squeeze Tucker's throat, viper-fast, while his "free" hand leveled the gun at Tucker's head. "Yeah. Try it, Blondie."

Tucker's eyes glittered. He locked in place, no longer reaching for me, but his chest bellowed with silent rage. He wanted to attack Bastard, but had to bite back on that instinct in order to maintain his brainstem and trachea.

His eyes shifted toward me, mutely asking if I was okay.

I nodded infinitesimally. My jaw already hurt less. That was a win.

"I just wanted you to shut up. I didn't shoot him, you stupid bitch," Bastard said.

Did he shoot Manouchka and her unborn baby instead? Oh God, oh God.

Slowly, I raised my head and squared my unbroken jaw. I had to see what had happened to her and if I could help.

If the mother dies, you have four minutes to perform a crash C-section.

Chapter 13

I'd never done a perimortem C-section before, never even heard of another student witnessing one, but I'd assisted a few live Caesarian sections.

If anyone was going to cut open a dead woman's belly, it would have to be me. Or Tucker. Or both.

I took two steps toward the broken bathroom door. Bastard had busted it in half.

The bottom part had propelled into the bathroom, perpendicular to the frame. The top half, I had to duck under, bracing myself against the sudden whiff of a coppery smell that might have been gunpowder, but could easily have been blood.

Please don't be blood.

My prayers achieved one thing. Bastard didn't stop me from entering the bathroom.

Maybe Manouchka was already dead, but I still had to know if I'd have a chance at saving her or her baby.

It took me a second to compute the blue-gowned figure quivering at two o'clock, behind the toilet.

The figure was moving. It was covered in dust and shards of glass?—no, plastic, I thought, as my shoes crunched into the room—but it wasn't obviously bleeding.

She wasn't bleeding.

Manouchka was alive.

I stared at her, unbelieving. I guess I'd thought it was too much to wish for, that Bastard would shoot Stan and June, but then not execute any of the three of us remaining.

I did not understand Bastard. Was this his form of mercy? Was he such a bad shot?

Still, I was wordlessly grateful that he'd concentrated his fury and destruction on the transparent shower stall directly opposite the door, which was now a gaping hole of shattered plastic.

No bullet holes in the wall, though. So he must've been strong enough to kick down the door and then bash in the shower stall with his bare fists and his boots.

I didn't want to think about what that meant, except that I didn't have to do a perimortem C-section.

I glanced down at Manouchka's huddled form and said, in French, "I'm here to help you."

"She's not Casey," said Bastard, from behind Tucker, whose feet now hovered barely outside the ruined bathroom door, within arm's reach. "I saw her in the toilet. She's just some nigger."

My breath hitched. I thought maybe Tucker's did, too.

It wasn't enough that Bastard had stolen a persecuted group's religious costume, shot two innocent hospital workers, terrified a pregnant woman, smacked me around, and held a gun to Tucker's head. Now he was tossing out racist slurs.

The only good part was (and you can tell that I'm a die-hard optimist. Oops. I will most likely die hard, thanks), forewarned is forearmed.

Bastard didn't like black women.

So he wouldn't like yellow women like me, either.

Maybe he liked white men, though. Maybe he wouldn't pull the trigger on Tucker quite as easily. That put Tucker on the most-likely-to-survive list.

And, for what it was worth, Bastard hadn't killed Manouchka. Yet.

Manouchka began rocking from side to side, as if the pain in her body would not allow her to stay still and silent any longer, even if it might cost her two lives.

"I could help her, if you'd let me," I said over my shoulder, to Bastard. I wanted him to think he was in control, the Grand Poobah granting favours. That way, maybe I could manipulate him into doing what I wanted.

Bastard barked, "I need you to deliver my boy. Get out here."

My body stiffened. Torn between competing needs. Should I capitalize on his request and ask him to move me and Tucker into another room, supposedly to deliver Casey's baby?

We'd abandon Manouchka right when she needed us. But it would also drive the gunman away from her.

Medicine is all about risks and benefits. I bet Manouchka would rather deliver the baby herself on the cold bathroom floor if it got her free from this madman.

I opened my mouth to say okay.

The intercom crackled in the outer room. A woman's voice cut in. "Are you all right in there?"

She didn't sound like the clerk we'd had earlier. That one had an old woman's warble. This one sounded much younger, and very calm for someone asking if any of us had survived.

Bastard said, "What the fuck?"

"It's the intercom," said Tucker. I saw his feet pivot as he probably pointed toward the grille and the red button in the wall at the head of the bed in the main room. "Press that if you want to talk."

I glanced at Manouchka. She was definitely panting now. Her sides heaved.

I edged toward her. Her bum pointed toward the ruined wall, and I needed to get to what we call the business end. (The head is the "office end," where the partner usually hangs out.)

Bastard said, "Are they fucking listening to us?"

"Only if you press the red button," said Tucker. "It's like a walkie-talkie. They can't listen in unless you press the button."

"Why are they talking, then?"

"Because they heard you breaking down the door," said Tucker. "They want to make sure we're alive. If they think we're dead—"

He didn't complete the thought, but I did. Would they storm in? Would Bastard panic and start shooting us, as well as the cavalry?

I took a few more small steps toward Manouchka, murmuring in French, "It's okay," even though it obviously wasn't.

"Why should I talk to them? They didn't help me find Casey," said Bastard, not unlike a toddler. Boo hoo.

"Maybe they could," I said. I spoke more slowly and carefully than usual, instead of my usual rat-a-tat style. While Bastard mulled that over, I crouched over Manouchka and said, "*Bonjour.*"

What a foolish thing to say. It wasn't a good day. But she still hadn't answered me. And I couldn't see her face. She was balled up, head down, into the tile. She must be freezing.

"That's a good idea, Hope," said Tucker, but I could still see his feet. He and Bastard hadn't maneuvered their way over to the intercom to press the button and communicate with them to make it so, even though I'd invoked the magic Casey word.

The intercom crackled again. "Manouchka? Dr. Zee? Dr. Tucker?"

I wanted to yell, *I'm here.*

Instead, I told Manouchka, "It's me. Dr. Sze. I'm here to help you with your baby."

If anything, she curled into a tighter ball. For a second, I thought of a mimosa plant's delicate leaves coiling up when touched.

I laid a careful hand on Manouchka's back.

Her breath seized, but she didn't scream. I didn't know if that was a good sign or bad.

Bastard said, "I don't like some chick blabbing at me. Maybe I should just take this out."

His feet twisted to the right. Toward the intercom.

My free hand jerked into the air, as if to stop him. The intercom was one of our only links to the outside world. I couldn't get my hands or eyes free to check my phone, plus the battery could die any second. If Bastard severed the intercom lifeline too, I might seriously lose it.

My phone.

Bastard wasn't watching me. And I had to deliver Manouchka's baby any second now. But in the meantime, I slid my phone out of my left breast pocket and stared at my messages.

Ryan: *I love you.*

Ryan: *Just heard. OMW.*

Ryan: *ILY.*

Dad: *Hope, hang in there. We're coming.*

Mom: *You're on TV!*

I had to smile. That sounded more like my little brother, Kevin. And my mom didn't text me, so I assumed he'd grabbed her phone.

Ryan: *I hear the police have surrounded the building. I'm at Anderson Rd. ILY.*

My hands were shaking. I only had a second, at most, but I sent the same message to all of them: *ILY.*

I love you.

It was 8:29 p.m. I was a bit hazy on the exact minute I'd first stepped into the case room to say hi to Manouchka, but I couldn't have been kidnapped for more than an hour. Ryan said he was on the outskirts of Ottawa, but it was really a two hour drive in.

He'd said *I'm at Anderson Rd.* First person singular. He hadn't waited for my family. They must be driving in separately.

Which, considering my mother, was a smart move. She was probably still packing me an extra blanket and making hot chocolate.

The last thing I needed was Ryan in a pile-up, trying to get to me.

At least it hadn't been snowing this morning.

But what about my family? Were they really going to hold a vigil outside the building, in the freezing cold? What if the police cordoned off the whole block?

I thrust that thought from my mind and dropped my phone back in my pocket. I loved them. I couldn't worry about them right now, or I'd lose it.

Before Bastard could shoot the intercom, Tucker asked one question. "Is that wise?"

Even in the midst of chaos, my mind clicked on to the word *wise*. If he'd said smart, Bastard might have taken offence. But wisdom? We don't talk much about wisdom, except for the three wise men, once a year.

Then I saw Tucker's body buck as Bastard jammed his foot between my man's. "You telling me what to do? You think you're running the show here?"

I jumped to my feet, ignoring the throb in my temples.

Don't you dare hurt Tucker.

Bastard, shoot the intercom. Heck, shoot a hole in the wall big enough for us to break into the next room. But don't you touch my man.

Before I could confront him, Tucker beat me to it.

"Never," said Tucker. "You've got the gun. That means that you hold all the cards."

I stopped two feet away from him. Tucker was standing very still, with his hands by his sides. I couldn't see the gun, which meant it was above the waist, behind the half-door. Probably pointing at Tucker's head, since that was Bastard's M.O.

I could tell from Tucker's body language that he wanted me to get the hell away. Even his words were a double message, reminding me not to play the hero.

But I wanted to. I wanted to charge at them and kick Bastard in the goolies.

I was getting a taste of how Tucker must have felt, watching Bastard hold a gun to my brain. Answer: crammed with impotent rage.

Too bad that, contrary to stereotype, I'd never taken up martial arts beyond an intro class or two.

I would have dearly loved to scream, "Haiiiiiiiii-YAH!" and jump-kick-fly-beat Bastard into the ground.

But he held the gun.

He held the balance of power.

Hang on. What about the flip side? If Bastard no longer controlled the gun, he wouldn't be the boss anymore.

If we could just get that g-d gun away from him.

"Damn straight. So shut it," said Bastard. His voice sounded compressed, like he was struggling to control himself.

He'd never spoke like that before. It made me question his tenuous grasp on sanity.

My fantasies shriveled. I forced my body into immobility. As in, I tried not to breathe.

It was so quiet that I heard Tucker swallowing his own saliva.

My heart clutched.

And then I heard a tiny moan from the floor.

Chapter 14

Slowly, it percolated through my brain that the sound had come from below me, behind me, and to my left, from behind the toilet.

Manouchka.

I'd forgotten her for a moment.

Bad doctor.

Bastard's gun appeared below the broken door. He couldn't possibly have a proper view of us, because the top part of the door was still attached, but his muzzle rotated toward us.

Threat received.

I inched my feet toward Manouchka, not daring to make much noise. She still hadn't acknowledged me. Maybe post-traumatic stress had kicked in. Was that how it worked? Too bad Tucker couldn't tell me.

"I'm here to help you, Manouchka. I'm a doctor. Dr. Sze. You met me before, remember?" I tried to sound as compassionate and welcoming as possible, but my dry throat caught, and I coughed the last word.

Manouchka didn't answer me.

I thought something was really wrong with her. Besides labouring at gunpoint, I mean.

Regardless, the baby was coming. I circled around to the business end.

Manouchka's hips shifted under her pale blue gown, briefly pointing her bum toward me. I got a good look at the distinct dark patch on her rear end, which made the thin material clung to her buttocks.

"What the fuck is wrong with that bitch?" Bastard said, even though it didn't take a MacArthur Genius Award to figure it out.

"She broke her water," I said, shivering involuntarily. "Things will move a lot faster now."

For whatever chemical reason, the amniotic fluid accelerates the labour. If she'd been at six centimetres an hour ago, she must be at eight, or even ten centimetres now. And if she was at ten, she was ready to push.

"Shit," said Bastard.

For once, we were in agreement.

Manouchka couldn't deliver a baby head-down on the bathroom floor. Well, she could. But it was already inhumane, how long she'd held on, soundlessly, while Bastard shot her nurse and busted into her room, and people jabbered in a foreign tongue. Meanwhile, her baby had signalled its unstoppable intention to enter this terrifying world.

I know that babies are born in wartime, or enter the world during earthquakes and tsunamis. But Manouchka might have emigrated from another country, seeking asylum and a new way of life, only to find herself struggling not to deliver a baby at the feet of a maniac. It was almost incomprehensible.

But she was tough. She'd hidden herself. She'd kept quiet as long as possible.

This was a risky business, though. If she moved, Bastard might suddenly decide he hated her black face and drive a bullet through it.

I imagined her crouched there, legs trembling, her baby's warm amniotic fluid leaking down her thighs.

She shouldn't risk his ire. But I could.

I said, "Ben, she's in labour. May I check her?" Scrupulously polite. Just like Tucker.

It flitted through my consciousness that once this baby was born, Tucker and I would no longer hold a Get Out of Jail Free card. Bastard might execute us.

But until then, he needed us. Because, judging from the rigidity in Bastard's legs, he had no desire to deliver this baby himself.

Fierce gladness flashed through me, that we could make Bastard uncomfortable, even if he was the one armed and dangerous. Probably, like most guys, he loved sex but had to leave the room if girls started joking about their period.

Bastard managed three words. "Make it quick."

Another idiotic thing to say. You can't pull a lever up to maximum so that the baby can be delivered in 15 minutes, or it's free. But I ignored that.

"I can help," said Tucker.

My heart thumped twice.

If he would just let Tucker go. If I could stand shoulder to shoulder with him, sense the warmth of his arm against mine. Failing that, if I could look into his eyes and catch his nod of agreement before I clamped the cord and he cut it.

I wouldn't have to wing it. We could guide each other.

It would transform me.

Funny. Yesterday, I would've hurried around the hospital, jockeying with Stan, trying to deliver my quota of babies, complaining if the cafeteria closed before I grabbed supper, and now I was *ravie*, as the French would say, at the mere thought of working alongside Tucker.

You know how Oprah's always going on about gratitude for the small things in life? As a hostage, living minute to minute according to a lunatic's whims, I finally understood what she was talking about.

Life before today had been *fantastic*. If only I'd realized it.

And if Bastard gave me the gift of Tucker, I'd practically kiss his sweaty toes.

'Course, part of my anticipation was purely practical. I've only delivered four babies in my life, all of them under the guidance of an experienced obstetric doctor. I could really use a partner in crime.

I shifted to the left, and suddenly, I could make out their top halves through a crack in the door frame. Tucker stood facing me, only a few feet away from the broken door, trying not to grimace as he kept both palms at shoulder height.

Bastard loomed close behind him, his body relaxed, but his gun jammed deep into Tucker's back.

"You stay right where you are, motherfucker," said Bastard. "You're the one I'm aiming at right now. You do anything weird, I'm pulling the trigger. Then your girlfriend gets it. And then the black bitch. I'll save an extra bullet for the baby, if I have to. Hands up."

Bastard managed to annihilate every buzz of gratitude, "girlfriend" notwithstanding.

I watched Tucker's hands extend even higher in the air, on either side of his head, and I wanted to kill Bastard. Especially when Tucker's fingers trembled.

I know sometimes I get an involuntary tremor. Usually at the worst times, like when a surgeon says, "Let the medical student try the next stitch."

I thought maybe only I'd noticed, because I was so closely attuned to Tucker, but Bastard laughed and said, "Now who's scared." Bastard chuckled a little to himself before he drove his right hand, his gun hand, forward.

My head jerked up. I couldn't see exactly where it landed, but Tucker's upper body rocked toward me, hinging at the waist. He suppressed a grunt.

"Who's the baby now? Who's going to cry waa-waa?" Bastard taunted. While he spoke, he insinuated his body closer, almost like a lover, spooning Tucker's hips with his crotch.

Tucker tried to jerk away from him, and his hands slammed the top half of the door.

The wood creaked under the impact.

Bastard chuckled. "Are we gonna have two babies in the room now?"

I had to do something. Manouchka moaned behind me, and I called, "I'm coming, Manouchka!" but I couldn't rip myself away from Tucker. The air between the two men felt dangerous. Menacing. Either Bastard would fire, or Tucker might explode. Either way would spell death for my man.

Chapter 15

I bent double and started wheezing.

It's a high-pitched, strained out-breath. I don't have asthma, but I get quite a bit of practice at imitating it, because whenever parents bring in their children and say they have trouble breathing, I reply, "Do they sound like this?" and put on a similar performance.

Right now, even a few seconds of whistling like a train strained my dry throat. I'd have been better off imitating stridor, which is rasping on the in-breath, but I couldn't suddenly switch sounds. It would tip my game. And the name of the game was saving Tucker's life by distracting Bastard from his killing spree.

Since I was folded in half, under the remains of the door, I was now fully visible to both men, or at least to Bastard, who had more freedom of head movement. I hadn't stepped toward them, which might seem too aggressive, but I was quite the noisy sideshow.

Bastard didn't move away from Tucker. I assumed he was still boring his gun into Tucker's neck/back/other unacceptable region, but he called, "What the fuck is wrong with you?"

"I need—" I gestured in front of my face, pretending to hold an inhaler and squeeze it. Asthma is so common, he'd probably have seen someone use an inhaler before, even if he didn't have asthma. Unfortunately, because of the remaining door bit, I had to stay hunched over. At least it made me more red-faced and desperate-looking.

"Oh, fuck," he said. "Where's your puffer?"

Ah. Puffer. The more common word for an inhaler. He knew what I was talking 'bout. "In. My. Call. Room," I wheezed.

"Stupid bitch."

I nodded, wide-eyed, gesturing at my throat.

"Fuck! Shit!" and he fumbled in his burqa with his left hand, still keeping his gun hand on Tucker.

I jerked, ready to duck down. Not that I could dodge a bullet, because he could easily murder me at his feet, but instinct gripped me.

I was trying to distract him from blasting a hole in Tucker's head, but Bastard might decide that we were too much trouble and assassinate both of us. A two-fer.

Bastard was still trying to grab something from inside his burqa, using his non-dominant hand. I couldn't see properly, because Tucker's body blocked most of my view, but he must have had a slit in the material to access his real clothes, or maybe a pocket inside the burqa itself, because he didn't have to lift up the floor-length covering. He just shifted his arms around a bit before he tossed something blue that hit the floor with a rattle.

A silver-topped Ventolin puffer in a blue dispenser.

Our kidnapper had asthma.

This could be useful.

"Try not to touch it," he said, which made no sense, because you insert the inhaler in your mouth.

I was stuck. I have this thing. I know this sounds crazy, because he could blow our heads off at any second, but I'm a bit grossed out by cold sores. I don't have them, and my risk of getting them is low because I hardly ever kiss anyone besides Ryan. Before I share a drink with my friends, I always ask about herpes. A total buzz kill, I know, but since a lot of them are doctors, they understand.

Also, I've never had to use an inhaler. No one in my family has asthma. Eczema, yes. We're often itching and scratching. At this exact moment, thanks to the drier winter air, I already had a rash on my hands, and a bit from the elastics around my ankles and waist, exacerbated by the stress of getting kidnapped. But none of us wheezes. The closest I've come is imitating taking puffers, for patients, but I've never actually put one in my mouth.

And now I'd have to share one with a killer. One that had fallen on the floor, no less.

Slowly, I bent over, still wheezing. I semi-deliberately fumbled the puffer. If the police burst in now, Tucker and I would be home free, and a real doctor could deliver Manouchka's baby.

The inhaler plunked on the ground again.

The cavalry did not arrive.

"Those are expensive, bitch! You putting me on?"

Oh, crap. My heart rate zoomed to 200. He had better instincts than I thought.

I dove for the inhaler, gasping and wheezing. For better effect, I should probably rasp out a *thank you*, but I couldn't bring myself to do that. Yet.

I stood up, trying to look as helpless as possible, while I uncapped the inhaler and held it to my lips. At least he was watching me instead of Tucker.

Bastard said to Tucker, "Open the door."

Tucker stepped forward and reached under the broken door to flip the lock from our side before he pushed the door remnant open, easy as you please.

Manouchka half-screamed.

"I'm. Coming," I wheezed at her, but I was staring at Tucker in Bastard's chokehold. Tucker's eyes looked like dark holes bored into his face. I'd never seen him so white. And his natural colour was pretty pasty to begin with.

Behind him, Bastard watched me with the gun rammed against Tucker's occiput.

Now was the time to open my mouth wide for the killer toilet puffer.

Don't think about herpes.

Don't think about hepatitis A. Or B or C, if he bled on it and you have a cut somewhere in your mouth.

You can deal with disease if you don't get your head blown off.

First things first. I exhaled as much as my lungs and tachycardia would allow.

I pushed down on the little blue canister, puffing medicine into my mouth and trying not to gag. It tasted a little bitter, but more than that, like the erasers I used to nibble on the top of my pencils. So, gross, even without worrying about infectious diseases.

I sucked the Ventolin into my lungs and held my breath for one. Two. Three. Four breaths—

Bastard shouted, "What'cha doing, bitch?"

I coughed and gagged again, expelling my breath. "I'm—counting to ten!" I said, barely remembering to wheeze in time.

"You're supposed to take two puffs, stupid!"

"No! You're supposed. To take. One puff. At a time and. Hold it. In. Your lungs!" I wheezed for effect, but this was ridiculous. I was giving a murderer asthma teaching. Better not to teach him and let him wheeze to death.

His brow furrowed. He seemed to be thinking it over, but then he heard voices in the hall and dragged the gun away from Tucker to aim it at me. "Just take your medicine and deliver the baby, bitch!"

Tucker opened his mouth, but Bastard brought the gun back on Tucker's forehead and said, "Not one word, Blondie."

I took my next puff, counting to ten as quickly as I could while Bastard's calculating eyes fixed on me.

I exhaled, still wheezing a little, and said, "I'm. Better now."

"You better be. C'mon, bitch. Go get the baby."

Aww. You talkin' to me? You shouldn't have.

I re-capped the inhaler and handed it to him, but he shook his head. "Put it in my pocket, bitch."

Right. He only had one hand, what with the gun and all. That didn't mean I wanted to touch him. I picked the puffer up with my fingertips, but then I realized his burqa was hanging down like a curtain. I couldn't access any of his pockets unless I reached inside the slit (not happening) or pulled up the hem (also gross).

Bastard shot me a crooked grin. "Get it in, bitch. I'm waiting."

Well. I wasn't going to fumble blindly inside the burqa. That was disgusting.

So I held my breath as I used two fingers of my other hand to draw his burqa up from the floor.

"That's it. You know it. You know where to put it."

Was it just me, or did that sound like a double entendre?

I glanced at Tucker's grim face.

It wasn't just me.

But I'd managed to raise the burqa above his hips, so I shoved the puffer into his right pocket as quickly as I could before I let the material drop back down to the ground.

Tucker exhaled in relief.

I took a few steps toward Manouchka, feeling light-headed and a little breathy, for real. Ventolin makes your heart race, your hands tremble, and your potassium drop slightly. Although most people who have asthma are otherwise young and healthy and can handle the side effects, I was hungry and on edge, which made me more brittle.

But Manouchka needed me. She was on all fours, on the bathroom tile, panting now.

Uh oh. I'd never delivered a baby on all fours. You have to mentally spin the anatomy around 180 degrees, which I'd have trouble doing at the best of times.

I started talking to her. I didn't want to croon like Bastard. I tried to keep a level tone, although my voice trembled, and I couldn't think of all the words in French. It was like my brain kept putting on the brakes every few words. "Manouchka. It's me. Dr. Hope Sze. You remember, I came to say hi earlier?" That sounded so stupid, I pressed on. "Your water broke. The baby's coming. I'm going to help you."

"*Non*," she said, low and drawing the syllable out and flat. At least she was talking.

I could sympathize. She'd used up so much of her self-control already.

"Why," she groaned in French, but I didn't think it was aimed at me. More a general why-me-Lord kind of expression.

I could see her legs shaking underneath the gown, and now that I was within arm's reach, I could see and smell the slightly bloody amniotic fluid puddling on the tile.

Wait. That wasn't just blood.

It was hard to say, in the dim light cast all the way from the lamp in other room, but blood sends out long tendrils. It's kind of mucousy. It likes to mix up with the amniotic fluid. But there was something else, more like yellowish flecks in the fluid.

This baby had meconium.

In the days before fetal monitors, there was one sign that the baby was in trouble, and that was meconium.

Chapter 16

Meconium, in case you don't know, is a polite word for baby poo.

Fetuses pee in utero all the time. They drink it and pee it out, over and over. It's normal.

They don't chew food like us. They don't have to. Mom is providing all the oxygen and nutrients. So they just store whatever minimal amount of poop they make in the first nine months, and the majority of them will push it out once they hit the bright lights and big city of the real world. That meconium will creep out of the rectum like a greenish black sausage, but that's the good news.

Because if they start pooping during birth, it's a distress call. It means they're not getting enough oxygen. And then, because they're still floating around inside of mom, practicing inhaling and exhaling, their caca gets into their lungs, and they can come out breathing fast, sometimes developing a fever and getting sicker and sicker.

I've only ever assisted healthy deliveries.

Sure, they had a few crash C-sections when I was a medical student, but the women sailed into the OR for neat, sterile surgery. Aside from the surprising difficulty of manually extracting the baby from the uterus (once, an obstetrician let me try, before I gave up and a nurse pushed the baby out instead), it was a joy.

But I've never wielded a retractor, let alone a knife, in a C-section.

Even if I felt up to it, we had no anaesthetic, except for a bit of Lidocaine in case we had to repair a vaginal tear.

I had to get the baby out the usual way.

I made sure to approach Manouchka's backside carefully, not treading on the small puddle of her amniotic fluid.

For a second, I wished Bastard would slip on the fluid, or on June's blood smeared in the centre of the main room, and hit his head. But with our luck, that would just set off his gun. And then he'd shoot us all in revenge.

"I'm a doctor," I repeated to Manouchka, in French. "I'm here to help. Let me get you out of the bathroom."

She stared at me, her eyes glazed.

That worried me. I'd seen that look before. In babies who have pneumonia, struggling to breathe, too tired to talk or cry, just gazing in the distance like a marathon runner, trying to stay alive. In a man with a heart attack, holding on his chest, his face furrowed in pain and his chest heaving.

She moaned. She must not have gotten an epidural, what with the panic going on.

I didn't have any medications for her, except for that bit of Lidocaine on the crash cart. Where's the chloroform when you need it?

I kid, I kid. Except then I could have tried to use it on Bastard.

"You'll feel better after you deliver," I told Manouchka. In French, a delivery is an *accouchement* and a miscarriage is a *fausse couche* (false delivery). So it sounded like I was trying to get her to lie down, or *se coucher*.

She groaned again.

She was probably ready to push right now, on the bathroom floor. I'd never checked her cervix, so for all I knew, she'd been eight centimetres when I'd said hello. Now the baby wanted out, and Manouchka was trying to hold it back.

I needed to check her. I said, "I have to wash my hands. Then I'll check the baby." The last thing she needed was a puerperal infection, or an infection in her lady bits.

I waggled my hands at Bastard and mimed washing them at the sink.

He said, "Hurry up, bitch."

Right.

As I stepped to the sink, I considered trying to get the fetal monitor back on her, because it would be a much better sign if the baby's heart rate was okay.

But Manouchka started rocking back and forth on her hands and knees in a way that screamed business.

Plus, I wasn't one hundred percent sure how to drag her over to the bed, get the belt on her, hook her up to the monitor, and convince Bastard to dance Tucker over to the screen in the main room so he could yell out the tracing to me. Just thinking about it made my head ache more.

Get the baby out. Now.

I bent at the waist to access the sink right behind the door, neighbouring the toilet. No Jacuzzis at St. Joe's, but at least I could access the cold, glorious water just by turning a tap. What a miracle.

I washed my hands, scrubbing between my fingers, and a quick scrape under my nails, in case Bastard wouldn't let me walk back across the room to grab some sterile gloves.

My throat ached. Touching water made my dehydration worse. I wanted to stick my mouth under the tap and drink, but I told myself, *You can do that later. After the baby comes out.*

I dried my hand on some white paper towels, fantasizing about sucking the water out of them—that's how desperate I felt—before I focused back on Manouchka, whose head was practically bowed down to the floor. Yes, the baby was coming any second now.

I glanced at Bastard and said, "May I have some sterile gloves and gel?"

Bastard repositioned his gun on Tucker's head and his arm around his neck before he met my eyes. The skin around Bastard's eyes gleamed with sweat, even in the dim light. His Adam's apple bobbed again, and he said, "What the fuck are you talking about?"

Tucker managed to nod at me. Even as a hostage, with his neck locked and the gun rubbing him a new bald spot, he was signaling me, *I got this.* He said to Bastard, in an only slightly-choked voice, "Sterile gloves, so we don't contaminate the baby. Lubricating gel, so we don't hurt the mother. We also have sterile gowns and face masks. Could I get those for Hope?" He tried to twist his head to his right, toward the delivery cart against the wall of the main room.

"You're not going anywhere," said Bastard.

"Could I get them myself?" I said. I'd never delivered a baby bare-handed, even though they used to do that all the time, I guess.

"No way," said Bastard, so I started to tiptoe around to Manouchka's nether regions, which she pointed toward the destroyed shower, away from the men.

Tucker's quiet voice cut through the air. "Please. You don't want this baby to get an infection, do you?"

"Aw, hell," said Bastard. "I'm coming with you. And if you try something funny, or if one of those bitches makes a run for it—"

"Gotcha," said Tucker, which probably wasn't the best choice of words, but he pointed at the hand sanitizer on the wall near the bathroom door, silently asking for permission to use it.

"Christ," said Bastard, but he two-stepped with Tucker and let him squirt his palms.

Bastard relinquished his neck hold only to seize Tucker's arm with his left hand and shove the gun into his back. It was strange seeing Bastard applying the same grips that he'd used on me while he growled, "I've got your covered. Don't even think about it."

"I'm not thinking," said Tucker. He sounded calmer already, now that he wasn't getting a gun noogie anymore. He crossed over to the delivery cart and said, "I'm unlocking the wheels. That way, I can just roll it over to the bathroom."

"Whatever!" said Bastard, but he watched Tucker nudge the little wheel locks. Bastard followed on his heels as he pushed it in front of the ruined bathroom door.

I liked that. It felt like Tucker was giving Manouchka some privacy to give birth, so she wasn't as exposed to Bastard's eyes and gun. And if/when the cavalry busted in, we also had a shield.

A shield only a little over waist-high, mind you, but it felt like some protection, since Manouchka hunkered down on the ground.

Tucker stopped about two feet away from the door, leaving us enough room to elbow our way out and dash for the exit if we needed to.

I liked the way my man thought.

He ripped open a pack of gloves for me and laid them out on the cart, even emptying a pack of Muco gel on the paper cover that had enveloped the gloves.

Nurses help you like that. If I had to open the gel myself, I'd contaminate my sterile gloves. Tucker had obviously paid attention. He always paid attention. Even though it was a tiny thing, it made me love him even more.

When I reached for the gloves, though, he shook his head and ripped open a blue gown for me.

I reached my arms through the plasticized polyester sleeves. Tucker tied the strings around my neck and waist. I couldn't help thinking that some men get to zip their women into ball gowns, but Tucker got me into a surgical gown with a gun at his back and a baby practically at our feet.

He held each glove at the wrist so I could plunge my hand into it, wiggling my fingers into each slot.

It sounds like a long time, but actually, he got it all done in less than a minute.

Just one more reason to adore him.

Even Manouchka moaned a little less with Tucker nearby. Thank God he'd imprisoned himself with us.

Bastard said, "What's the hold-up? Quit dicking around!"

Ugh. The less he spoke, the better. But since he was the one holding the gun, Tucker held his hands up and walked backwards, away from us and toward Bastard, saying, "Everything's ready to go" while I turned to Manouchka and her meconium baby.

Chapter 17

Newly sanitized, with my sterile gloves in the air, I stepped toward the toilet and frowned. I said to Manouchka in French, "Do you want to deliver in the bed?"

"Noooooooooon," she groaned, turning her face toward the toilet paper dispenser on the far wall.

So be it. We were lucky to have made it this far alive.

Belatedly, I wished I'd asked Tucker to either turn on the bathroom light or flip open the back end of Manouchka's gown. Otherwise, I was going to contaminate my gloves as soon as I tried to expose her vagina. But there was nothing I could do about it except take a step backwards and hit the light switch with my right elbow.

Manouchka cried out as the yellow fluorescent lights flickered above us. I squinted, too. The light was like an assault on my previously dilated pupils. But I had to see. Well, I didn't have to—I'm sure experienced doctors and midwives could deliver blindfolded—but five deliveries, belatedly including the one on my psychiatry rotation, did not anoint me into that exalted crew.

I sucked in my gut to make myself as skinny as possible while I scooted between the toilet and the shower wall remnants, trying not to step on Manouchka or her amniotic fluid.

The thin, foot-wide puddle partially hidden under Manouchka's big belly did indeed contain yellow-green meconium as well as blood. Gah.

I tip-toed past it, toward her hind end. She shifted a little bit, to let me in between her bum and the toilet, but not much. She was losing control now, less interested in accommodating me than in getting the baby out.

I said, "Um, I need to expose the...region." I'm not sure how to say things tactfully in English, let alone French. "Could you lift up your gown?"

She moaned and shifted her hips from side to side.

"I can help," said Tucker.

Bastard said, "You've helped enough, motherfucker."

I squatted sideways, grinding plastic shards under my soles as I sank between the wall and the toilet, as I used my left elbow to nudge the gown above her waist.

"I'm going to check your cervix. I'm using my right hand to touch you," I said. I can speak French fluently, but trying to speak medically makes me sound pretty stilted.

My index and middle fingers were already covered in sterile goo. I used those to reach into the small gap between Manouchka's legs.

I heard Bastard suck his breath in. I had to smile to myself. He might wave a big gun around, but if I said the word vagina, he didn't know what to do with himself.

Something to file away for later, along with his blue puffer. Bastard's Achilles heels: asthma plus fear of birth canals. Not sure how to work that, unless I could sic a giant set of women's genitals on him and set off a fatal asthma attack.

"I'm touching your thigh with the back of my left hand," I told Manouchka, belatedly rotating sideways so my left shoulder could venture forth and risk contamination first. I always narrate internal exams, and in this case, the more I could scare Bastard, the better. "Now I'm separating your thighs."

For a second, Manouchka started to slam her legs together, but she forced herself to relax a few inches.

I shifted forward between her legs and I maintained her legs open with my left forearm before I started to touch her with my right hand. Honestly, the labia always feel like a bunch of folds between the legs, but in advanced labour, when the vagina gapes open, I tend to plunge my hand in and start poking around.

In this case, I couldn't see anything, from my back-hurting angle, but my fingers marched past the labial folds, sank into the vaginal mucous membranes—not what I was looking for. I wanted to feel the baby's head and the circle of the cervix.

Now, some skilled people can practically tell time in there. *Okay, here's the anterior fontanelle...baby's facing this way...I've got a nose...the baby wants to be called Adam...*

Not me. I'm a newbie. Luckily, my index and middle fingers ran right into the baby's head no more than two inches inside her vagina.

The baby was coming now.

I pressed her left hip with my left elbow, trying to angle Manouchka away from the toilet and toward the far wall. Really, I'd like her to deliver in bed. Not because I was King Louis XVI who wanted to watch my mistresses give birth (apparently, that's how it came into fashion to have women give birth lying down), but because we were stuck in the dirtiest, most cramped corner of the germ-infested hospital. But I couldn't make her walk across the room now. So I just said, "Push!"

Manouchka glanced over her shoulder at me with hazy eyes. She didn't bear down. I'm not sure what bearing down looks like, exactly, on all fours, but I'm pretty sure it's not hanging out with your mouth open and your back swayed.

She was losing it, at the worst time.

"The baby needs to come out now," I said, in French, trying to draw her eyes on mine and take her out of her cocoon. "Push."

She shook her head. Her ponderous belly swayed from side to side as well.

"Please," I told her. "Your baby will get sick." I didn't want to tell her that it was already sick.

"Get it out so you can get my baby," called Bastard.

My shoulders tensed, but I ignored him. He could shoot us, or not shoot us, but right now, I had a job to do.

I needed Manouchka to help me, though. Why was she so out of it? When I first met her with June, she'd been tired and pushing, but alert. Was she shocked by the bloodshed, or could it be something else?

Like eclampsia?

I've seen pre-eclampsia, which is not only high blood pressure in pregnancy, but evidence of kidney impairment (swollen hands and eyes, protein in the urine). But full-blown eclampsia is a medical emergency because the woman starts seizing. Plus, I seemed to remember that eclampsia was more common in black women.

Holy fucking shit.

Chapter 18

What if she started seizing with a baby on its way out, on all fours, in the bathroom?

I knew the treatment was magnesium, but it wasn't something we kept tucked in a corner of a room just in case. I'd have to order it. Someone would have to bring it to our room, Bastard would have to allow it through the door, and we'd have to load it in a syringe.

Manouchka didn't even have an intravenous lock. It's part of our "look, we're family-friendly, just like midwives" policy. Normal childbirths don't require IV's. Too bad her birth had done a 180.

I'd already seen Tucker insert IV's like a champ, but did we have any saline locks or IV bags and poles in the room? Probably not.

Focus, Hope.

I squinched my eyes shut and shook off the doubts. She wasn't seizing yet. I didn't see any signs of high blood pressure, if only because she wasn't wearing a BP cuff. If she seized, Tucker and I would deal with it. But until then, *get the baby out.*

"Manouchka!" I snapped, before I consciously gentled my voice. "Listen to me. Push your baby out. Now."

She shook her head and lowered her head toward the ground. But at least that meant that, if I wedged myself with my bum practically inside the broken shower stall, her hind end was relatively front and centre for me for what I assumed was her next contraction.

I started massaging her perineum, that skin between the vagina and rectum. One of the obstetricians was very into that. He said that it reduced tears. The one woman I massaged with him didn't tear, so maybe it worked, but what I really wanted was to bring Manouchka's attention back to her baby through the power of touch. Even with my limited experience, I was pretty sure that with a few good pushes, she could get this babe out.

I used my lubricated fingers to stretch her vaginal opening, drawing the elastic skin toward me, moving from 2 o'clock to 10 o'clock and back again.

Manouchka tried to inch away from me, but I said, "Please! Your baby's coming!" I could see the infant's creamy brown skin now, surging toward the air, and maybe even a little bit of hair, under the harsh fluorescent light, although her body cast a shadow. "*Poussez! Poussez, poussez, poussez!*"

She gave a mighty effort that pushed her bum toward me, but then she sagged forward. Her contraction was over.

I bent over her head. "You're so close," I told her quietly, intimately, as if were just the two of us. No men, no gun. I was trying to recreate the spell she'd woven with June. "Your baby wants to see you. I could see the hair."

Her head perked up. She could hear me. I was getting through.

"Your baby wants to come out now. I want you to try as hard as you can on your next contraction. I know you're tired, but if you can just get your baby out, I can help it breathe."

"And then he'll kill it!" she shouted.

Even if Bastard didn't understand French, her tone was clear.

She was right. I tried to keep my voice steady. "Yes. Maybe. But he might kill us either way. Your baby...needs more oxygen." It was hard to explain meconium without getting too technical. "I can help your baby once it comes out. Can you push?"

She shook her head, but the next contraction hit. She lowered her head and started to pant while I massaged her perineum again. And then I remembered one other thing.

I called to Tucker, "Turn the incubator on." I'd forgotten to do that, with all the excitement.

Tucker's brown eyes lit up. He started to turn, but Bastard cocked the gun at him and said, "Where d'you think you're going, buddy?"

I turned back to Manouchka. The baby's head abruptly came down enough that I glimpsed and felt the crown of the head. I yelled out loud with joy, but when she gave up, the baby's head shot back up the vagina.

Still, a vast improvement.

She crouched on the tile floor, legs shaking.

"Good! That's it! Good job. One more push like that, and you should get the baby out."

Meanwhile, I could hear Tucker educating Bastard. "We'll need somewhere to keep the baby warm."

"What the fuck?"

"The baby's weak. We need to keep him or her warm, just like inside mom. I have to turn on the incubator. You can come with me."

"You're not going nowhere!"

"It's right there." Tucker pointed at the incubator directly to their right, at the far end of the room. "I just need to turn it on. I should check the equipment, too."

"You go where I say you go, motherfucker!"

I prayed that Tucker could reason with him.

Manouchka cried out in terror, and my heart clutched. She was losing faith, and part of me wanted to throw myself in front of Tucker like a human shield. Bastard hadn't shot anyone in the past few minutes, and he seemed to believe that he had to clamp down on Tucker to prove his manhood. Danger, danger.

But Manouchka and the baby were my priority now. We had to get the baby out.

"We'll take care of him here, if we have to," I told her. "I can deliver him and place him on your stomach." That's standard, at St. Joe's. Deliver the baby and place it right on Mommy's tummy to cut the cord, unless the baby's in respiratory distress.

If the baby wasn't breathing, I had 30 seconds to dry it, suction the nose and mouth, and stimulate it.

But if I remembered my resuscitation properly, after those 30 seconds, I'd have to bag the baby.

Or was it intubation first, since the baby had passed meconium? That sounded right. Stick a tube down the baby's throat and suction out all the yellow/green/black stuff.

Oh, crap. Tucker better remember the algorithm better than I did.

Regardless, I needed a warm, safe place to safely assess the baby's condition without causing an infection.

But if I had to resuscitate this baby on mommy's belly, hunched over a toilet, I'd do it.

Tucker was telling Bastard, "If we practice on this baby, we'll be even better at helping yours," and I prayed that he'd go for that.

Meanwhile, the next contraction hit Manouchka.

She curled over, fighting the pain, before she arched her back with a scream.

I bent over her and yelled, "Push! Push! Push! You can do it! Yes, Manouchka! That's it! GoGoGoGoGo!" The last bit was in English. Even French people say GoGoGoGoGo.

I thought I heard the guys moving out of sight, crossing around the corner to the incubator, but I couldn't spare a glance at them because the baby's head started to ooze out.

Because Manouchka was on all fours, the baby's head came out facing me instead of the ground, the way they do when a woman is lying in bed. I jerked in surprise before I smiled at the forehead emerging.

My first instinct was to keep massaging her perineum, but with the head sailing toward me, it would squish my fingers. I gave up and used both hands to catch the baby.

I'd already had one episode where the medical student thought I was going to grab the baby, and I thought he was going to get it, and the baby nearly hit my thighs before I caught it and scooped it into the mother's lap with a bigger-than-usual smile, saying, "Here you go!"

Manouchka grabbed her own knees and curled her chin toward her chest.

"Yes! That's it, exactly!" I'd forgotten to coach her on that part, but either the nurse had told her earlier, or Mother Nature had kicked in with a vengeance. Manouchka was bearing down and forcing that baby out, probably oblivious to my cheerleading.

The baby's eyes, nose, and bluish lips were now squeezing toward me.

I wasn't panicked about the baby's colour. In my limited experience, they all look a bit cyanosed during delivery, but pink up shortly afterward.

Then the whole head emerged, and I realized that the umbilical cord was wrapped around the baby's neck.

Chapter 19

I'd seen this once before, but I had no equipment on me.

"Tucker! I need two clamps and a pair of scissors!" I yelled. "Cord around the neck!" Even while I spoke, I shoved a finger between the umbilical cord and the baby's neck. It was just loose enough allow my finger, so as long as I kept it here, the cord wouldn't strangle the baby. No wonder the poor thing had started pooping in utero.

"I'm on it," Tucker said.

"What is it?" said Bastard, and for once, he wasn't swearing.

"Push, Manouchka," I said, keeping my finger inside the cord. I could feel it pulsating with the baby's heartbeat.

I felt like the kid with his finger in a dike. I'd reached out for the cord automatically with my right hand, so I'd have to catch the baby with my left, but that was better than nothing. And, at least with Manouchka on all fours, the baby couldn't fall far.

Manouchka's head jerked, drawing my attention to her.

Don't seize on me. Don't you fucking seize on me with the cord wrapped around the baby's neck.

"Baby's in trouble," said Tucker, and I heard him grabbing stuff from the delivery cart. Thank God he was the one on that. I didn't know what was where, on that cart. I just prayed that he'd had time to warm up the incubator, in case the baby stopped breathing.

Tucker hurried to my side, ripping open a tray wrapped in a green sheet. I glanced over and snatched the nearest pair of forceps, barely noticing Bastard, who barged into the bathroom behind Tucker, still waving around his ubiquitous gun.

This close, Bastard wouldn't miss, but if I went out, I'd go out saving this baby's life.

Manouchka squeezed out the baby's shoulders. There's usually a slight pause after the head, before the shoulders emerge, and that's when we clamp. But because I didn't have the tray beside me, we lost those few precious seconds. I'd have to do this on the move, like I was in a video game.

An instant later, the torso eased out, the baby's arms folded over its chest.

I moved forward to catch the baby's body on my gowned-up knees while I clamped the cord awkwardly, with my left hand.

Meanwhile, the rest of the baby was coming out, and I dropped the clamp to catch the baby with both hands.

Tucker's two hands shot forward, each wielding a metal instrument.

He clamped the cord an inch from the first and, with his other hand, severed the umbilical cord with scissors.

No going back now. The mom was no longer giving oxygenated blood and taking away deoxygenated blood from her babe.

Sink or swim time. But at least the baby wouldn't strangle on the cut cord.

Immediately, Tucker started suctioning the baby's mouth with a blue bulb suction, the way you're supposed to in a meconium delivery. Whaddaguy.

I didn't have time to worry about Tucker's non-sterile hands, because I was too busy catching the baby before it hit the floor. Face-up, with his skinny legs flexed at the hip, it was easy to see his reddish, swollen testicles and miniature, slightly bulbous penis.

A baby boy. Just like Casey's.

"Is he alive?" Manouchka called, her voice reverberating around the small bathroom.

"Yes," I said, but my eyes were surveying his chest, which was moving too fast. Bellows breathing, they call it, because their miniature chests are pumping away, hyperinflating and deflating fast enough to fan red-hot flames in a fireplace.

His face wrinkled up, and his mouth opened soundlessly.

Cry, baby, cry. Breathe and cry.

Tucker suctioned his little nose next. The nostrils were flaring even without the noxious bulb suction, but he was too small and weak to get away from two determined doctors.

Tucker and I both knew we had to get this baby under the lights. If his breathing didn't recover with this suctioning, we'd have to intubate him and suction the meconium out of his trachea.

"Let me see him," said Manouchka, pushing upward to sit on her bum, and after a second's hesitation, I placed the baby in her lap. That was the least I could do. But I murmured a warning, "He needs to breathe."

She touched his face. She stared into his wide, dark eyes as if she could see the world in them before she cradled him tightly against her chest.

The baby continued to gasp, but his arms folded up against his own chest and he seemed to fit against her.

Even with the baby breathing too fast, even with Bastard hovering over us with death in his eyes and in his hands, this was the most beautiful moment I could remember between a mother and a child. I would never forget that silent, desperate tenderness.

I wanted to hold them both close and guard them with my body.

The most maternal I get is with my brother Kevin. He's only eight, although his ninth birthday is coming right up. I had to grit my teeth to force back any tears, thinking about him and if I'd survive until his birthday next week.

If I died, he'd remember it every time he blew out his birthday candles.

Don't think that way, Hope.

I turned back toward the baby. He still hadn't cried. And even though they don't have to cry, that plus his obvious gasping made me too nervous to let them stay nestled up like that.

Tucker spoke first. "We need to help him breathe. We'll get him back as soon as possible. I promise."

Manouchka touched her baby's face. She murmured something in his ear, not seeming to hear us.

Tucker and I exchanged a look. We didn't want to have to fight her for him. She'd been through enough. On the other hand, we couldn't let her baby die on our watch.

Bastard cleared his throat. Even he didn't want to intrude, which just goes to show how holy this felt.

Either that, or he was politely warning us before he massacred us all.

I murmured to Tucker, "Wash your hands. I'll talk to her."

He cast me a slightly dubious look, but stood up and ran the water at the sink, while I told Manouchka, "Your baby is breathing too fast. He has...caca in his lungs. We need to get it out. We might have to put a tube down his throat."

"Non!" She held him against her.

I stared into the baby's eyes. He was gazing back at me, observing me from the protective cocoon of her arms, but still breathing harder and faster than I would like.

We all had to take an obstetric and neonatal resuscitation course, but none of them had prepared us for being held hostage while the mother refused to let us treat the baby. Maybe I could write an addendum on that, if we survived.

She offered the baby her breast. The baby's mouth opened, maybe to drink, maybe to sob. He managed to emit a weak cry that was almost drowned out by the sound of Tucker drying his hands on paper towels.

"See!" said Manouchka. "He's just hungry."

"Look at his ribs sticking out when he's breathing," I said. "Look at how round his nostrils are. He's using his stomach muscles. He's breathing, yes, but he's getting tired. And when he gets too tired, he'll stop breathing, and we'll have to breathe for him."

Tucker squatted beside Manouchka, blocking out the light beaming into the baby's face. The baby's mouth opened and closed while she tried to shove her breast in his mouth. I'm no newborn expert, but I didn't think he was getting any breast milk. Tucker said, in French, "Congratulations, Mama."

She hardly glanced at him. She kept her head down, gazing at her baby and hunching her shoulders. Her arms formed a cage to keep us away. But I thought maybe her cheeks rounded in a barely perceptible smile.

"You worked so hard to get him here, under the worst circumstances. What's his name?"

Aw, geez. Tucker was using his psych superpower again, establishing a rapport. Part of me still wanted to snatch the baby like a football and break for the incubator. But I watched her body shift slightly toward my man, and I thanked any random deity that Tucker was here. I've got the skills, or some of them, but it's no good if you alienate your patients.

"I haven't decided yet," she said to Tucker. "God will tell me."

So she was religious, probably Christian. Maybe not surprising at a place called St. Joseph's Hospital.

How could we use that to our advantage? I racked my brain for appropriate Bible quotes.

If only I could call a friend. Ryan could utter a dozen pithy phrases that would convince her to airlift the baby into the incubator.

Tucker said, "Yes. 'The wolf will live with the lamb; the leopard will lie down with the young goat. The calf and the lion will graze together, and a little child will lead them.'"

He said it in English. I'm not sure if Manouchka understood it or not, but I only realized it was a Bible quote because of the last phrase. It was in a movie starring Halle Berry about giving her son Isaiah up for adoption, so I even knew that it was from the book of Isaiah.

Maybe that's how Tucker knew it, too, since I'd never heard him talk about religion until now.

I hadn't heard the whole quote before, and I wasn't sure what to make of it, but it sure felt like we were hanging out with a metaphorical wolf. (Although, as an animal lover, I should point out that wolves are an important and respectful part of the ecosystem, unlike, say, most humans.)

Manouchka blinked at Tucker, and then she said, "*Un enfant...*"

A child. "Yes," Tucker and I said at the same time. If we'd been kids, I would have said, "Jinx." But we'd had enough jinxes.

Manouchka shifted from side to side and said, "It hurts."

She pointed at her belly, underneath her still-heaving baby. I belatedly realized that not only was she sitting on her sore ladybits, but she hadn't delivered her placenta.

Chapter 20

There's a normal gap between delivering a baby and delivering a placenta. After all, you want the placenta to keep up its good work as long as possible. It can take fifteen minutes or more for it to come out naturally.

Normally, we speed things up by applying gentle traction on the umbilical cord, and the placenta slowly detaches itself from the uterus and plops out through the vagina.

But this time, because we'd been so worried about the baby—I decided to call him Isaiah, in my mind—we hadn't considered her placenta at all.

"What's the hold-up here?" Bastard groused. "You got the kid out. Let's go find Casey."

My heart contracted. I'd forgotten about him for a moment.

Tucker answered, still squatting by Manouchka but gazing up at Bastard. "The baby's sick. We need to take care of him in the incubator. And Manouchka still has to deliver her placenta."

"What the fuuuuuuuck," said Bastard. But he wasn't pointing the gun at us, for once. He started pacing back and forth just inside the bathroom, hemming us in, but he wasn't directly holding us hostage.

Was it possible that one of us could grab the baby and make a break for the door?

I was seriously tempted.

The bathroom door was less than ten feet from the main exit.

And what if we split up, one of us with Manouchka and the other with the baby?

One of our two teams might make a successful break. Maybe. If Bastard was sufficiently distracted, with bad aim, and we ran like a tornado.

Too bad the bathroom didn't have a secret exit into the hallway, but this wasn't Harry Potter. One of us would have to dash out the bathroom door, past Bastard, and throw open the door to the hallway while carrying a newborn.

It was risky. Very risky.

Say Tucker tackled Bastard alone and managed to distract him for a few crucial seconds. Even so, Bastard could recover immediately and shoot all four of us, just pick us off, in less than a minute. Even if the cavalry was waiting right outside.

Pro scoop-and-run argument: this baby was sick. Tucker and I had done okay, but it would be even better to get him into warm, sterile conditions, in expert hands, with Mom at the ready to cuddle and breastfeed. To do that, we needed to get Isaiah and Manouchka out.

Stay-and-play argument: we did have an incubator and two doctors here who could bag or intubate this baby without any shots being fired. Short term, that was the safer option.

But how safe was it to stay cooped up with a psycho?

Should we bolt now, while we still had the nerve and energy? The longer we waited, the more Bastard would swing from erratic to deranged territory.

Meanwhile, Tucker spun his words around Manouchka like they were the only two people in the room. "He's beautiful. We need to take care of him. Will you let us help him breathe?" He was staring at her, so I couldn't try to telegraph my pro-running thoughts to him.

She was more likely to give her baby to Tucker than to me, and I didn't see him making a break with a newborn. Not if it meant leaving me and Manouchka here.

Chances were, either all of us would get out, or none of us.

I glanced at Bastard, at the broken doorway, and tried to measure the distance to the exit.

Manouchka groaned. "Just you," she said to Tucker.

Hey. Was she saying what I thought she was saying?

Before I could prickle, she groaned and handed him her baby.

Tucker gently scooped Isaiah in his newly-washed hands. I'd never watched him hold a newborn before, and my heart stabbed with pain, drinking in his sweaty blond head bent over Isaiah's skinny, flaring chest and his stick-like limbs. Tucker was a natural. He should have ten kids. He shouldn't be stuck with a murderer and me.

"Thank you. I'll take good care of him," said Tucker, and rocked back on his heels to balance himself before he rose up from his squat and faced Bastard, who blocked the doorway.

Bastard said, "I need you to look after Casey." He didn't sound really angry, more like he felt like he had to stand his ground. But that could be dangerous, too.

"I will," said Tucker. "Just let me get this little one settled first."

Bastard lifted his gun up. It was pointing at the ceiling, not at Tucker and Isaiah, but I gasped.

My mouth was still gaping open when Bastard aimed the gun at me. I pressed my lips together, and suddenly I understood the term "right between the eyes." It was almost like I could feel a bullet punching a third eye between my eyebrows.

Bastard said, "No funny business,"

"No funny business," I agreed. My dreams of sprinting out the door collapsed.

Bastard nodded agreement and shoved the delivery cart backwards to allow Tucker and Isaiah out of the bathroom. Bastard was still lined up with a good sight of both the bathroom door and the incubator, so even though theoretically he now had to split his attention between two different sets of people, I had no doubt he could perforate all of us before we all got out of gunshot range.

"Oh," said Manouchka. "It feels…"

I turned back to her, and she was hunkering down now, like she was hovering over a squat toilet, except it was the placenta squeezing out of her vagina and hitting the floor.

"Oh. Jesus," said Bastard.

"I've got it!" I said, scooping up the still-warm placenta. Normally, we throw it in a sterile, stainless steel bowl, but Tucker hadn't brought me one, just the clamps and scissors now scattered on the floor.

Maybe it was only in my mind, but the placenta filling my hands felt like it was pulsating with a rich warmth.

"That stinks," said Bastard, and he didn't sound too good.

I wanted to say to him, *You know what stinks? You potentially killing all of us. That smells worse than amniotic fluid.* Now I thought back on my innocent self, from an hour ago, worrying about mild odours in the birthing room. I wanted to yell at that Hope, *those were the good times! When you were free and no one pointed a gun at your head! Laissez les bons temps rouler!*

But I knew what was bothering him. I can't even describe the wet, earthy, amniotic smell of a placenta. Really heavy and dense, especially inches from your face. I've examined placentas before—one obstetrician likes to inspect them and makes sure there are no missing bits, and if the baby is post-dates, sometimes you see calcifications, like the placenta is getting elderly. It's always kind of fun to play with the ruptured amniotic sac where the baby used to live.

Normally, I'd do a cord blood gas, sticking a needle into one of the umbilical arteries and sending off the blood to prove that the baby got enough oxygen at birth. There are a lot of lawsuits in OB. Everyone wants the perfect baby, and disabled infants are expensive. Solution: sue the doctor.

But you need to send an arterial blood gas right away. I don't know exactly how fast, but a nurse or orderly always runs off in a panic. By the time we escaped from this hellmouth, any blood gas would be useless. Maybe I should just forget about the blood gas. If Manouchka sued us, I'd deal with it then. Lawsuits were for the living.

On the other hand, drawing blood might distract him. Especially since he hated blood and wombs. And a needle in hand could double as a weapon, if it had to. So I said, "Could I send a blood sample to the lab?"

"No one's going nowhere," said Bastard. He aimed his gun at Manouchka for a second before he trained it back on me.

Right. I was not going to brave a bullet over a blood gas. So now I didn't need the placenta anymore.

My first instinct was to dump it in the toilet, but that seemed sacrilegious and might plug up the plumbing. This placenta was a good double handful for me, smaller than a soccer ball, but still sizeable and dripping blood besides. St. Joe's pipes probably have trouble handling some bowel movements, let alone a placenta.

Bastard made a small noise, and I realized that the placenta might come in handy. He hated blood.

Maybe I could lob it in his face, like a bomb of hemoglobin.

Bastard's hand shook slightly on the trigger, and I dismissed that thought, too. If I pushed him too far, he'd shoot us.

Still, I didn't want to sling it in the garbage. It seemed as blasphemous as a toilet, even though I think hospitals do throw out placentas, unless the moms want to take them home.

So I tossed the placenta into the sink. It made a wet, smacking sound and blood spattered, spraying the white ceramic walls of the sink, the stainless steel faucet and a bit of the white wall as well.

Gah. So much for my germ phobia.

Bastard made a gagging noise and took a step back.

"Sorry," I lied. I turned back to Manouchka. "Are you okay?" For some reason, the chorus from Michael Jackson's "Smooth Criminal" reverberated in my head, but I tried to block it out. I really wanted to finish up with her and help Tucker with Isaiah.

She pointed to her crotch, and Bastard said, "Aww, God" and faded two more steps away from the doorway. Which gave us a little breathing room, but brought him closer to Tucker and Isaiah.

I had to finish up with Manouchka. Fast.

I said, "May I examine you?"

She sat back on her bum and spread her legs apart, revealing the clotted blood between them.

CHAPTER 21

Okay.

I'd just finished mentally making fun of Bastard for flinching, but I'm no expert at repairing birth lacerations.

I haven't seen that many, and the whole process seems kind of mysterious. The doctor picks up some dissolving suture, and the next thing you know, he's dipping a curved needle into the woman's vagina.

And maybe it wasn't a vaginal tear. Maybe her uterus was hemorrhaging. I'd have to get a good look, and ideally a good feel, to be sure.

"You okay, Tucker?" I called out.

"Yes," he said. "I intubated and suctioned him. He's coming around."

"Good job," I said, even though I was slightly jealous that he'd gotten to intubate a newborn. I've never done that.

Manouchka clutched at my hands. "My baby. My baby is okay?"

"Yes," I said. "Dr. Tucker's taking good care of him. Now let's take care of you. I just have to change my gloves, because these ones aren't sterile anymore."

Even as I was talking, I couldn't help dwelling on the fact that Tucker got the cool interventions and I got the uterus. That might sound like I'm hating on women, but the chances of intubating a newborn at a community hospital like St. Joe's are minuscule. We do rotate through neonatal care later in residency, but even so. I could sew up fifty vaginas before I so much as glimpsed a distressed baby, and even then, the other residents might shove me aside while they pulled the superhero moves.

I shook myself. There's no use keeping score when you're staring into the maw of death. I was losing it.

I turned back to Manouchka. "Could I get you into a bed?" I gestured to the wall blocking us from the bed next to Tucker, in the main room. "I want to keep you clean. And you're shivering." It was true. Her legs trembled, which is not uncommon, from the effort of labour, but her arms shook, too.

She looked sick. Not seizure-like, necessarily, but exhausted.

She hesitated before she made eye contact with me and jerked her chin. "*He's* there."

I glanced up. Bastard had only taken about three steps outside the bathroom door, so he was still standing guard on us in the bathroom, yet maintaining his direct line to monitor Tucker and Isaiah at the incubator. He blockaded all of us from the main door.

As if sensing our eyes, Bastard rotated his head toward us. "What's the hold-up, ladies?" he said, making me want to smack him. Again. Still.

"She's bleeding," I said.

"Well, fix it!" he said, but his throat convulsed as he swallowed.

Yep. Squeamish.

How could I use this against him?

Nothing came to mind, except that a bed sounded better and better for Manouchka. Not only was it cleaner and warmer than the frozen bathroom floor, but it brought us closer to her baby and Tucker, as well as the resuscitation cart.

In the meantime, though, I scooped the scissors and both pairs of forceps off the floor. They were dirty, but I couldn't just leave them there for us to slip on and stab ourselves.

"What's that?" said Bastard.

I showed him. The scissors were obviously bloody enough for him to spot from the hallway, and he said, "Jesus."

"We might need these," I said.

"For what?" he said, and I couldn't answer him, exactly.

A Kelly forceps is about as long as my forearm, mildly curved at the end to hold on to whatever you need, but each of the two "arms" is narrower than a skinny French fry. They're like metal fingers, really, designed to reach someplace so high or deep or narrow, your fingers can't make it. You can squeeze the handle part together when you reach the area you want, locking and clamping your tissue in place.

I've used them to separate muscle fibres when I'm inserting a chest tube. Obstetricians can use them to clamp the umbilical cords, as we had, although we usually apply opaque white plastic clips on the cord. Or we'll use the forceps to reach inside a vagina, uterus, or other segment of the abdominal cavity.

The metal clattered together as I bundled the instruments in my palm.

The scissors were more hefty than the dainty pairs you find on a fine instrument tray. The first time I cut an umbilical cord, I was surprised by how...chewy it was. You need a fair amount of force to first cut and then drive through that rope of tissue. Honestly, cutting the cord reminded me of the time my grandfather made me eat a pig's ear at a Chinese restaurant. My teeth just bounced and bounced off the cartilage before I managed to chew it into fine enough bits, swallow it, and swear to myself, *Never again.*

Anyway, I stooped and wrapped the instruments up in the formerly sterile green towel Tucker had thrown on the floor. I told Bastard, "They have to be autoclaved."

That part was true. You have to sterilize them before another patient will use them.

"What does that mean?" said Bastard.

"We have to clean them for the next patient. We don't want to give anyone HIV or hepatitis, right?" I looked him straight in the eye, willing him to connect the dots that the next woman could be Casey, or his sister, or his mother.

His lips seemed to move under the material of the burqa, almost in a silent snarl, before he backed away from us.

I tucked the bundle under my arm and used my other arm to help Manouchka off the floor. Her legs buckled once, but she grabbed on to me and levered herself into a standing position, even though I thought she looked a bit pale, under her melanin. She just didn't want to show weakness in front of Bastard. Probably a good policy.

"You'll be closer to Isaiah this way," I said, smiling and trying to distract her.

She frowned at me.

It took me a second to figure out why. "Isaiah. Your baby. I'm sorry, that's what I was calling him in my head. I mean your son."

She nodded and leaned her weight on me. We took a few shuffling steps.

She was a trooper, all right. I've never given birth in my life, let alone on my hands and knees, with a gun in my face. I squeezed her arm against my side—I didn't have a free hand because of the instruments—and said, "You're very brave."

She kept her head up, looking toward the incubator instead of me. I was just noise.

After a few steps, something on the ground caught my eye.

I spied a few spots of blood, smaller than a dime, but fresh blood. Not June's.

Manouchka was hemorrhaging.

Chapter 22

"Move it," said Bastard.

I pointed silently to the floor. Since we'd paused, a few more drops of blood dripped on the ground, directly below Manouchka. Now that I looked closer, I could make out blood tracking down her legs.

"*Je*sus," said Bastard, recoiling, even though he was at least three feet away from us, and June's blood was already smeared into the main room's beige tile floor.

What, like assassinating people was supposed to stay neat 'n' tidy?

Manouchka ignored him. She leaned on my arm. Somehow, it felt Biblical, like she was weary and in need of shelter. Which she wasn't going to get anytime soon.

I helped her toward the bed. It was only maybe ten feet away, but it felt longer, because of her fatigue and Bastard reluctantly moving out of our path. Unfortunately, he migrated toward Tucker and Isaiah, and I felt her tense just before she said, in French, "My baby."

Bébé sounds an awful lot like baby, so Bastard had no trouble translating that one. "Don't worry," he said. "I ain't touching your nigger baby."

Her head reared back like a dragon about to exhale flames upon him.

I smoldered, too, but my hand flexed a warning on her arm. He was still the man with the gun.

"How's the baby, Tucker?" I called, trying to sidetrack Manouchka as well as get a status update.

On cue, Isaiah uttered a weak, warbling cry.

"Great! His Apgar's 7 now. That's a lot better. He really pinked up."

Manouchka started toward the incubator, and I debated for a second if I should ask her to lie down first. I sympathized with her need to see her son. However, fainting in the middle of the room wouldn't do us any good.

"Maybe you could lie down and Tucker will bring him to you?" I suggested, but she lunged toward the incubator and said, "My baby. David."

Oh. I guessed it wasn't going to be Isaiah, then. Too bad. I kind of liked it.

She swayed like she was about to topple, and I nearly dropped the cloth-wrapped forceps and scissors out from under my arm. I lobbed them under the bed instead so I could grab her with both hands, from behind.

In the meantime, to my astonishment, Bastard had instinctively reached out to catch her.

I hugged her from behind with one knee between her legs, but Bastard clutched her from the front and side, so they were almost face to face and surprisingly intimate.

It reminded me of a much happier time when two campers had yelled "Sandwich!" at me before squishing me between them. Hard.

Basically, Bastard and I were making a Manouchka sandwich.

He was much taller than her, by at least eight inches, I'd say, and he stared down at her for a second with an unreadable expression on his face before she shoved him away and repeated, "*Mon bébé.*"

She seemed strong enough, so I took a step back myself.

Bastard let her go. He clicked his tongue and made a point of grasping his gun, but mercifully said nothing.

Tucker was already wrapping baby David up in a blanket, so he turned around, holding him aloft like he was the star ornament for the Christmas tree. "He's fine. See?"

Whatever hostility Bastard was working up ebbed with the sight of the newborn baby mewling in the air. We all sighed in relief.

"David," she said. She hadn't cried, but I could feel the tears in her voice, and it made me shudder inside, where Bastard couldn't see.

"Lie down, and I'll bring him to you. Special delivery, right to your lap. Okay?" Tucker grinned at her from underneath his matted hair, darkened by sweat. His French was tinged with more English than usual. He was secretly losing it, too. He was just a better actor than me. Good to know that he wasn't used to suctioning newborn tracheas every day.

Manouchka stumbled toward the bed, falling toward the dirty instruments.

I hauled her upright by grabbing her gown from behind, so it wouldn't be as personal as holding her by the waist. Then I knocked the instruments a foot under the bed with a solid kick. I know that's unsanitary, but so was the blood she was dripping on the floor, and they were her own instruments. I'd get them later. For now, I needed to sew up her coochie.

When she drew her legs up into the bed, I helped her lift the leg nearest to me and gaped at the streaks of blood on her inner thighs. It was a bit like *Carrie*, only X-Rated.

"It's that bad?" she said, and I tried to recover the inscrutable Asian card I'd missed out on at birth.

"No, no problem. I just need to, ah, give you a massage to help control the bleeding." I still had the same gloves on, but I didn't need sterile gloves for the external massage.

I braced her hip with my left hand and reached for the soft expanse of her abdomen with my right. Then I started grinding on her uterus through the skin of her belly like I was trying to knead a lump of floppy dough.

Usually, after you give birth, the uterus recognizes that the baby is gone and starts shrinking back down to size. Nursing the baby helps release oxytocin, which contracts the uterus too. But since we'd whipped David away, he hadn't really had a chance to nurse, and she'd started bleeding.

"What are you doing? I want my baby." She started to squeeze away from me.

"Your uterus is too, um, big. Loose," I added in English. I was startling to struggle with my French worse than Tucker. "I need to massage it. That way, it will close up again and you'll stop bleeding."

"Is it dangerous?"

"It can be," I said, not wanting to lie, but I couldn't figure out how to sugarcoat it.

Tucker to the rescue. "Most women do well with the massage," he said, winding around to the head of the bed and smiling down at her from the office end. "Do you want to see your son, David?"

She fixed her eyes on David and opened her arms, so Tucker successfully distracted her while I mentally ticked off the post-partum hemorrhage algorithm.

One. Two large bore IV's. She didn't have any. I could try to put one in, and Tucker definitely could, but only if the nurse had left the venipuncture kit in the room. In the emerg, most rooms are stocked with equipment, but I've also seen nurses carry a small blue basket of needles, gauze, Opsite dressings, and tape from room to room. I wasn't sure which way OB swung.

Two. Group and screen her blood. They may have done that when she arrived, or as part of her prenatal blood work. Either we've documented the mom's blood type, or draw it immediately. Unfortunately, boxed into this cage, I didn't have access to her record, but maybe I could ask the intercom when I got a hand free. Again, Bastard would probably block them if they actually tried to deliver her blood, but if we needed to cross-match her some units, we'd have to start now.

My kingdom for a CBC (complete blood count, not Canadian Broadcasting Corporation, in this case).

"What the fuck is going on?" said Bastard.

"She's bleeding. I'm trying to stop it. Can I call for help?" I lifted my chin at the intercom, even as I kept pressing on Manouchka's stomach.

Bastard made sure not to gaze too far south on Manouchka, but he steadied the gun at my own midsection. He said, "Don't even think about it."

Out of the corner of my eye, I thought I saw Tucker move back toward the wall and hit the intercom button with his shoulder.

I could've been mistaken, since I immediately dropped my eyes down to Manouchka's belly, but my man was thinking again. If he'd accomplished his goal, the outside world could hear us and figure out the best time to bust in.

In case he hadn't managed, I glanced over my right shoulder. I'd just remembered another way to alert the cavalry: the code rope near the incubator.

They showed us the code rope on orientation. I forgot because I haven't seen a code yet, and maybe because I was getting delirious with fatigue, but the idea is that if you're resuscitating a newborn, instead of running over to a phone and pressing 5555, you can just yank on the cord and keep on bagging/tubing/compressing that child.

I assumed Tucker hadn't yanked it while working on David, probably too mindful of Bastard's watchful eye, but he might've managed to alert the authorities now.

Thank heavens.

I don't know how call bells work, exactly, but I think the patient either pushes a switch on a rope or the intercom button and it lights up at the nursing station. The secretary or a nurse will see that room 4392 needs help and press their own button at the desk to say, "Yes?" Or sometimes the nurse has to go to the patient's room to shut it off.

Either way, if Tucker had managed to push the button, he'd activated the intercom, and now they could hear us.

He brought the authorities ever-closer to tearing us away from this madman.

In the meantime, though, I still had to save this woman's life. And based on the blood slowly streaming out from between her legs, I'd have to step up my game.

Chapter 23

I tried to knit my thoughts back together.

Post-partum hemorrhage. No IV, no blood tests, no blood, no use with the external massage.

I gave Manouchka's abdomen an eleventh-hour drumming, hammering down on the uterus through the belly, hard enough that Manouchka's breath puffed out in protest, and she squeezed David, who uttered his thin, new baby wail.

Shoot. Or rather, don't shoot.

Tucker offered me a crooked grin and raised his voice to be heard above the ruckus, "How's it going?"

"She still seems floppy. I'll have to do internal massage." One hand inside the vagina, one hand compressing the belly. Sort of a one-two punch to the uterus, telling it to tighten up while we bring on the drugs.

Speaking of which, step four. Oxytocin. And five, Hemabate. Useful, useful drugs. "Can you get me some Oxytocin and Hemabate? And some IV equipment for yourself?" Once again, I wished for the Wayback machine for the good ol' days when they used to install IV lines in every labouring woman.

"We can do Syntocin IM. Ten units instead of five," said Tucker. He pointed at the delivery cart and raised his eyebrow at Bastard.

"Yeah, sure," Bastard muttered. "Just shut that kid up. And don't go anywhere."

Manouchka hugged David to her chest. He settled for a second before he started crying again.

His mewling seemed to bounce off the ceiling and walls so they could reverberate in my ears an extra time or ten. Even I gritted my teeth, and I wasn't a killer. As far as I know.

We'd have to keep David quiet before Bastard lost his shit even more.

Manouchka cradled her son to her chest, gazing at Bastard and then at me, pleading.

I belatedly realized her problem. "Um, she needs some privacy to nurse. Could you, uh..." I glanced at the thin bit of curtain slumped against the wall. Most of the curtains in the Family Medicine Unit get stuck halfway, but even some privacy was better than none.

Bastard followed my gaze. "No fucking way. Who knows what you cunts will get up to back there."

The c-word? Really? I blinked at him, but I wasn't really surprised that he'd broken out the most vile words while he vetoed some more basic human rights.

Fortunately, when I turned back, Manouchka had dragged a sheet over her chest and now struggled to arrange David one-handed underneath all the cloth.

I wanted to help her. I've read about breastfeeding, and I vaguely remembered something called the football hold, which is good if you've had a C-section, but I'm fairly useless in real life.

I cleared my throat and called to her above David's intermittent bawls, "Good job. You can squeeze your breast and help aim it at his mouth." I only knew that move because a nurse was counselling a new mother when I popped in on ward rounds yesterday.

David's howls faded. His tiny body relaxed. I heard, or imagined I heard, miniature lips smacking.

"There you go, Manouchka. Good job." I could never be a cheerleader. I felt like a fool, encouraging her when I had no real idea what was happening under that blanket, but I literally had my hands full with my last-ditch external massage.

I cocked my head at Tucker, who had ripped open the delivery cart and lifted out a clear glass vial not unlike the Lidocaine ones we use in emerg, except this one had a green bar on the label that I could spot from the bed.

Oxytocin. Also known as Pitocin. Either way, the drug to make the uterus contract. Praise be.

Thank God we kept drugs in the room. It made sense. When a woman bled, we needed Oxytocin now, not after running down the hall to input her name into the locked drug system. But this was my first post-partum hemorrhage, and the nurses were so good at magicking things up, I didn't know where they located them. Oz, practically.

I allowed my shoulders and hands to relax for one gorgeous second just before I asked, "You've got Hemabate, too? Just in case?"

"No. That's in the post-partum hemorrhage kit, at the nursing station."

Too much to wish for. I said, "Let's start with the Oxytocin. And toss me a new pair of gloves."

"Aye aye, captain." Tucker lobbed another sterile set at me.

I caught them. I would have liked to wash my hands again, but I trashed my old gloves, settled for a quick Purell from the wall dispenser, and got gloved up again.

Oh, no. "I need—"

"Me," said Tucker, crossing to my side and squirting more gel on to the sterile side of the paper glove wrapper.

I mouthed, *I love you.*

His eyes flared, and he mouthed it back and took another step toward me, but Bastard said, "Fucking doctors with their fucking thumbs up their asses."

Tucker turned back to the cart, unwrapped a syringe and shook the bottle before he ripped open a needle.

Bastard's voice cut through the room with a new and dangerous note. "What the fuck are you doing?" Before Tucker could answer, Bastard took two steps toward him and snatched Tucker's arm with his free hand. "No needles. Don't you fucking dare."

I barked in disbelief. "We're trying to save this woman from bleeding to death. That's how we give the medication."

Too late, I realized how wrong that sounded when Manouchka bleated from the bed. She definitely understood more English than she was letting on, which made me the bad guy, even though I was trying to save her life. I tried to apologize with my eyes while Bastard blustered,

"I know what I'm talking about. No needles, if you know what's good for you."

"Shit!" I said. I try not to swear in front of patients, so I was 0 for two, but this was unbelievable. "You want rivers of blood to pour out between her legs?"

Manouchka choked.

I said, "*Je m'excuse*, Manouchka." I tried to throttle back my temper, but Tucker beat me to it. He dropped the needle and said to Bastard, who was still gripping his left arm, "You want Casey, right?"

"That's what I'm telling you. You're wasting my time." Bastard shifted his gun. At this exact moment, he wasn't pointing it at Tucker—it was more at the incubator—but my heart clutched anyway. I wasn't willing to get shot over Oxytocin. Not if I could stop it the old-fashioned way.

I shoved my hand inside Manouchka's vagina. I'd never actually done this part before, but I knew the theory. If you press on the uterus through the abdominal wall, the flaccid uterus just ping pongs around in the abdominal cavity. But if you secure the uterus with the other hand on the cervix, you can make sure those muscle fibres get a good rubdown, contract under the pressure, and *stop bleeding*.

Two millimetres into her vagina, my fingers immediately sank into a deep tear.

Chapter 24

As I advanced my fingers into Manouchka's spongy vagina, I couldn't kid myself about the size of her vaginal laceration.

It was like my fingers had fallen into a pothole. Or, since it was such a long tear, it was more like a trench. A World War I ditch of blood and soft tissue.

My heart battered my throat. I forced myself to breathe, to try and think logically.

No one talks about this, but pushing a baby out, 90 percent of the time, it's okay. Minor tears at the most. The superficial ones, you can just let heal on their own. Bigger ones mean a few stitches. But the fourth-degree tears are the ones where you can rip your vagina into your rectum.

I'd sewed up a few of these lacerations, with the help of the consultants, but my brain kind of switched off. They'd say, "Sew here," and I'd sew. The woman would always ask, "How many stitches?" and the doctor would hedge, "It's kind of hard to say, because the stitches are running together." (They're running sutures, where you keep sewing without tying a knot and cutting the thread in between each stitch—I'm sure you can imagine how challenging that would be inside a vagina.) But whenever we have to sew the vagina, it's usually a big job. Like, at least ten bites of suture.

I'd never repaired a vagina on my own before.

But I wasn't on my own. I had Tucker.

I calmed myself and surveyed Manouchka's private parts, as if I could check the tear with X-ray vision as well as my fingers.

If her perineum were a clock, the tear would be at six o'clock. It felt deep because the swollen mucous membranes enveloped my fingers, but she couldn't have torn any deeper than a centimetre.

My finger pads crept forward, pressing south and meeting spongy resistance. That was good. I definitely wasn't just falling into the empty cavern of her rectum. This was not a fourth-degree tear.

Finally, just when I reached the full length of my second and third finger, the tear grew shallower and ended.

I moved side to side to check, but this was the end of the road.

Massive phew. My shoulders sagged in momentary relief.

Tucker was talking to Bastard behind me. "Once we save this woman and her baby, we can find Casey. She's waiting for us. But right now, we need to do it right. You wouldn't want doctors who wouldn't save a woman's life, do you?"

Bastard paused to think about it.

Tucker waited for him, managing not to swear and/or scare the patient. Good thing one of us was still lucid.

The intercom crackled, but I ignored it. With any luck, the cavalry could hear us, but they wouldn't tip their hand until they were ready to rumble.

RUMBLE. Please, cavalry, come and rumble this man before he murders us.

On cue, the operator cut in through the hospital loudspeaker. "CODE BLUE, FOURTH FLOOR. *CODE BLEU, QUATRIÈME ÉTAGE.*"

"What the fuck is that?" said Bastard.

So Tucker had pulled the code rope after all. My gaze zinged toward Manouchka's. Her eyes widened and her hands seized on David, even though, from the way his head was lolling, I thought he was asleep and definitely breathing better.

I told Bastard, without turning around, "They must have heard that David was in trouble and started the code team. The pediatrician will come and resuscitate the baby. Sometimes the obstetrician helps. The obstetric nurses are very good at codes, they're the ones who—"

Bastard snapped, "No one comes in here."

I kind of expected that, but it felt worse when he said it out loud, especially when he walked toward me, suddenly sure, with the gun aimed between my breasts. "No one comes in here except Casey. No one leaves. This is my turf."

Tucker opened his mouth and drew in his breath to speak.

I glanced at him, which made Bastard turn around. He jerked the gun right toward Tucker's open lips.

My man snapped his jaw shut, fixing his gaze on the weapon.

"You tell them to fuck right off, or I'll kill them. And you. And everyone else."

My heart ached. My ears rang. I wanted to cry. *Tucker, don't die. Ryan, I'll never see you again.*

But then *I thought, No way. I get to see Ryan again. This isn't how it ends. That bastard doesn't get to decide.*

And Kevin, my little brother? He can't just have his sister knocked off in a hostage-taking. This is Canada.

I almost laughed at myself right then. Like our national reputation as peacekeepers could keep all the crazies out. But if that was all I had to cling to, I'd take it.

"Stop that fucking code!" Bastard shouted, so Tucker pushed the call bell clipped on the bed and said, "This is Dr. John Tucker. The baby in Case Room One had meconium and has been successfully suctioned and is no longer a Code Blue. I mean, Pink. Repeat, the baby is no longer a Code Pink."

The young woman's voice answered him. "Thank you for the update, Dr. Tucker. Could we send staff in to assist you?"

"No one! No fucking one!" Bastard screamed, loud enough that the woman could hear him, because she said smoothly, "No additional staff required at this time. Understood. Who is speaking now?"

"Are you talking to me?" said Bastard.

Manouchka groaned, and more blood spurted out from between her legs and over my fingers, so I remembered my call of duty and advanced my hand inside her vagina while Bastard called, "I'm the one who decides here! I'm in charge!'

"Thank you for talking to us. My name is Olivia."

"I don't give a flying fuck what your name is. I need Casey Assim!'

"You're looking for a patient, is that right?"

"For fuck's sake!' said Bastard, and verbally tore her a new one while Olivia tried to soothe him and my hand retreated from Manouchka's already-torn one.

They talk about fisting. Personally, I've never done it or experienced it—until now.

My fingers had been too short to reach up to her cervix, so after I withdrew them, I slowly advanced my entire hand inside her vagina. Intellectually, I know that a baby is much wider than my arm, but it surprised me that I could insert my right hand and wrist inside her lady parts.

Heck, I probably could have fit *two* hands, except that Manouchka was whimpering and tensing her legs.

And that was just with her poor, ripped vagina. How could I reach all the way inside her uterus and start scooping away any stray flesh?

Then I remembered one of the obstetricians telling me, "I don't always insert my hand inside the cervix. That's only necessary for retained placental products. Otherwise, the key is internal uterine massage."

"The placenta!" I said out loud.

"The placenta," Tucker repeated. "You're right. I've got to check the placenta. After I give the Oxytocin. All right, Ben?"

It was the first time he had called Bastard by name. I held my breath.

Bastard said, "No fucking way," but he was still swearing at Olivia, and during the confusion, Tucker stepped back to the cart, ripped open the needle, drew up the Oxytocin, and quickly plunged it into Manouchka's deltoid muscle with hardly a second to wipe an alcohol swab over her skin first.

Chapter 25

Oh, God. Tucker had violated Bastard's 'Thou shalt not use a needle' commandment.

Manouchka flinched, but she didn't make a sound. She understood that we had to do this as covertly as possible.

I barely breathed.

Bastard was now yelling at the intercom, "You get me someone who knows his ass from his armpit, and I'll think about it!"

Tucker jammed the needle into its pink sheath, permanently covering it and insulating himself from a needle stick injury before he shoved the used syringe in his back pocket. Then he said to the still-arguing Bastard, "May I check the placenta in the bathroom?"

"Shut up, dickweed!"

I twitched, trying not to watch the bulge in Tucker's scrubs, which was opposite the usual one. The needle was on him. If Bastard caught him with the syringe, would Tucker be able to talk his way out of it? He'd never make it unnoticed to the sharps container next to the incubator, so he'd either have to ditch it in the bathroom or carry it around as permanent evidence.

On the other hand, he'd finally given Manouchka her medication, and I was delivering her internal massage at long last. If Bastard wouldn't let him check the placenta, I'd have to go for it the old-fashioned way.

Reaching forward, I grasped the rim of her gaping cervix between my scissored index and middle fingers. I could easily slide one, two, three or more fingers inside her the cervical os. Probably my whole hand could fit inside. David had done his job well.

Manouchka lifted her hips off the bed when I touched her cervix, but she bit her lip and didn't cry.

They say the cervix isn't well innervated, that it doesn't carry pain fibres the way other organs do. Maybe this would be okay.

I took a deep breath and inserted my first two knuckles past the cervix, inside her uterus, but Manouchka moaned.

"I'm sorry," I said in French. "I want to stop the bleeding."

"It hurts," she said, rolling her eyes up to the ceiling.

Either she hadn't gotten an epidural (which made sense, since she had no IV and could walk to the bed), or it had worn off a long time ago. Either way, she didn't want my fist to go deep space nine on her. Neither did I, but I had to.

Sweat smarted my forehead. I'm not a big sweat-er, but my sterile gown was heavy and I was a bit panicked. You don't want to deliver the kid and lose the mother.

"If a piece of your placenta is stuck to the uterus, you need me to take it out," I told Manouchka. "It will bleed, and your uterus won't shrink down the way it's supposed to. I also still need to sew your vagina and stop that bleeding."

Tears slid down Manouchka round, brown cheeks. She shook her head at me.

Oh, God. She clearly didn't want this. I didn't have consent to insert my entire hand inside her uterus. But I was trying to save her life. Did she understand that?

"The uterus. Where the baby—David—was living for nine months. It was his home, and the placenta was feeding him. But if the placenta got ripped, and you still have a piece inside, your uterus will stay floppy and bleeding—"

"No," she repeated again, clearly.

What would a bioethicist do?

I licked my dry lips, tasting the blood. "Tucker, if you get me some Lidocaine, maybe I could try a local injection and it wouldn't hurt so much."

"Just give her internal massage for a second without scraping the uterus. I'll check her placenta."

"If you can," I said, glancing at Bastard's back. He was facing the intercom as he argued, like he was squaring off against an invisible opponent. "It's in the sink."

"Shut up!" said Bastard, railing at both me and Olivia, but I couldn't be bothered while I kept one hand deeper into a woman's nether regions than I'd ever gone before. I was two seconds away from torturing her by scraping her endometrium with my nails and fingers.

"I've got to go to the bathroom to check the placenta," Tucker told him, and spun on his heel.

I admired his shoulders and his confidence, even as the rest of me cringed. *Don't shoot him.*

"I'm coming with you!" Bastard hollered at Tucker's departing back, and I ripped my eyes away from Tucker—*he's alive, let him go, concentrate on your patient*—and focused on the right here, right now, between my two hands. There are certain organs that seem very meaty: bloody, firm, and hard to control. One of them is the liver. Two others are the uterus and the placenta.

Manouchka said, "Stop this. Let me go."

"I can't, not until you stop bleeding," I said, but since Tucker was probably splaying the placenta in the sink, checking for any missing chunks, I backed out of her uterus, letting the mouth of the cervix hug my fingers.

She sighed, and her back arch flattened out on the bed. I'd been hurting her. Whoever says the cervix isn't well-innervated probably doesn't own one.

But I couldn't stop now. I stabilized her cervix by clutching its rim, pinching the flesh with my thumb and index fingers while my left, my weaker side, massaged her abdominal wall as deeply as possible.

Maybe that was a mistake, because she tried to snap her legs together, only I was between them, so she couldn't quite close them, just batter my shoulders while I yelled, "Please! Let me help you!"

"The placenta is intact!" Tucker yelled from the bathroom.

"Oh, thank God," I said out loud, which seemed to be some sort of cue to Manouchka, because she started to pray at high volume.

It seemed appropriate.

I said, as calmly as possible, "I don't need to go inside your uterus. Dr. Tucker thinks your placenta came out with all the pieces still attached.

I have to hold on to the cervix, the tissue at the opening of your uterus. If you let me keep massaging you, most women will stop bleeding with this kind of massage." I was saying "massage" an awful lot, but it conjured up visions of white towels, heated stones, and water fountains instead of bloody organs.

The medication should kick in anytime too. Go, Oxytocin, go.

When Tucker returned, with Bastard tracking him closely with his gun, I abandoned my pride and said, still grinding away on Manouchka with both hands, "Tucker, how do I know when to stop?" The only good thing about a retained placental product is that if you find it, you know your job is done. I was pummelling on her two-fisted with no idea when I should quit.

"When she stops bleeding."

But I had my arm inside her. Wouldn't that cork her up a bit? I didn't know how to ask that politely, so I kneaded even harder. Her praying kicked into a higher RPM, and I said to her in a high, strained voice, "Please look at David. Isn't he cute?"

Finally, I withdrew my inner hand a little, praying *no blood no blood no blood no blood.*

More blood trickled out.

I swore.

Manouchka glared at me.

Tucker said, "You getting tired? You want me to do it?"

"No." I wasn't quitting until I was really scuppered. I went back in, pressing in earnest, so hard that she cried out and my heart dropped and Bastard said, "Do you really know what you're doing, bitch? You better not hurt Casey like that, I'm telling you," but I kept going, going going, letting my hands talk for me, letting them feel that yes, the muscle of the uterus was starting to contract a little. Maybe it was my desperate massage, maybe the drugs had finally kicked in, but I felt a difference.

I said, "That's it, now. Let me."

Manouchka relaxed a smidgen.

This time, when I pulled out my hands, I knew the blood would stop. And it did.

She still had that tear, though. Maybe partly thanks to my Herculean efforts, the front of the laceration was now V-shaped. Like, at least three centimetres wide. I'd already measured it as long as my index finger, or about 8 centimetres.

I stared at it, my shoulders sagging. You don't have to sew up a vaginal tear right away. I could just pack it. But I didn't want to leave anything unfinished, especially when bullets could fly at any moment. I started glancing around for suture material.

"You want me to do it?" said Tucker, appearing on my left side.

I was the one with the gloved hands. I should pick up the needle and keep on going. But you know, when he said that, I suddenly wanted to stop playing the almighty hero and let him take over.

"What. You don't know how to do it?" said Bastard, from behind Tucker.

"I stopped the bleeding," I told him. "Dr. Tucker is excellent at suturing. We specialize in our different territories. Manouchka deserves the best care." Also, I couldn't help thinking that if Bastard considered both of us essential, we were more likely to survive as a duo.

Bastard stared at me with flat eyes. I found myself holding my breath, staring him down, willing him to believe me and my Rasputin-worthy gaze.

After a minute, he sighed. "You guys are fucking useless. I could skin a pig before you guys even picked up a knife."

Please don't, I thought, but didn't say.

Tucker shouldered his way forward until he was nearly touching me. I thought I could feel the heat from his body, like he was an oven. I swayed toward him while he said, "It's also a question of good hygiene. Dr. Sze should have the opportunity to wash off the blood and disinfect herself."

Disinfect myself? I took a gander down at my own body.

I looked like a horror show. I'd earned a solid wall of blood up my right forearm, plus more blood had trickled past my elbow. No wonder Tucker had suggested gloves.

Bastard's eyes flickered up and down, taking in my scary movie impersonation. Then he took a step back before he bellowed at me, "Get clean, bitch! What the hell is wrong with you?"

Chapter 26

Bastard aimed the gun between my eyes, but for the first time, I noticed a tremor in his hand. Either he was tired, he hated birthing blood, or both.

Was that good news for us? Maybe. Maybe we could now overpower him.

Or maybe not. I could picture him getting too edgy, riled up, blowing up, and unleashing another torrent of bullets.

I held my hands up like we were in a shoot 'em up Western. Which we sort of were, I guess, except no horses and an orgy of real blood.

I jerked my head at the bathroom, hating myself for asking for permission, but at least I didn't have to beg him with words.

After a second, Bastard lowered his gun and said, "Go on."

Wow. I almost didn't recognize him without the omnipresent muzzle threatening to split my skull.

Manouchka's breathing sped up. She hadn't liked me between her legs, but she didn't want me to go, either. I tried to tell her with my eyes that I'd return to her side as soon as I could.

She closed her eyelids, as well as her legs, and shook her head.

I couldn't blame her for not believing me. I couldn't promise that I'd keep on breathing for the next five minutes, let alone protect her and David, but I'd do my absolute best.

Me and Tucker both. I hesitated for a second, because my man was within kissing distance. I almost gave in to the overwhelming need to at least snatch his hand and squeeze it one last time.

Well, I guess that wasn't the brightest idea, since I looked and smelled like an abattoir, but...you know.

I backed away from Tucker and edged toward the bathroom, with my back to the delivery cart wall, so I didn't have to turn my back on Bastard.

I loved the idea of even a few seconds to myself, away from his jackhammer eyes. I only wished it didn't mean separating from Tucker and Manouchka and David.

Tucker hadn't stirred from Manouchka's side, but he wasn't suturing her yet. He was watching me with the occasional quick side-eye at Bastard, like he wanted to throw himself between us, and maybe he would.

My man would literally take a bullet for me, I realized all over again. He would take a beating, he would take a bullet, whatever he had to do.

So would Ryan. I would stake my life on it.

It's one thing to have one guy who loves you, truly loves you, more than he cares for himself. There are guys who will fuck you, guys who will flirt with you, and any guy is willing to copy trigonometry homework. But to find two soul mates at the same time?

The best of times, the worst of times.

I mouthed at him, "I love you."

Bastard said, "Move it. Christ, bitch. You stink."

I wanted to blow him a fake kiss. I imagined my bloodied glove raised in the air. If I slowly brought it to my mouth, pretending to smooch it, it would probably make him faint. But before Bastard dropped, he might pull the trigger, so that kind of Hollywood show-off wasn't worth it.

Instead, I bent my head forward and slowly, deliberately sniffed the gory glove on my right hand.

I heard Bastard catch his breath, which only made me prolong the show, moving my head up and down, stroking the latex-free barrier coating my fingers. I could feel the ridges of dried blood that had coagulated under my touch. It didn't weird me out. I've done it dozens of times, half-consciously.

Then I said to Bastard, enunciating each word, "You're right. I do smell like blood."

I turned my back on him and walked to the bathroom with slow, purposeful steps and my head held high. Like I wasn't a prisoner.

He might have lifted the gun. He might have pointed at me. My shoulder blades twitched in warning. But facing away, I couldn't see his weapon, and like Hammy Hamster used to say, *If I can't see you then you can't see me.*

I made it to the bathroom alive.

I didn't close the door. I wasn't going to push him that far, although I really would have liked to pee in peace.

I pulled off the besmirched, formerly sterile gown, bundling it tightly to make it fit in the soiled linen cart. If we were trapped here a long time, we'd run out of room for garbage. We'd turn into our own landfill site.

I started to strip off the gloves. The trick was to turn them inside out at the seam to ensure that the blood didn't brush my skin. First, my left fingers plucked the opening at my right wrist, the dirtiest glove, turning it inside out so that the cleanest side was exposed and balled in my left palm, before my right fingers peeled my left glove off, neatly turning it into a bag for the first.

I tossed the glove ball in the garbage. Two points.

"What's taking you so long, bitch?" hollered Bastard.

"I had to dispose of my garments. Now I need to wash up, but the placenta's in the sink," I called back.

"What?"

"The placenta," I repeated.

"What?"

Bastard stomped his boots toward me, but instead of flinching, I beckoned him closer, all the better to display the placenta still plopped in the porcelain.

I'd tossed it in shiny side up, with the Saran wrap-like membrane enveloping it present-style, but Tucker had turned it over so that he could inspect it for any loose tissue, exposing the seeping flesh.

Everyone always says the placenta looks like liver, but I guess it depends if you've ever ripped open a liver. The side of the placenta that spends nine months adhered to the inner wall of the uterus always seems more raw and ragged, with pools of blood mixed in with the meat. The post-dates placentas have visible islands of calcium—not Manouchka's—but hers had something even better for my purposes.

Like I said, the amniotic membranes usually look like cling wrap. If they don't break, that's what makes the 'caul' over a baby's face that they used to associate with ESP. I've never seen a baby born like that, although the fleeting thought reminded me of Mme. Bérubé, a patient's wife who claimed to read palms.

However, in Manouchka and David's case, the torn amniotic membranes, stained yellow and green by meconium, sagged to either side of the placenta like too-big elephant pants.

Bastard gagged. And not just a little gag, but one with a bit of gargle in it.

Oh, this was good. "We don't have anywhere to put it, and it's in the way of me washing up," I said, as if I didn't notice anything untoward. "We normally place them in a stainless steel bowl." After that, I imagine a nurse whisks the bowls away and bundles the placenta up for the pathology lab. Since we were trapped in our own closed system, that wasn't going to happen.

"Get rid of it," he said, in a strangled voice.

"I'll grab a steel bowl," I said. "It's on the delivery cart."

He backed away from the bathroom, looking a little pale around the eyes for a white guy. "Just do what you gotta do, bitch. And do it fast."

When I passed by the bed, Tucker was already trimming his sutures. I guess it takes longer to discombobulate a kidnapper than it does to repair a second- or third-degree tear. He gave me a look: *Are you okay?*

I gave him a slight nod. I wanted to convey to him, *More than okay. We might be able to figure something else out from here.* But my plan was still coalescing in my head. All I could do was mouth again, *I love you.*

His face relaxed. And then a smile sliced across his mouth, and it was extraordinary, how even the room air seemed to lighten before he mouthed, *I love you, Hope.*

I wanted to explain to him that I still loved Ryan. That hadn't changed. But it was too complicated, so I just beamed back at him before I gave Manouchka a reassuring look.

She closed her eyes instead of responding.

Then I ransacked the delivery cart, opening every drawer, searching for the stainless steel bowls. When I'm in a hurry, I have trouble finding stuff and have to open drawers two or three times before the nurse kindly points out the object in front of my nose and asks if I was looking with my "man eyes."

"Bottom drawer," called Tucker, and of course he was right. I thought, *What would I do without this guy? Honestly. Would I just join Stan on the hall floor?*

I liked that Tucker was here, but it worried me that I was becoming too dependent on him, like a dumb-ass helpless maiden. Maybe I should have insisted on doing it all. Simultaneously deliver David, intubate and suction him, stop Manouchka from bleeding to death, sew up her tear, and freak out our jailer.

Then I stopped myself. No one does it all alone.

The best thing for women who give birth in a hospital is that you have access to a highly-skilled team. The nurses can triage you, welcome you to the case room, check your cervix, coach you through labour, put in an IV, massage the uterus, push the baby out of the uterus during a C-section, and do countless other tasks. The medical student can do the history and physical exam and deliver the baby in a pinch. The resident can do that, plus ripen the cervix (med students can do this too, but it's a grey area to me), and once they're senior, do the crazy stuff like crash C-sections, embolize arterial arteries, reanimate crashing pregnant women, and basically act as extra hands for the staff. That's not even counting the OB/gyn, the head guy or girl with the biggest tool kit of all.

Sure, Hollywood would make me do everything solo, because it's more dramatic, but medicine is not a solo art. Especially in residency.

Ryan would have helped me, too. He stays calm, grounding me, while he makes suggestions. Even now, my phone must've buzzed five or ten texts through, although I didn't dare check the screen for fear that Bastard would smash it. A phone in pocket was worth two in pieces. Or something.

In the meantime, I unwrapped the cloth covering the cool, steel bowl and crossed back to the bathroom to pitch the placenta inside. "It's still a little warm," I said to no one in particular.

Bastard said, "No one's interested, bitch!"

I am, I thought. *I'm very interested, Bastard.*

But I was careful not to look him in the eyes or let my mouth move. I couldn't give the game away. Because I'd finally worked out my own small plan.

Chapter 27

Meanwhile, Tucker called from the bed, "I'm all done."

He probably wanted to distract Bastard, but Manouchka responded first. "Is everything okay?"

"Yes. Your body will heal nicely. You did very well under...difficult circumstances." Even Tucker's tact was under strain.

"*Merci, Docteur,*" she said, with deference I hadn't noticed with me, but that's par. Guys are still automatically given a plus one (or ten), even in 2012.

"I'd better see if Dr. Tucker needs help," I told Bastard, taking a step toward the doorway. I held the placenta bowl in front of me like it was my own pregnant belly.

Bastard snorted. "I don't know why you two need so much help. Buncha losers." But he and his gun swung sideways, into the main room, to give me enough room to get out.

Placenta power.

Across the room, Tucker met my gaze before his eyes dropped to the steel bowl that most people would have abandoned in the bathroom. Say, inside the shattered shower that no one was going to use.

Would he understand the method to my madness? Maybe I was overplaying. Well, probably. But I didn't want to molder here forever, or until Bastard got too bored or edgy and started firing again. I'd mapped out only a few weaknesses for him. Better exploit them sooner rather than later.

Say, right now.

I advanced toward the bed, willing Manouchka to look at me. She was resting her cheek against the top of David's fuzzy head, but when I waved the magic placenta bowl, the movement caught her eye, and she glanced upward.

I mimed at her to cough. Meaning that I moved a hand to cover my mouth while I silently jerked my abdominal muscles and expelled a silent breath while Bastard was still fixated on the placenta slopping around in the bowl.

Manouchka stared at me like I was plum crazy. Maybe placenta crazy.

"Be careful with that, bitch. Jesus Christ." Bastard pushed the gun at me, but he was clearly eyeballing the flesh swilling in front of me.

"Sorry!" I said, and switched the bowl exclusively to my left hand—the hand closer to Bastard—while I explicitly pretended to cough, fisting my right hand in front of my mouth.

Then I jerked my chin at her and widened my eyes, willing her to join in. If she didn't play along, all was lost.

Manouchka grimaced.

Please, Manouchka. Pretty please with freedom on top.

At long last, she cleared her throat and gave an unconvincing ahem.

I blinked at her, raised my eyebrows, and ventured a small but definite nod, mentally urging her, *Encore! Encore!*

A plea that works in both English and French. Maybe bilingualism would help. Couldn't hurt, anyway.

Tucker, the most multilingual of us all, watched the drama silently while he gathered his sharps together and told Bastard, "I need to get rid of these."

"Hurry up, Blondie."

With the back of my brain, I realized that somehow, Tucker had managed to get Bastard's permission to use anaesthetic while I was in the bathroom. And if I knew him, he'd dispose of the other syringe at the same time. Brains, I tell you.

But in the meantime, I had to get Manouchka on board. I raised my eyebrows at her, pleading.

This time, she managed to cough enough that her upper body jerked, made more obvious by the fact that David's tiny body jumped with hers, like he was a ship rocking on the ocean of her body.

Still, David kept sleeping. Only a baby could sleep through a hostage-taking.

"Are you okay?" I said loudly, in French. "You look a little short of breath."

"What's going on?" said Bastard.

"It's amazing how well Manouchka is doing, considering her...health problem," I told him in English, before switching back to Manouchka in French. "You lost a lot of blood. We'll have to clean it up, since we don't want anyone else to get infected."

"What are you talking about?" Bastard's head whipped up at the word *infected*. He didn't need any translation on that one.

"I really couldn't say," I said, in my blandest tone.

"Tell me, bitch!" He took a step toward me, his hand lifting like he wanted to smack me, but I accidentally-on-purpose raised the placenta bowl as a buffer, and he dropped back two feet.

Bastard's eyes darted wildly around the room before locking on Manouchka. More specifically, his gaze dipped toward the bed sheets, twisted and saturated with blood. Tucker had done the best he could, and had thrown away the disposable piqué pad already, but the blood stains remained.

Fortunately.

I tried to meet Manouchka's eyes in a trust-me-I'm-a-doctor way.

She glared back at me.

This would have worked better if Tucker were engineering it, with his charm and his hail-old-buddy ways, but I'm the only one crazy enough to dream these things up. If he caught on, though, we could work as a team.

"We do have patient confidentiality," I told Bastard. Too late, I remembered how Stan had died, and I stumbled over the last word. Bastard didn't care about the Health Insurance Portability and Accountability Act. He cared about the shortest line between him, his woman, and his baby.

I changed tactics. "More importantly, you know that Canada is a country of immigrants who have helped make our country great." I must've ripped that line off of the politician of the week, but I soldiered on. "Unfortunately, the cross-migration sometimes means that diseases can spread more effectively through all parts of the world."

"What are you talking about?" Bastard said slowly. It was the first time he'd spoken in a measured way and quite possibly the first time he hadn't sworn at me.

He didn't want to hear another word. So naturally, I had to deliver it.

"Have you ever heard of Ebola?" I asked.

Manouchka swung forward in the bed, her entire body stiffening. Her mouth opened in protest.

Tucker took two quick steps back to my side, but I couldn't spare either of them a glance.

I laid my hand on the bed's footboard, trying to reassure Manouchka non-verbally, while my eyes lasered in on Bastard's.

I was gambling here. The only blood-borne diseases I usually discuss with patients before transfusions are HIV and hepatitis.

But HIV is treatable right now—not curable, but treatable—and hepatitis C is common among IV drug users. Hep C is more transmissible than HIV, so I'm always careful to glove up among hep C carriers, but it wouldn't surprise me if one of Bastard's cronies had it. Hell, he might test positive himself. You can treat hep C with some antivirals, although I'm sketchy on the details.

Neither disease carried the same pound-for-pound terror-weight as the unknown and brutal menace of Ebola.

"No fucking way," snapped Bastard, but he was hyperventilating.

Ah. He had heard of Ebola.

I'd read *The Hot Zone* as part of my med school keen-ness, which gave me a little background. Not much, and not rigorously based on evidence, but a spoonful. Enough to make Bastard's flesh creep. "I've never heard of another disease where you cry blood," I said conversationally. "And your intestines can liquefy inside your own body. Can you imagine?"

Bastard's gun zoomed toward the bed, aimed between Manouchka's breasts. She stared back at him in mute panic. He could kill her and David in the next breath.

Shit. He might shoot now and ask questions later, especially if I got him too revved up. Time for damage control in my most impassive voice. "So the last thing we need around here is more blood. You definitely can't shoot them."

Bastard's gun arm raised and lowered again. He could make the same calculations I had: spraying the Beauziles' insides all over our small area would definitely contaminate us all.

"We should isolate them," I said. "And I should get rid of this placenta. It has a gigantic blood supply from both the mother and the fetus. Like, 650 cc's every minute."

"Jesus," said Bastard. He licked his lips, and I could practically hear his neurons synapsing: *black person. Scary. Bloody. Must have Ebola.*

"We should stay calm," I said. "Just because someone's visited Africa doesn't mean she has Ebola. But of course, she already has a fever of 38.1 degrees Celsius and abdominal pain"—never mind that the pain was because she was in labour and had ripped herself open—"and a bit of a cough." Coughing isn't how you usually spread Ebola, but he didn't need to know that. "If she develops vomiting and diarrhea, especially if it's bloody, well...the virus can live inside blood at room temperature for days at a time."

Tucker stepped beside me. I didn't look at him, but his hand dropped to the foot of the bed, beside my own. His skin was paler than mine, but his hand was steady and his voice was firm when he spoke. "Yeah. Ebola is horrifying. You can bleed to death just through your IV site."

I wondered how he knew that, but then again, most of the time, I wondered what was going on inside Tucker's brain. In a good way.

Bastard licked his lips again. He was scanning the room, as if he could see the virus haunting him.

I had to bite the inside of my cheek to stop myself from laughing inappropriately. The Ebola virus is so small that if you blew it up to be as thick as a piece of spaghetti, a single strand of human hair would be the width of a gigantic redwood tree, or twelve feet.

If I laughed now, Bastard would reward us with a skull and crossbones.

I managed to squeeze back any giggles by staring at a bit of dirt under Tucker's left thumbnail before my face stilled and I made eye contact with Manouchka.

"Have you travelled recently?" I asked her in French. I added, in English, "Say, to West Africa."

Her lips rounded. She watched my face and Tucker's for a beat too long. My heart contracted before she slowly nodded.

"I hope your fever hasn't gotten any worse," I said. "Now that you've finished labouring, maybe you wouldn't mind wearing a face mask. Do you think you could handle that?"

She stared at me.

Of course. I'd slipped back into English.

"We don't have any masks in the room," said Tucker. "They're at the nursing station. I could go get one."

"Shut the fuck up," said Bastard. It sounded like the words were being squashed out of him, one at a time.

We obeyed. We waited, with me looking at Manouchka and thinking, *That's it, you're doing it perfectly, keep it up.*

"Are you shitting me?" Bastard finally managed to drag out.

"Everybody stay calm," I said. "We don't know if she has Ebola or not. But she does have a fever, with a cough, and she recently came back from West Africa."

Out of the corner of my eyes, I could see Tucker nodding thoughtfully before he said, "Ebola is spread through direct contact with vomit, diarrhea, and saliva. If we're going to be stuck together, we'll have to do our best to isolate ourselves."

"Ebola!" said Bastard. "I haven't heard about that in years."

"I just read about it in the Lancet," I said. "I'm happy to show you on my phone, if you want. It's also called enterohemorrhagic fever. People vomit up blood—"

"I get the idea," Bastard snapped. "Shut the FUCK UP!"

We did.

It was so quiet that I could hear Bastard breathing before he started pacing his half of the room, muttering and swearing to himself.

It was a very delicate balance.

The next biggest wild card was Manouchka. If she screamed, "I don't have Ebola, you racist whore!" it could launch a catastrophe.

The third unknown was David. He could wake up wailing and set Bastard off.

I held my breath.

Manouchka didn't speak. I could feel her eyes on me and Tucker. I could hear her breathing, and the groan of the mattress as she shifted in bed.

She coughed again. A good, loud one this time.
Bastard started to wheeze.

Chapter 28

At first, his wheezing was subtle. Mostly, he was struggling to exhale.

In medicine, we call this prolonged exhalation. When the airways seize up and clamp down, it's hard to move air around. Sometimes, to try and make parents understand their child's constricted airways, we ask the caregivers to try exhaling through a straw. It takes them longer and they have to put out ten times the effort, so they feel first-hand what their kids are going through. Especially if they try and *inhale* through the straw like I did.

I glanced at Bastard out of the corner of my eye, not wanting to make a big deal out of it. Guys, especially, don't want you to leap up and down on them and yell, "Are you okay?" In guy-speak, I think that translates into *Are you such a wimp that you need me to help you?*

I did feel a little bad. The first line of the Hippocratic Oath, which I swore at med school orientation, is "Do no harm."

But that wasn't enough to stop me. Because we were fighting for our lives here, and I'd use every weapon possible to save me and Tucker and Manouchka and David.

Right now, my weapons were my ears.

I wanted to gauge the severity of his asthma attack.

Tucker didn't make a sound. He was waiting for my cue. And I was watching Bastard.

When I started medicine, I was surprised that some of the best wheezing you hear is with your ears, without a stethoscope. Right now, I still had my stethoscope wrapped around my neck. It's almost become a part of my body when I'm on call, like my glasses.

But I didn't whip the rubber tubing off my neck. I was concentrating on the high-pitched squeal of Bastard's breathing.

Another big part of med school is listening. Instead of jumping in, jabbering away, thrusting your cold stethoscope on a patient's chest and ordering a dozen expensive tests, they steer you toward paying attention to what the patient has to say. Revolutionary concept, I know.

Subtlety is not my strong point. I'll tell you what I think, without blinking and without sugar coating.

But I can listen.

I wanted Bastard to feel like he was in control here. He was the big man, the big cheese, the one literally calling the shots.

The one who could hang himself, if he offered himself enough rope.

Out of the corner of my eye, I noted his chest starting to heave underneath his disguise.

He rubbed his forehead with the back of his hand, but I could tell he was just smearing the burqa around, trapping the sweat under the material as he gasped.

Perfect.

He gripped the material around his waist and wrenched it upward to rip off his burqa. "It's too fucking hot in here."

Since he still had the gun in his right hand, he struggled to strip one-handed. As a guy with probably zero experience ridding himself of floor-length clothing, except a bed sheet on a long-ago Hallowe'en, he managed to expose his bulging gut, hidden by a black shirt, and well-worn jeans, but couldn't get his gun arm's elbow out. "Shit!"

You know, I *could* assist him.

Nah. I watched him flail, unwilling to relinquish his gun and too proud to ask for help.

It felt better than a dozen kitten videos on YouTube.

Who's the bitch now?

However, all good things must end. Once he managed to get the gun arm out, it wasn't such a stretch to pop his head under and unroll the burqa inside out over his left arm.

Bastard flung the material on the bloody floor and got enough breath together to boss me around. "Clean that...shit up." He paused to wheeze, "You can use this."

I hesitated. Transforming myself into Cinderella, pre-prince, mopping blood with a burqa instead of sweeping ashes, hadn't been at the top of my menu.

Still, I kept my head down and staring at the garment rippled on the floor, as if I was considering his generous offer, but mostly avoiding an accidental glance at Bastard's naked face. I've heard that when the kidnappers don't worry about you identifying them, it's because they're about to kill you.

I said to his black boots, "What we really need is a disinfection system. With bleach. Otherwise, we're just smearing blood around. And I ought to dispose of this." I swung the placenta toward him, only a few small inches of movement, but enough to make Bastard take a step back and shout, "Watch it, bitch!"

"Sorry," I said, lowering the bowl. "It's kind of heavy. And slippery. Where would you like me to put it?" I took a step toward him, even though Manouchka's bedside table was to my diagonal right.

"Fuck...you!" he snapped, although now he was gasping between words. "Get. That out. Of. Here!"

"Does that mean I can open the door to deposit it outside?" I asked. Really, I wanted to bolt, but I wasn't that stupid. He was in the mood to shoot.

"No!" he hollered, and sucked his breath in.

I stopped. And waited. While he wheezed.

I didn't tell him to take his inhaler. He was a big boy. And honestly, if he had to concentrate on staying alive, we could probably get the gun away from him.

Tucker stirred beside me. I wondered if he could migrate behind Bastard. If I kept Bastard's concentration on me and the magical placenta, Tucker could jump him.

But how long should we wait?

Emphysematics are usually old, skinny smokers or ex-smokers, sometimes oxygen-dependent, often north of sixty years old. They get a lung infection and slowly crumble over days to weeks (often, they've been in hospital so many times, they try to avoid coming back, but that just means they're sicker when they cross the emerg doors). We hit them with bronchodilators, steroids, and antibiotics for secondary infections.

Asthmatics are usually much younger. Often still smokers. They've got more reserve. But if it's bad enough, a severe cat allergy can unleash a tsunami of an attack that kills them.

However, chances were that Bastard was a regular asthmatic. It would take a long time for an asthmatic to tire. Like, hours if not days. They weren't sick to start with.

And most of them had the sense to take their puffers.

Bastard coughed, wheezed, and coughed again.

His neck looked stringy because the sternocleidomastoid muscles heaved for breath. He was panicking.

I remembered a surgical resident remarking, "It's terrible to watch a child who can't breathe. It's worse than someone bleeding to death." The surgeon agreed.

Bastard glanced at me. I was still trying to keep my head down and pointed away from him, both deferential and advertising that I was not a threat or a witness, no siree, with the placenta as a barrier between us.

Still wheezing, he aimed the gun at me. His hand trembled, but out of the corner of my eye, I thought I saw his finger flex on the trigger.

CHAPTER 29

First I squeezed my eyes shut. I felt like that famous photo from Vietnam taken at the exact moment where one officer shot another man's brains out.

The bullet didn't come.

I was still breathing.

For a second, I kept my eyelids sealed. I didn't want to trigger this guy off. Ha ha, another bad pun. Freudian slips worked in mysterious ways.

What if my last thought was a bad pun?

I shifted my head to the right and peeked at Tucker then. I refused to go out of the world thinking stupid thoughts. I'd rather my last view was of him.

He met my eyes head on.

I caught my breath. I don't think he'd ever meant more to me than at this exact moment. Both of us freaked out, sweaty, on the edge of execution—didn't matter. Only he mattered.

I didn't think I could carve the yearning out of my eyes, so I didn't try.

He stared back at me the same way.

Neither of us said a word.

Still wheezing, Bastard walked right up to Tucker with his gun hand up. He didn't stop walking until that arm reached across the foot of the bed, diagonally across my chest, so his gun pressed against Tucker's sternum.

I yelped. I know it sounds girly. I couldn't help that, or the little voice squeaking out of my throat that said, "Stop!"

Bastard kept the gun braced against Tucker's chest while he fumbled in the front right pocket of his black jeans. He was using his left hand, so he looked awkward, like he was either doing an ironic white boy dance or trying to dislocate his own shoulder.

"Shit. Come. Help me. With this. Bitch," he wheezed.

I broke away from Tucker's side, literally letting Bastard come between us, but you know how they say money talks? Forget that. Firearms talk. They order. They compel.

On the upside, *mein Kommandant* was still panting. I shifted the placenta on my left hip—the three of us were too close for me to dare put it down, although I would have liked to bonk Bastard on the head with it, like in a movie—and slowly stretched the free fingers on my right hand toward his inhaler.

I have to say, even though I hated this guy and wished he would fall unconscious so that we could step over his body on our way out the door, my insides twitched.

Any wrong move, and he could kill Tucker. Just like that.

I wanted to kill Bastard.

(Do no harm.)

Harm the motherfucker.

While I leaned forward, the placenta wobbled in the steel bowl, slopping toward him.

"Stop. It!" he wheezed, but he was struggling. The medically-trained part of my brain automatically noted the ruddiness in his face and the veins bulging in his neck before I remembered to jerk my eyes southward.

Too late. I'd memorized his eyes already, angry brown orbs scanning the room, but I got a flash-quick impression of them glaring from underneath low-set, bushy eyebrows and a rapidly retreating hairline, partially disguised by him shaving his hair close to the skull.

Otherwise, a potato face that I wouldn't have considered threatening if I'd stood next to him on the subway, although I might've noticed his hooked nose and weak pink lips. He'd already been hit by five o'clock shadow, and I have to say, he was kind of dark-skinned for someone who liked to holler the N-word.

In other words, his face had seared itself into my retinas. I was now officially a dead woman.

Bastard's left hand curled into a fist while his right hand pressed the gun into Tucker's chest so hard that I wouldn't have been surprised if he managed to indent the bone.

It must have hurt, but Tucker maintained an eerie rock-like silence.

And then Bastard's hands began to shake.

Holy Christ. I snapped, "Don't worry! I've almost got it!" as I dug the inhaler out of his pocket, my fingers slipping in haste.

Bastard's left hand shot out and clenched my right wrist in a death grip.

I needed stoic lessons from Tucker. I gasped and instinctively twisted away in the same second that he snatched the puffer.

The placenta wobbled in its bowl before it plopped out toward Bastard's crotch.

"Shit!" He twisted away from me and Tucker, backpedaling a beat too late.

The placenta thumped on the ground between our feet. It didn't score a direct hit on either of us, but tiny drops of blood fountained out on impact, spraying our shoes and legs.

He screamed and started to kick it away before he computed that he didn't want to make any contact with a potentially Ebola-laden organ, so at the last second, he tried to kick *past* it.

That just made him overbalance on to his ass, squeezing off a bullet as he dropped.

The sound, so close to me, in the confines of this tiny room, deafened me for a second.

Nothing hurt.

The shot echo reverberated in my clotted ears, but no part of my body screamed with pain or drenched the linoleum with blood.

It took me a second to calculate that I had not been hit.

But maybe someone else had.

The first thing that penetrated my ears was the sound of Manouchka wailing.

I slowly turned to my right, toward my man, dreading what I might find.

Chapter 30

Tucker was lying on the floor. On his stomach.

I hit the ground beside him. I didn't care what Bastard did to me.

I didn't care that my shoes were slipping on the fresh placenta juice and trying to stick to the partially coagulated gore.

I didn't care that a bullet might slam into my skull any second.

I didn't care that Manouchka's screaming pierced my half-deafened ears. If she was screaming, she was alive.

I did care that the baby screeched his tiny, piercing newborn cry. See above.

Vaguely, I realized that I was screaming too. It didn't matter.

I hit the ground on my knees. The tile floor smacked into my patellas, and it felt good. I wanted to feel the pain.

I reached for his shoulders, to roll him over and start CPR. Maybe I should check for bullet holes first, but I grabbed him.

And then Tucker rose up on his elbows and hissed, "Hope!"

I stared at him. It took me a second to realize that he was alive and talking to me. Those brown eyes, the whites tinged with red and circled with exhaustion—he was alive. Blinking.

His mouth was moving.

He was talking with no obvious difficulty.

I scanned his body, checking for wounds. He was smeared in blood, but maybe it was from the floor.

Tucker grabbed my shoulders and threw me down on the ground with him.

I let him. For a second, I stopped thinking about anything or anyone else. I was just so goddamn happy that he was okay that I lay on the bloody floor with him, the tile chilling me through my scrubs, my glasses knocked askew, my stethoscope tumbling off my shoulders, and he said, "I love you. Never forget that. Okay?"

"Never," I said, and I kissed him like I'd never kissed anyone before. One single, desperate, end of the world kiss, his mouth branding mine with heat and pressure that blotted out any other thought or sound, before something rammed into Tucker's body.

His entire body shuddered with the impact, but he clamped down on to my body to protect me.

I ripped my mouth away from his while I tried to figure out what was happening. Bastard loomed above us, his boot smashing into Tucker's ribs again, hard enough that he probably broke two of them at once.

Tucker grunted and tried to roll us both under the bed. I was still in shock, so I resisted for a moment, and this time Bastard's boot caught my side.

Son of a bitch. He might be wearing cheap black boots, but he wielded enough force behind them to knock me breathless.

I couldn't cry. I just gasped for breath.

Tucker folded himself around me, encasing me like human armor, while Bastard said, "Get up. You stupid. Fucking. Doctors. Or I'll start shooting you. In. The. Crotch."

What a bizarre thing to say.

Tucker didn't move. I could feel, even without him speaking, that he would not desert me willingly. But I didn't want him to get shot. And the way we were wrapped together, Bastard could easily kill both of us with a single bullet, if it penetrated deep enough.

I said, "I love you." Then I twisted my shoulders, signalling that he should let me go.

Tucker didn't move.

He smelled good, you know? You wouldn't think it would be possible, with us sweating at gunpoint, delivering babies and rolling around in blood and amniotic fluid. But underneath all that, he still smelled a bit like lemon soap and himself. I let myself close my eyes and inhale that tiny hint of Tucker before Bastard said, "I'm counting to three. One."

Like we were children. But I ignored Bastard's madness so I could talk to my man. "Please, Tucker." This wasn't how I wanted us to die. The in-his-arms part was good, but not the assassination-in-front-of-a-mother-and-newborn part.

"Two."

I started struggling. Tucker was bigger than me. He's not a big guy, maybe five foot ten and an average muscular build, but let's face it. He could win a wrestling contest with me any day. And he was still holding me down.

I started to panic. Like, if Tucker clung to me and refused to let go, pinning me down, weighing me down, so even if I wanted to obey Bastard, he'd shoot us both (in the crotch!) to punish us for not getting up, but I *couldn't* get up—

—and then Tucker levered himself up on his knees, but kept a hand on my chest while he maneuvered his legs on either side of my torso, still guarding me. He muttered, "I love you" in my ear before he turned around to face Bastard himself.

Tucker had sat up without any problem. I noticed that, with the hind part of my brain, still cataloguing any possibility of injury. He rose to his feet quickly, smoothly, placing his body between me and Bastard.

He hadn't been shot. Yet.

My first instinct was to try and block him back. You know that game where you put one hand out, and he puts his palm on the top of your hand, and you put your other hand on top of his, repeat, making a tower of hands, until you end up just whapping each other and laughing?

I wanted to do that, running ahead of him, but then he'd run ahead of me, and on and on. No laughing.

As soon as I moved, Bastard's eyes and gun flicked to me, so I hesitated on my knees, while Tucker's breath hissed out between his teeth.

We couldn't both be heroes. That might kill us.

But I'm not used to anyone else sticking around when the shit hits the fan. Before this, at the eleventh hour, I've always faced down the murderers solo. I've gotten used to risking my own life, but I wanted Tucker to get out of here and make beautiful babies. Preferably with me.

I still wanted a dark-haired baby with Ryan, too. That hadn't changed.

But right here, right now, I wanted to do the rescuing.

David warbled a teeny newborn cry.

I spared him and his mother a glance. Manouchka watched us with wide, terrified eyes. No obvious bleeding or signs of difficulty breathing. I didn't think she'd been shot.

I couldn't make out David's form. Then I realized that not only did she keep him cradled in her arms, as I'd expected, but she'd covered him up with a pillow.

Strange. A bullet would pierce a pillow. But maybe she was thinking *Out of sight, out of mind.*

Or maybe she wasn't thinking.

Please, please don't smother your baby, Manouchka.

David was sobbing, so he still had air, but I twitched and tried to tell her with my eyes, *Let him out!*

Bastard wheezed. I flashed toward him automatically. He spotted me from behind his puffer—no use pretending I wouldn't identify him now—and took a quick shot of Ventolin with one hand while his other trained the gun at my face.

He inhaled the Ventolin, nice and easy. Calmer now that he could breathe. And definitely not amused. "You rolling. Around. In Ebola now, bitch?"

Speaking in longer phrases now, too, I realized with the automated segment of my brain, the doctor part that kept on working, even when the rest of me was frozen with fear and this-can't-be-happening.

"We're all contaminated," I said. There was no point in denying it. Maybe he'd be so grossed out that he'd let us go.

He nodded and took another hit of Ventolin. He was mulling it over. I wondered if he'd hurl us out in the hall like human garbage. That would be the best solution.

The intercom crackled, and Olivia's disembodied voice cut through the room, "Are you all right?"

"I didn't hit anyone," said Bastard, slowly and clearly. "But I will, if you don't do exactly what I say."

CHAPTER 31

Bastard sounded different now. More confident, like he'd made up his mind about something.

Tucker's shoulders twitched. He'd noticed it, too.

Bastard went on. He was slightly short of breath, cutting off the ends of his words, but he didn't sound like he was in the midst of a fatal asthma attack. "I've got one bitch here they say has Ebola. Get her and her kid out of here."

"We can do that," said Olivia, in a neutral voice.

My heart thumped. That was better than I'd imagined. He was kicking Manouchka and David out! And maybe me and Tucker, since we were marinated in blood too…

"I'm going to shove 'em out. But if you try and bust in here, I'll kill the two doctors. First the boy, then the girl."

My heart screamed, even as my brain registered, *Well, at least we know what order we'd die in. That's something.*

Tucker took a half step forward before Bastard pointed the pistol (or whatever it was) in his face, and Tucker backed off.

None of us wanted to die. I was still grinding my knees into the floor.

At least Manouchka and the baby could escape. I glanced at her, but she was staring at Bastard like she could absorb his every word through her eyes. I got the feeling that she wouldn't dare believe in freedom until she'd slammed and locked St. Joe's outer doors behind her.

"That's the first thing," said Bastard.

"You're releasing Manouchka Beauzile and her baby. We will not interfere. We're awaiting further instructions," said Olivia in the same even tone. I definitely got the feeling that she was a professional.

I'd wondered where the police were. Everything in Montreal was disintegrating—last month, a nurse was in a hospital elevator when a cable snapped and it plunged several stories, miraculously leaving her unharmed; parents were visiting a school when a pane of glass fell out of a window and nearly hit them; and one poor woman was eating sushi with her fiancé to celebrate her birthday when part of a building sheared off and pulverized her.

But we do have a police force. Hell, I've got two of their phone numbers. Maybe one of them had texted me, and I could answer if I could just convince Bastard to let me pull out my phone laden with Ryan messages.

But I didn't dare. I needed to spend my favour tokens with extreme vigilance, and even though I would dearly love to hear from my dearly beloveds, my main priority was survival. A phone is not survival.

Maybe the professionals had silently massed outside. Maybe they'd storm the room.

I liked that idea, except the part where hostages usually get caught in the crossfire. I've heard that most hostages die at Get Out of Jail Dead time.

For the most part, hostage-taking is pretty banal to look at. Just a lot of sitting around getting pistol-whipped. But when someone's trying to get in or out, hoo boy. That's when the bodies start flying.

I voted for Bastard just getting rid of our contaminated selves.

Bastard snapped, "Where's Casey?"

"Casey Assim," said Olivia. Even over the intercom, her tone was not quite a question.

"I know what her name is, bitch. Where is she?"

"We're setting all available personnel on task, sir."

"You mean you don't have her yet? You just sitting there with your thumbs up your butts?" Saliva sprayed out of his mouth. I flinched.

Bastard didn't notice. "What am I paying your taxes for?"

I had to bite the inside of my lip and keep my teeth pressed into the tender mucous membranes to stop any other sort of reaction. If this guy worked and paid legitimate taxes, I'd lick that placenta.

Olivia continued, "We just need some more information, sir. What's her birthday?"

I chewed my lip. The skin was flaking, and my throat ached. I needed a drink, but I had no idea when or if I'd ever get to touch water again.

"Her birthday." Bastard flung his arms wide. I winced again, watching the gun, which he held tightly in his right hand. It splayed out toward the exit door before he brought it back to his side. Yay. His side was a marked improvement over one of our heads or hearts. "Why, you want to buy her a present?"

Even I had to wonder what they were playing at. It did seem like basic information they should have unearthed a long time ago.

"It's part of how we identify the patients, sir."

"What, you can't find her? You want me to come out and get her myself? I can do that!" He lifted his gun once more, aiming it at Manouchka and David. "You want me to start blowing these people away until you figure out how to bring me my woman? I can do that."

My God.

Manouchka huddled over David, half-knocking over the pillow, while I sprang to my feet and tried to bar Bastard from his side of the bed, but Manouchka twisted away from me, too.

I didn't mean to scare her. At least the pillow was out of smothering range. I jerked my body straight, trying to form as large a barrier as possible.

Bastard transferred the gun to my forehead.

You know that Dirty Harry pose where the guy is standing back and his gun is out to the side, ready to fire? Like that.

"Don't you fucking move, bitch," he said. "I only need one doc, and you said the other guy is better at stitching."

Tucker started to shoulder me out of the way, but I held my ground and told him, "Sorry."

"Is that Dr. Sze?" said Olivia. She pronounced it like the letter C, which is close enough. I know I shouldn't care about stuff like that now, but there you go.

"The Chinese bitch who delivered the baby," said Bastard, but before I could process that charming description, he pointed the gun at Tucker. "I got some blond guy who stitched up her twat, too. Any wrong moves, and they both buy it."

I wanted to laugh. Twat stitching. A vital skill to add to your c.v.

I was giggling in the face of death. Keeping up my spirits. Or maybe just cracking up.

"Dr. John Tucker," said Olivia. "Both excellent resident doctors who will help Casey, once we locate her for you."

I breathed a little easier. She was reminding Bastard of our names and ranks and skills. That felt good. They were at least somewhat on the ball.

"Where is she!" shouted Bastard.

"We'll locate her very shortly, sir. In the meantime, you mentioned that you would like to release Manouchka Beauzile and her baby?"

"Yeah. Get rid of the niggers."

My heart ached. Manouchka started rocking back and forth in the bed, indenting the mattress, while she cradled David. Bastard's right arm twitched toward her, but I didn't think he would shoot them. Not really. Not if he was even slightly scared of Ebola. And everyone should be scared of Ebola.

"We can arrange that, sir. We can let everyone know that she and her newborn will be coming out of the room and no shots are to be fired."

"That's right. You try to pull anything, I'm bringing down these doctors and every cop I can get."

"No problem, sir. We'll ensure that the area is secure for the Beauzile family, right away."

Bastard moved again, but it was just him raising up his Ventolin puffer with his left hand while he swept his right arm, making the gun's muzzle move across us in a loose arc.

We all held our breath and listened to the hiss as he pressed down on the canister and the gasp as he inhaled the medication.

"I'm sending the bitch doctor to the door behind them. You try and gas us, or shoot us, you're shooting her."

I gulped. Montreal is known for many things. Fine food, exquisite wine, historical architecture, art, and joie de vivre. But expert marksmanship is not one of them. If the cavalry tried to attack Bastard, more than likely, Tucker and I would kick it in the crossfire.

Bastard grinned at me. I noticed that one of his back teeth was silver before I wrenched my head away to gawk at his body instead.

He was chunkier than I'd realized. Now that he'd stripped off the burqa, I figured he was about 200 pounds. Mr. Potato Head and Mr. Potato Body, only made remarkable by the gun now threatening Manouchka and her baby.

His next words jerked my attention back to his flabby, pink lips. "Get out, niggers."

Chapter 32

Ah. The bigot's call to action.

Time for me to lead Manouchka and David to freedom.

And possibly get ganked in the process.

I tried to smile reassuringly at Manouchka while I took a millisecond to breathe.

Once Ryan tried to introduce me to Buddhist philosophy. I think it was because I showed zero interest in Christianity, and it was a gateway discussion, but anyway. He said Buddhism was about concentrating on one thing at a time.

True dat.

I forced myself to concentrate on the air zipping in and out of my nostrils and thought, Okay. Instead of spazzing out about how unstable both Bastard and the Montreal security system could be, I'd keep my eyes locked on one step at a time. Not "Will I get free? Will I get shot?" But *Let's see if, at this exact moment, I can guide Manouchka and David out of this hellhole.*

And really, I'd rather be doing something. Even at gunpoint, I'd rather move around than freeze in position with my arms crossed and my teeth clenched.

I glanced at Tucker. He stared back at me. I could feel him willing me to be calm, to be stable, to do this right.

I could handle that.

Manouchka sniffed and huddled David against her chest. "Are we leaving?" she asked me in French. Her voice shook on the last word, but she sat up straight. Like a queen.

"You and David are leaving," I said, also in French. My lips widened, but I know the smile didn't make it to my eyes.

"Thank you," she said, with dignity.

She tried to heave herself out of bed and winced. The Lidocaine must be wearing off, or maybe it was never much good in the first place. My heart melted at her bravery. Nerves of titanium, that woman.

I offered her my arm, but she wouldn't take it, even though her arms were full with David, making it difficult for her to balance, and she must've been aching from the waist down.

Bastard clicked his tongue. Still, even he didn't have the gall to yell at a woman who'd just delivered a baby.

It seemed like an hour, but it probably only took a minute or three for her to shift one buttock, and then another, inching her way to the edge of the bed so she could dangle her legs.

Finally, she consented to take my arm with one fingertip and hop to her feet. I heard her breath puff out, but she didn't cry out at all, and she kept her face blank.

Tucker reached to assist her, or us, but Bastard pointed the gun at his ear and said, "You stay right where you are, buddy."

David had sunk back into a deep sleep. I marveled at his teeny chest, heaving up and down, while his eyes stayed mostly-closed and 100 percent oblivious. I've heard about sleeping like a baby, but here was the living proof. Thank goodness. The less he remembered of this, the better.

Manouchka steadied herself and promptly released me so that she could continue to support David with both arms.

I knew better than to offer to hold him. First of all, she wouldn't let him go, and secondly, this was their one collective chance at escape. If it were my baby, I'd kill anyone who tried to come between us.

Bastard stood at about one o'clock, in line with the incubator and guarding Tucker, so I made sure I was on Manouchka's left, shielding her slightly, as we walked toward the door.

Bastard had ordered me to open it, to maximize the chance of me catching any stray bombs, but for now, I tried to drop back a little, so that I could block her slightly from our greatest immediate threat.

She held her head high as she walked, no, marched, away from Bastard. Didn't even glance at him. No thank you for letting her go, no curses for calling her a nigger. She treated him like he was irrelevant, and even though I didn't look back, I imagined Bastard's eyes smoldering and his thumb rubbing the gun's trigger.

Tucker cleared his throat. I caught my breath, wondering if he'd engineered some brilliant move for all of our deliverance as soon as I cracked open that door.

The second passed. I started breathing again, shadowing Manouchka and David, one footfall at a time. The chances of any of us manifesting a miracle right here, right now: unlikely. This ain't Hollywood.

I didn't hear any cavalry outside. I know stealth must be one of their specialties, but I didn't detect anyone tiptoeing in the hallway, or shifting weaponry around.

Still. We should be prepared to hit the floor. I wondered if I should signal Manouchka, but she motored to the exit fast enough that I sped up my stride.

My eyes focused on that door. The crack of light spilling from underneath it seemed like heaven to me. The promise of a brightly-lit space, open and relatively free of blood and gunfire.

I ached to thrust open the door and run for it. A mad dash toward liberty and justice. I'd just scream, "Come on, guys! *Viens t'en!*" and sprint like we were World War I combatants trying to scale Vimy Ridge.

But I knew I couldn't do that, because Manouchka couldn't outrun me. She and David would bring up the rear and die, horribly deserted.

So when we were a foot from the door, I said, in English, mostly for Bastard's benefit, but also for any lurking cavalry members, "I'm reaching for the doorknob, to let Manouchka and David go." And then I glanced at Bastard. I hadn't wanted to do that, hadn't wanted to ask him for permission, but I did it instinctively, and hated myself in that moment.

Bastard gave a miniature nod.

Manouchka grasped the door handle first.

Chapter 33

The door handle was a bar, easier to grip than a knob, even with a babe in arms.

But David started to slip, and when she clutched him with both arms, I opened the door. What Bastard asked for, Bastard got. For now.

I did it slowly. No sudden movements that might trigger off either Bastard or the cavalry. I flexed my arm, drawing the door inside, while I squinted at the growing light at its edge.

You know the poem about the exquisiteness of a tree? Nature was beyond my reach, right now, but I burned for the paradise unfolding before me. The fluorescent lights, the relatively fresh air, the grotty telephone just a body-length away in the nursing station, the unseen-but-they-have-to-be-here police, and Ryan's presence.

I know it sounds strange, since I hadn't checked my phone or heard anything since Manouchka delivered her baby, but I sensed Ryan was nearby, or at least closer than he'd been. Which was both a great and terrible feeling.

I'd rather he was safely stowed away in Ottawa, but I swear he was either outside the hospital or making his way toward me.

I wanted to fling my body toward his.

But Tucker hung back in the shadows, his life at the mercy of a madman.

It was one of the hardest things I ever did, but I announced, "Everything looks okay," and stepped to the side, within the room, holding the door open.

Manouchka and David escaped alone into that lovely brilliance.

I peeked through the door jamb. My eyes had adjusted to the light, and my throat burned as I lingered on the threshold to nirvana.

Yes, the heretofore unrecognized glory of soiled linen bins, and the alcove with the broken ice machine dispenser, and most of all, the cavalry that must be, had to be trumpeting toward us, even though the nursing station across from me looked suspiciously empty.

I imagined that around the corner, massing the stairs and blocking the elevators, lurked officers with guns and canine units and high tech equipment, just waiting to break me and Tucker free.

They had to be. Someone had carried June away. True, that could have been hospital personnel, but we'd been here long enough for the Canadian version of the SWAT team to kick some motherfucking ass.

Through the gap, I watched Manouchka dash down the hallway to her left. I'd assumed she couldn't run, but she sprinted like Donovan Bailey in the 100-metre race, with David tucked securely under her right arm while her left arm pumped in the air.

I watched her go.

Bastard said, "Close the door, bitch."

Manouchka hit the ward doors, and then she was out in the elevator lobby. Free. Away.

I released the door. It clicked shut behind her.

She was safe. Or at least safer.

Bastard crossed the room and slammed the wooden door with the palm of his hand. The walls reverberated with the force of his blow. He pointed the gun at me. "There. Now the Ebola bitch is gone."

I glanced down at my bloody scrubs, not to unnerve him this time—my heart was still fleeing down the hall with Manouchka and David—but more out of confusion. If she was contaminated, we were all contaminated.

Bastard surveyed me from hair to sneakers. My heart thumped when I realized his eyes paused not just at the blood stains, but at my breasts and hips. He wrinkled his nose and said, "Clean yourself up."

"You mean—" My heart pounded. He'd let Manouchka and David go. Could he free me, too?

He jerked his chin to the right, to the destroyed bathroom. "Wash up and get rid of your clothes."

"But...I don't have a spare set of scrubs in this room." The way he checked me out, I'd just as soon keep my biohazardous greens.

"You had that blue thing. You know, the one that you tied around your neck when you delivered the baby."

"I think there's only one gown per room," I lied. I've gowned up occasionally at the same time as the OB/gyn, but they try to ration them. They're expensive.

"She's right," said Tucker.

Bastard waved his hand at the cart. "Just put one of those yellow things on. I saw some other chick wearing it. They keep them on the wall and throw 'em away. I bet you got tons of those."

He meant isolation/infection control gowns. I licked my cracked lips, trying to think rational Buddhist thoughts. On one hand, I wanted to distract him from Manouchka and David as they made their way to safety. Bastard's sudden interest in my personal hygiene pretty much guaranteed their escape.

On the other hand, I felt off-kilter. Somehow, the fact that half of us had managed to break free had made me fantasize that maybe Tucker and I could bolt, too. Instead, Bastard seemed to be getting more nuts.

I tried to grin like this was a massive joke. "You mean those disposable gowns? They're made out of paper." I don't know what they're made out of, exactly. They feel like soft, thin, plasticized paper towel. They're translucent yellow and they don't tie all the way around, just gape at the back, the way patients hate because their bums poke out when they're trying to walk down the hall with their IV's.

You've got to put two gowns on, one tied in the front and one in the back, to get any privacy. I doubted that was what Bastard had in mind. And that wouldn't work because the material itself is see-through.

"You heard what I said, bitch. I don't want that black bitch's blood on you when you deliver my boy. Now do it, or I'll kick you in the hall and shoot you in the head."

Well, at least then I'd escape into the hall for a whiff of freedom before I went splat.

The whole thing made no sense. We still had a placenta rolling around the floor, albeit half under the bed, plus old and new blood splatters from both June and Manouchka. What good would it do to clean me up if I'd trot right back into what looked like a snuff film set?

When I silently surveyed the mess, Bastard gestured at Tucker and said, "He'll mop up the room and then he'll clean off too. You shower first."

A shower. The mere thought of immersing myself in water, suds and steam made me want to sing the Hallelujah Chorus—

—except the part where I'd then have to traipse around the room dressed like a downmarket version of Lady Gaga. I mean, I'd do it for Tucker solo, although the yellow isolation gowns are no sane man's idea of foreplay.

But Bastard? Even though he was supposedly on a cleansing kick for Casey and his baby, I didn't trust him.

Still, I took a step toward the bathroom. Toward freshness. Clarity. Everything this man was not.

I just wished that I could search for a pair of scrubs first. That wasn't worth the risk of getting shot, though.

Tucker murmured, "I'll look for you."

He'd figured out what I was thinking, somehow. I glanced at him out of the corner of my right eye and clenched my hand, trying to convey that I loved him and thanked him. Always.

Then I slipped into the bathroom and tried to swing the intact half of the door closed before I hesitated. It would keep Bastard out, but what if Tucker needed me?

"Keep the door open, bitch!" Bastard hollered.

Well, that decided that. I lifted my hands off the wood. Tucker muttered something, but Bastard was already there, hauling the half-door open and looming in the entry before he jabbed the gun at my breasts. "Keep the door open, or I'll shoot you here and lock your body in the bathtub."

Ugh. I thought of Bluebeard's wives, sliced into bloody bits. Or the more modern equivalent, men who had dissolved their wives' bodies in bathtubs filled with acid.

Goosebumps rose on my arms, and I had to clench my teeth to stop them from chattering.

Bastard glanced southward, down my body, and I realized that my nipples had sprung to attention.

Totally involuntary. I wasn't turned on, the room wasn't particularly cold, but there it was. Or rather, there they were. I'd worn a light bra today—can't really stand those things, so I pick the most minimal ones possible, especially when I'm on call.

I wanted to cross my arms, but he'd moved the gun close enough that I was afraid I'd nudge the muzzle with my elbows.

I froze.

Bastard exhaled slowly. He wasn't wheezing now. And his eyes darted between my breasts, ping-ponging from left to right like he was a thirteen-year-old who'd never seen any before.

This man wanted me to shower with the door open?

In slow motion, his left hand began to raise in the air, rotating outward to cup my breast.

I checked my impulse to jerk backward. Or yell. Or hit him. None of these were an option now.

Instead, I snapped, "I'm contaminated."

Chapter 34

"What?" Bastard's eyes hiked up to mine.

We stared each other full in the face.

No use pretending that I hadn't memorized his potato features. I'd signed and sealed my death warrant long ago.

And right now, I was past caring. I just wanted us to survive, if only for the next few minutes.

One minute at a time, I thought. Like Buddha Ryan might coach me.

"I'm covered in blood from Manouchka and June," I said, trying to keep my voice even instead of edgy. "I've got to wash it away."

He checked out the stains on my scrubs, but that started up the boobie hypnosis again.

This was ridiculous. Barely anyone pays attention to my breasts, ever. They're so small, one of my supposed friends joked that they'd been put on backwards. Why on earth would he be so taken with them, when he claimed he was on a mission for Casey?

My brain clicked into gear, and I said, "I wouldn't want to hurt Casey and your baby. With all this blood."

He jerked his head from side to side like a dog tossing water droplets out of its ears. "Casey," he repeated.

"Yes. The woman you love, who's having your baby." Casey might not want to hear this, but I needed to employ every weapon right now, including storytelling, like a Scheherazade on steroids.

"Casey. My baby."

"Right." He was a bit red in the face, as well as dumbly repeating my words. Maybe he was starting to lose it, too? Perhaps shooting people and holding hostages was taxing work, and he was starting to get tired and slow. One can only hope.

I smiled at him, because his thoughts seemed to be staggering in the right direction, but then he fixated on my lips.

Ryan once told me I had a sexy mouth, right before he did something X-Rated with it. So this was *not* the kind of attention I wanted.

Maybe *I* should pick up the burqa.

In fact, that was a great idea. Not that I wanted to share clothes with the guy, but I'd rather do that than get raped. So I said, "I'm cold."

"I can see that," said Bastard, his gaze drifting down to my chest again.

For a second, something flickered in my hindbrain. I've seen other girls use their looks to get ahead. It's never been an issue for me. Not because I'm so heinous-looking, I think, but because it's only in the past few years that Asian beauty has gone mainstream, that I've outgrown the "Flat nose! Four eyes!" comments, and because I'm really focused on school, not beauty pageants. I mean, Montreal has rained men down on me, but Ryan and Tucker are the exception, not the norm.

Just my luck, if I suddenly transformed from a forgettable duckling into a swan while being held hostage.

But far more likely that Bastard was hopped up on adrenaline and wanted to jump anything with ovaries but no Ebola.

I said, in a high, strained voice, "I'm just going to make sure I can find a change of clothes, okay?" while Tucker advanced toward the bathroom doorway and said to Bastard, "Maybe I can give you a hand."

"Don't move," said Bastard, but from the way he twitched his head to the right, he was talking to Tucker, in the main room.

Tucker paused, but his dark eyes were fixed on mine, telegraphing, *I'll get you out of this.*

I shook my head slightly and pointed back his way, toward the delivery cart. "All the gowns are in the room. I'm going to go find one."

"I already looked, Hope." Tucker sounded grim. "I don't even see any disposables. You'd have to change back into your scrubs, if that's all right."

"Let me have a look, okay?" I said, grinning at Bastard like a Hallowe'en skull before I thought to lower my eyes and glance up at him beneath my lashes. Hell, it works in cartoons.

After a long minute, Bastard said, "I'll come with you. You can wear one of those yellow things."

I'm telling you, if I get out of here, I am *never* looking at those MRSA isolation gowns the same way again.

But at least he twitched his body out of the way so that I could edge past him without giving him a lap dance.

Tucker stared at me as I passed by, and I tried to communicate, *Trust me. I've got a plan.*

Sort of.

I poked around in the delivery cart, but Tucker had already searched it, so I lifted a few cloth-wrapped shapes half-heartedly and said, "Hmm. I definitely don't see the yellow ones you like."

"Stupid fuckers," said Bastard.

"Let me check around the bed," I said, and when he didn't say no, I carefully migrated to the side of the bed and scooped the burqa off the floor. "I'll just put this on, and I'll be fine."

"It's too big," said Bastard, but I was already fighting my way into it. It was like a bag, really, with the mail slot for the eyes, plus sleeves.

I aimed for the eye hole first. I was trying not to panic, because I couldn't see, and I could smell him in the cloth.

Stale sweat and cheap deodorant and marijuana and beer and just the primal nastiness of wearing a murderer's disguise. Plus whatever blood and amniotic fluid it had stewed in on the floor. But I forced myself to calm down. Better this than swallowing his semen.

I swam my way through the material until I got to the eye hole, and then I flapped into one sleeve, and then the other.

Bastard started cackling.

I probably looked ludicrous. The sleeves were what felt like half an arm too long, and once I figured out the bunched-up hem and ushered it past my waist, it fell to the ground in a pool of material. He must've thought I looked like a kid dressing up like a black ghost for trick or treats.

Even Tucker bit his lip like he was trying not to laugh.

"I'm six foot two," said Bastard.

Okay. Taller than I thought. A foot more than me, not counting my quarter inch (Hope and the angry quarter inch! Could we make a musical about this? Bastard was even a drag queen, technically!).

I guess we were all teetering on the brink. Whatever you wanted to call it, Bastard started laughing, a stupid hee-haw that tugged at the corners of my mouth, and Tucker shook his head and smiled at me while he mouthed, *I love you.*

I love you, I mouthed back, and then it occurred to me that neither he nor Bastard could see my lips move. I might be kissing the same fabric that had caressed a killer's mouth, but at least I had the freedom to mouth *Die, motherfucker* from behind the cloth.

Which felt surprisingly good.

Bastard finished laughing, and then he said, "You look stupid. Take it off."

Ugh. I hated that I had so little control over my own body that I couldn't even wear his cast-offs without permission.

"Now. And take a shower," he said. From the look in his eye, he was looking forward to it.

Chapter 35

The burqa wasn't working its magic yet. It's supposed to help you keep your chastity because men won't be tempted by your shape, but I guess these operative scrubs were just too, too sexy. I had to create a new game plan.

Bastard gestured at Tucker. "Your boyfriend's gonna use that thing to mop up in here anyway." He held out his hand for the burqa.

I considered resisting, but that hadn't worked out for anyone else so far.

The only thing that worked was outwitting him with Ebola. So I had to use that, had to gross him out, and remind him that I, too, was unclean.

I started prolonging my exhalations. I'd play the asthma card again while I figured out what to do.

Bastard dropped his eyes down to my chest once more. This time I was heaving, not in a come-hither way, and covered by heavy cloth. Still, it made me a little nervous, and I was already claustrophobic and a bit hot in the burqa, so it was easy to start wheezing. Just at the end. But definitely high-pitched and noticeable in the close confines of this room.

"Aww. Your asthma's acting up again?" said Bastard, in a concerned voice.

I nodded my head. The burqa material bobbed up and down with me, but even the head part was too big. It drooped over my eyes. I shoved it back.

"I guess you'll be wanting this," said Bastard. A grin crept across his face. He dug the puffer out and showed it to me with his left hand.

He still had the gun in his right, but he was a little distracted by his own awesomeness right now.

If we were going to attack him, now was the time. Right?

I took a step forward, but the burqa material rippled, distracting me. If I was going to fight, I'd have to practice in this thing first.

"Here, kitty, kitty," said Bastard, shaking the puffer at me. It rattled, and he laughed. Oh, he was having a grand time. Too bad nobody else was.

Tucker said, "Dr. Sze."

"Shut up, motherfucker," said Bastard, without turning around. Clearly, he wasn't swayed by the fact that I was a doctor. Hell, maybe it would encourage him. At least, naughty nurse fantasies seemed to be pretty common. "I'm talking to her. And I'm telling you, Doctor Zee, that if you want this, you gotta do something for me."

Like delivering a baby wasn't enough? "You want me to find Casey and deliver your son?" I said, playing dumb in order to reactivate fond memories of his baby mama.

"Yeah. That," he said.

"Okay—"

"And take your top off," he said.

My eyes shot back to his, startled, and he licked his lips and grinned. "Your bra. Everything. You gotta get naked for your shower anyway, right?"

"No," said Tucker, even before I could.

Tucker walked around and stood in front of him. Between us. "She's a medical doctor and deserves to be treated with respect."

Bastard laughed. "I'm treating her with respect, buddy. If I hadn't, I'd already have her bent over."

This was not happening. I unlocked my lips. "What about Casey? I think I heard something." I remembered to wheeze, but not too badly. I didn't want him to believe this was a life or death issue in case I got distracted and forgot to wheeze.

"What?" Bastard's grin stretched across his face, wide enough to show a metal crown on his bottom left. "That old trick? You think you can grab the puffer out of my hand while I'm not looking? Dream on. And take that shit off. I bet you look all right under there."

At least he wasn't drooling. Yet. "I'm serious," I said. "Let's talk to Olivia." I took two steps toward the head of the bed, and the intercom, but Bastard grabbed me by the right arm and said, "Don't make me rip this thing off of you."

Ah. The arm squeeze. I felt my hand veins bulge with a dreadful familiarity. I could sense the pressure in my arm, but not watch my veins react, through the burqa.

"Let her go," said Tucker. His voice sounded strangled. He was looking at Bastard, so I couldn't see his face, even if the burqa didn't keep dropping a curtain over my eyes.

"It's okay," I said. "I just want to talk to Olivia. I bet she has more news. OLIVIA!" I hollered, and Bastard's hand clamped down like a live snake bracelet, but the intercom crackled to life.

"Did you call me?" came Olivia's calm voice, and somehow that broke the tension in the room, like a teacher suddenly bringing us all to order.

I sagged inwardly with relief, but what I said was, "I thought I heard something. Do you have any news about Casey Assim?"

"We've located her place of residence," said Olivia.

Bastard released my arm so he could yell at the intercom. "You found her fucking house? What kind of detectives are you? I need you to bring me my woman and my baby. Is that so hard?"

Olivia said, "We're doing our utmost, sir. We've contacted her family members."

"I'm her family, goddamn it! I'm the father of her child. Don't you get that? Are you so fucking stupid?" He kept railing at her, and I thought, *Good. Vent. Get it all out, so that you don't need to rape me to prove what a fucking man you are.*

Tucker backed toward me, circling around Bastard and coming up on my right side, trying to cut between me and the bed. He was obviously eyeing Bastard, who stood on my right but slightly behind me, shouting while wielding the almighty gun. "Do you even know where Casey is? Huh? Do you have any fucking clue? Because if not, these doctors aren't doing me any good. I could kill them any second. You think of that, bitch?"

Tucker turned sideways, but he couldn't quite wedge between me and the bed. I didn't dare move, because that would draw attention to both of us, but when Tucker's right arm slipped forward, I clutched his hand in my left.

Tucker squeezed back so hard that it hurt. I knew what he was thinking. This was his line in the sand. He'd watched Bastard break down two doors. He'd watched him shoot June. He'd watched him threaten Manouchka and David. He'd watched Bastard hold me at gunpoint. He'd watched Bastard backhand me.

But he wasn't going to let the guy strip me and fuck me. He would die first.

Chapter 36

Tucker tightened his pressure on my hand even further. I wouldn't have thought it was possible, but for a second, he reminded me of Bastard.

I closed my eyes, willing myself to breathe through the pain.

This was so surreal. I was draped in a killer's burqa, holding hands with Tucker, while the madman threatened to kill both of us.

At least we'd saved Manouchka and David.

Olivia spoke next. "Those doctors are valued members of our team."

It sounded like she was reading a script, and maybe she was. My heart dropped. If she wasn't good at playing Bastard psychologically, he'd freak out. Sodomize me, shoot both of us, who knew.

Bastard barked out a laugh. "They're on *my* team. If you get Casey here in the next twenty minutes, and they deliver my baby, I'll let them live. If you don't, I'll kill 'em. Simple as that."

"We need the doctors alive," said Olivia.

"Did you hear what I just said, bitch? They're alive."

"We need you to show us. Right now," said Olivia.

Bastard paused to compute that. "Didn't you hear the girl yelling?"

"I need to hear both of them," said Olivia.

"Are you getting me Casey?"

"We're doing our utmost, sir."

He snorted. "Prove it."

"We know that you were living together at 2363 Giroux Road, Apartment B6, until three weeks ago. We know that she left that apartment—"

"Ancient history," said Bastard, although I wanted to hear it. Why had she left the apartment, and where did she go? Bastard had so few Achilles heels. One of them was Casey. Another was his son. We'd have to exploit them in the next twenty minutes in order to survive.

"She talked to her sister this morning."

"Tara?" Bastard sounded distracted.

"Yes. Tara, at 9:19 this morning."

"What did she say?"

"We don't have a recording of her call, just the record of her cell phone usage."

"So where is she using it, bitch? I know you've got a GPS and shit like that. Why aren't you using it?"

"She's not using her cell phone right now."

"Probably the battery ran out. Stupid cow," he said, but with some affection. You know how they complain that rappers are always calling women bitches and hos? I guess I finally met someone where that's true. 'Cow' was a step up for him.

"We're finding her, sir. We're holding up our end of the deal. Now we need you to hold up yours. We need proof of life for Dr. John Tucker and Dr. Hope Sze."

"Fine," said Bastard, and let go of my arm so he could swing his left fist at Tucker's face.

Tucker ducked. He hadn't let go of my hand, so I was jerked downward and sideways by his movement, before I belatedly caught my footing. I yelped.

Bastard said, "Jesus. I'm just messing with ya."

Tucker didn't take his eyes off of him as he slowly straightened his legs, keeping his knees soft. Ready for a fight.

WTH?

My brain calculated one thing: Bastard had jumped the shark.

True, I doubt many people in their right mind start shooting and kidnapping hospital people in the first place, but at least he'd been consistent until the last twenty minutes or so. In some ways, it worried me more that he was regaining his sex drive and telling supposed jokes. What other lines would he cross next?

Bastard chuckled, oblivious. "Now say hello to the nice lady."

Tucker squared his shoulders. He interlaced his fingers with mine, which meant letting go of me for a second, but only so that he could weave our fingers more tightly. I thought that was symbolic, but before I could make a whole metaphor out of it, Tucker started speaking. "This is Dr. John Tucker." His voice was firm. He took a breath to search for the next words. "Dr. Hope Sze and I—"

"Shut up, Blondie, and let the chink speak for herself."

Tucker's teeth clicked closed. He didn't like that one bit.

Neither did I, although the slurs had lost their shock value a long time ago. "This is Dr. Hope Sze," I announced. If we said "doctor" enough times, maybe it would help ward off evil. My voice sounded weird, echoing in my own ears within the burqa. "Dr. Tucker and I promised to deliver—"

"Shaddup. They don't need your life story," said Bastard.

I breathed a little more easily within the confines of the material, though. I'd rather he told me off than ripped off my clothes.

Of course, those two things weren't mutually exclusive. I just prayed that invoking Casey, even subconsciously, would have some protective effect.

"We do need to know if you're in good health," said Olivia.

"Physically intact, psychologically stressed," Tucker replied immediately.

I thought that summed it up, but Bastard said, "I'll fucking give you stress, Blondie. Quit holding hands with your girlfriend and scrub that floor. I want it nice and clean for my woman." He raised his voice and his head toward the intercom. "You hear that, bitch? I expect Casey walking through that door in eighteen minutes. Clock's a-tickin', bitch."

Too many bitches. A girl could get confused. But this time, I was pretty sure he was talking to Olivia.

"Sir, we're doing our best. We hear you. The time limit is impossible."

"I already gave you all the time you needed. Hell, the nigger woman delivered a baby! What are you doing besides sitting with your thumb up your ass! I want Casey and my boy!" He lifted his gun and pointed it at Tucker. "Get on the cleaning, Blondie, or you'll be looking at the hole in your own head."

Shit. He was definitely starting to crack.

Tucker squeezed my hand one last time before he started to let go

I said, "Don't." My throat garbled the words. I clung to him. So much for me cast as the fiery, independent heroine. I just wanted him. "I can help you. Two hands—four hands—are better than two, right? Right. I can do spic and span. Where's the soap?"

"No, darling," said Bastard. His voice changed, dropped into throatiness. "You just take off that thing, give it to your boyfriend, and come lie on the bed with me. You're my insurance."

Chapter 37

I didn't move.

I held on to Tucker as Bastard backed toward the bed, his eyes looking me up and down, even inside the fucking burqa.

"And take off your shirt. Hell, take off all your clothes. You won't be needing 'em."

Even more than Bastard raping me, one thought echoed through my head: *I can't have Tucker see me naked for the first time like this*. It would have been bad enough for Ryan, to pollute the memories we'd built together. But for Tucker, when we'd been dancing back and forth so many times, fantasizing about each other, to end with me stripping down for a murderer…

It was killing what we'd built together. Sacrificing it on an altar of blood and pain, just so we could survive a few more miserable minutes.

"I'm covered in blood," I told him. "I'm contaminated."

"Shit," said Bastard.

"That bed is contaminated, too," I said.

"Fuck." He glanced at it in irritation.

"Plus I have my period." Might as well go for broke here. I read once, in *The Joy of Sex*, that grossing out your rapist is a good strategy.

"Jesus. What *don't* you have?" His gaze fell on my and Tucker's hands, still intertwined, although partially hidden by the too-long burqa sleeve. He said, "I told you to let *go*."

With the last word, his left hand karate-chopped toward us, smashing into our hands. My thumb took the brunt of it. Pain firecrackered through my hand, which spasmed and somehow let go of Tucker.

Just as Tucker reared back and kicked Bastard square in the crotch.

Bastard fell back with a grunt.

Tucker screamed, "Hope, *RUN!*"

Chapter 38

A split second.

They say that all the time, that's all you have, a split second.

Less than a breath to turn and rush for the door, abandoning my man in order to outrace a bullet.

I started to. Because he told me to. Because I wanted to live. Because I knew he'd just sacrificed himself for me.

I wheeled to my left, away from Tucker, away from Bastard.

Toward the door.

But I couldn't. I stopped after one step.

I couldn't leave Tucker, even if we both died.

I turned back to Tucker.

Bastard had raised his gun up. He was red in the face and had death in his eyes. It sounds like a cliché, but the bar had just been raised from "toying with you" to "premeditated murder."

I said, "Don't do it."

Bastard's eyelids hardly flickered in response. His gun levelled at Tucker, who shouted again, "Run!" But the note in his voice was futile. He knew I wouldn't run.

The agony in his voice seared through me, raising goose bumps on my arms. He would die for me, but he didn't want it to be in vain.

Still, I had to make our nightmare complete. I lifted my hands in the air and said, "I'll take the burqa off."

Bastard gasped, "I don't. Give a shit. About that. Anymore. He fuckin' *hit.* Me. In the nuts."

Must've been pretty hard, too, because his voice was hollow and I thought I could detect a sheen of sweat across his forehead. Good. He'd be less interested in using them if they were newly injured.

Bastard pointed the gun at Tucker's head. "Say goodbye, Blondie."

Tucker blinked before he stared at me, willing me to flee like a good girl.

Instead, I hollered, "Wait! I can make it up to you."

"No one can make it up to me, bitch." But he didn't cock the hammer. Maybe he'd gotten tired of killing people. He'd shot Stan and June right away, but he let Manouchka and David go. He wasn't just a brainless machine gun. I could appeal to, well, his baser nature.

That was all I had left.

We'd worn out the Casey card. He'd already set a time limit on her arrival, which was now ticking down to maybe less than fifteen minutes. If the cavalry was going to bust out, now was the time.

So now the trick was to lure him away from Tucker without having sex with him.

I knew this was a dangerous game. Even if Bastard's usual equipment was temporarily on pause, I remember a man, maybe a soldier, in Rwanda who raped a woman with a gun and shot it off inside her vagina.

Still, when you're a doctor on call, you just take it one hour at a time. If it's a really bad night, you take one minute at a time. You might not think that you can survive another eight hours, but eight minutes? That just might be possible.

I might be able to Mata Hari him for fifteen minutes. "You want me to get clean, right? So I'm ready for Casey and your son?"

"Yeah. Show me your tits."

Right. Mardi Gras at St. Joseph's Hospital. I took a deep breath.

"It's really hot in here," I breathed, trying to sound sultry. "I'm going to take it off anyway."

"Hope," said Tucker.

Bastard whipped toward him. "Shut your motherfucking mouth, or I'll blow it off." He turned back to me with a crooked grin. "All right, bitch. Entertain me. Show me your mouth."

My hands faltered for a second. I remembered how, on Reddit's Girls Gone Wild page, one girl had posted a picture of herself lifting her top, with the title something like, "Do you like small tits?" (I clicked on it for obvious reasons.) To my surprise, not only had the guys slavered over her breasts, but at least two of them drooled over her lips in the top left of the photo.

And her lips happened to look like mine.

So I wasn't crazy about revealing my naked face to Bastard, even though he'd already seen it before. In fact, it could be even more of an aphrodisiac that I was all covered up, so a glimpse of my arms or my hair would make him think he'd scored.

But this wasn't about me. This was about saving Tucker. Already, the energy in the room had dipped from murderous to...still powder keg, but at least now he'd shifted the gun between us, no longer aiming it directly at Tucker's forehead.

I didn't say I would take everything off. I didn't say I would fuck him. I was just taking off the burqa.

I picked up the hem and joked, still a little breathless, "Could I have some music?"

CHAPTER 39

Bastard laughed. "Would that put you in the mood?"

"Would it put you in the mood?" I countered. Somehow, it was easier to vamp within the confines of the material. He couldn't see my mouth twisting in disgust. He probably wouldn't have picked up on the sarcasm in my gaze anyway. I thrust one hip out, and his gaze dropped down to it.

Yep, his testicles were feeling better.

Should I strip sooner, before his throbbing balls recovered from Tucker's shoe?

Or later, to draw this out as long as possible?

Later, I decided. Tucker would do his level best to kill Bastard if he dropped his pants. So I needed to delay that moment as long as possible, for all of our sakes.

Bastard chuckled. "I like you, girl. Hell, let's get some tunes."

"I could use my phone," I said, my body suddenly on the alert. If he let me access my technology, I could check my texts. I was willing to bet my eyes that Ryan had posted something useful as well as supportive.

"Naw. That would ruin the show." He snapped the fingers of his stray hand. "Blondie. Get on that."

I tensed. Forcing Tucker to play the music for me to strip for this inglorious SOB might just shove him over the edge.

Bastard tilted his head up. "Let's see. Something good. You got 'Girls, Girls, Girls'?"

Ugh. I'd heard that on the radio the other day. Changed the station. I also thought it sounded completely ludicröus (get it? Ludicrous with an umlaut, in honour of Motley Crüe), since I was the only female in the room. Girl, Girl, Girl doesn't have the same ring to it.

Or "'Cherry Pie'? You know that one, by Warrant?"

How old was this guy, anyway? The only reason I knew that one was because once, at Ryan's church, they played it when a bad guy swung on stage, before he was saved, of course.

"No, wait. The one where she's on her knees." Bastard eyeballed me. "That's what I want."

Chapter 40

"I don't have that one." Tucker's flat voice cut through the testosterone haze, but Bastard didn't flinch.

"That's the one I want," said Bastard. He took a half step toward me, and I had to fight not to move backward. I totally would have done it, except it'd ruin the illusion of me flirting with him.

I was so bad at this. I'd dated Ryan for four years, then basically only did school, before getting touched by Aphrodite as soon as I landed in Montreal. I would have traded back every ounce of sex appeal at this point, just to have Bastard treat me like one of the guys, except he probably still wanted to whack Tucker.

"I bet I could download it!" I said brightly. "Just let me get out my phone."

"I bet you could download anything," said Bastard, taking another step toward me, close enough that the smell of his sweat clogged my nostrils, and I tried not to gag. Dang. I'd never thought of download in a dirty way before.

Bastard was still talking. "No phone for you, though. Blondie can take care of it."

"What's the name of the song?" said Tucker. I could tell, without looking at him, that he'd decided a song was a better delaying tactic than anything else.

Bastard sneered. "You're a doctor, but you don't know shit about good music."

"I can get good music, if you tell me what song you want. Or I'll have to search for it."

"It's about a girl who's giving him a blow job and begging for it," said Bastard, his tone dropping.

"By Nickelback?" Tucker inputted the information into his phone with sluggish fingers.

"Jesus, you're slow," said Bastard. "I could have your girlfriend's mouth around my dick before you press enter." He turned his flat eyes on me. "As a matter of fact..."

Oh, God. Not my favourite activity at the best of times. If Bastard tried it on me, I would literally puke. And I wasn't sure that would stop him.

"You wouldn't want Casey to see that," I said, which was not a good segue, but I was desperate. "She's coming any second now, right? That's what you were asking for."

Bastard snorted. "What she don't know won't hurt her. I've got the rest of my life with her and my kid. I might as well get one more freebie before I'm up with the ball and chain. And you're better than nothin'."

Gee. Thanks. "Um, really, I think—I know—she'd feel betrayed if she came in the room, about to have your baby, and you were messing with another woman. You'd lose her forever." *Because otherwise, she'd want to spend forever with a kidnapper and murderer. They're so attractive.* "Not worth the risk."

"I'll decide that," said Bastard, but his tooth-flashing grin told me he wasn't pissed off, he was already imagining his happy ending. "Now get on your knees."

I was still wearing the burqa, so for half a second, I considered it. Was that part of the burqa design, that you kept a barrier of material between your mouth and a passing penis?

As if reading my mind, he added, "And take off the potato sack. It's killing the mood."

"Hey, I have an idea. Do you have that song on your phone?" said Tucker.

"'Course I do."

"Why don't you bring it up for us? I still can't find it."

"Jesus, numb nuts. What the fuck is wrong with you? Is that what you're like with your girlfriend, taking ten minutes to figure out where your dick is?"

Tucker flinched, and Bastard paused for a second. "Wait a minute."

My heart thudded. Whatever Bastard was thinking, I could guarantee it wasn't good.

Bastard jabbed his thumb at me, but he was talking to Tucker. "You're fucking her, right?"

Tucker paused. "We…" He glanced at me.

I turned red. With rage, but also with shame. If I'd known we'd end up here and now, hell, yes, I would have fucked him a hundred times over.

"Shiiiiiit." Bastard glanced me up and down. "I saw you kissing her. So what the hell happened?"

I licked my lips under the burqa and said, "It's not relevant."

"Bitch, what's *relevant* is whatever I say is *relevant*." He rolled the last word on his tongue in a way that made me feel self-conscious about my vocabulary.

Should I pretend to have another asthma attack? But he'd just force me to perform sexual favours in exchange for a puffer.

Bastard turned back to Tucker. "You've never fucked her, you poor shit."

Tucker didn't answer. His hands clenched before he forced his fingers to extend.

"I could blow you away and her away, and you've never gotten into that slit. That's so fucking sad, man."

I forced myself to breathe. He was trying to upset us. It was working. But we couldn't annihilate him if he got us on the wrong track. I tried to signal Tucker with my eyes that I loved him, that this was bullshit, but he wasn't looking at me. He was staring directly at Bastard.

"That makes it even better," said Bastard. "You're like a fucking eunuch, and I just met her. And I'm the one who's going to fuck her brains out while you watch." He snapped his fingers at me. "I'm not going to ask you again, baby. Take off the potato sack, or I'll take it off you." He grinned. "Maybe you'd like that. You've been waiting for a real man all this time. Am I right?"

I glanced at the door. If I was going to run, I should have run when Tucker told me to.

Back to the original algorithm. If you can't run, hide.

If you can't hide, fight.

So fight.

This guy was bigger and stronger than me, but there were two of us. It was as if we were dogs tossed in the Coliseum to fight a bear. He was a giant savage with bigger weapons, but we were fast and we could work as a team.

If he would work with me. Because Tucker was still staring at Bastard.

Tucker was so good at psych, it had never occurred to me that it could work both ways. Maybe he was more vulnerable to words, even when spoken by a lying, treacherous numbskull.

Also, the back of my brain whispered, maybe Tucker was incapacitated because he'd spent the past five months offering his heart to me while I pranced around with other men. Even for someone as cocky as Tucker, it had to take a beating on his ego.

Maybe I was the one who'd been holding Tucker hostage. And Ryan.

Maybe I was the bad guy.

Shit! I shook myself. Now I was doing it. Doubting myself.

We couldn't afford this.

Especially not when Bastard grabbed a fistful of material between my breasts and said, "Get naked, sweetheart."

Chapter 41

Tucker took a step forward and said, "She's mine."

"Your what?" said Bastard, a tiny smile playing at the corners of his lips, a miniature, mocking smile that made me want to slap him around. He was such a little fuck. If we could separate him from his weaponry, we should be able to take him down.

"My everything," said Tucker, and his words were so bare, it took a second for them to penetrate Bastard's brain, and the grin fell from his face while he worked them out.

I should have focused on survival, but my heart gnawed at me. I didn't want to be Tucker's everything. Didn't deserve to be. Not unless he could share me with Ryan, and I'd never seen either guy share more than a handshake. Even that was grudging.

Tucker deserved a good and gorgeous girl who'd hang on his every word, be forever faithful, and bake him apple pies every Christmas. But for some stupid reason, he'd latched on to me.

"I don't see your name on her," said Bastard, which struck me as another little kid thing to say. *You can't sit there. That's my chair!* vs. *Well, I don't see your name on it.*

"It's there," said Tucker, quiet but sure. "We were working on a case last week, and one of her patient's wives read my palm."

I started for a second. Mme. Bérubé read his palm? I'd never heard about that. She never told me, and Tucker is not one to keep a secret. Or so I'd thought.

Bastard snorted. He didn't let go of the burqa. His hand still rested between my breasts. "You believe in that shit?"

"I don't believe everything," said Tucker, "but she's the real deal. She has quite a following. It's an honour for her to read your palm."

"Well, what did it say?" said Bastard.

Tucker didn't look at me, but I could feel his attention and the way he kept tabs on me out of the corners of his eyes. "She said that my love life is crooked."

I twitched. Mme. Bérubé read my palm. She never talked about boys, but if she did, I'd probably have the most crooked line out there.

Bastard snorted and torqued his fist a few more degrees. "That you? You bent?"

I didn't like the sound of that, but Bastard was laughing at his own joke too hard to care.

"She described Hope to me. Smart, funny, stubborn. Beautiful." His voice cracked.

Bastard stopped laughing. "That could be anyone."

Tucker kept talking. "You see this line?" He pointed at his hand. Bastard unclenched the burqa a tad so he could lean toward it.

"You see how it has a break in it? She told me, 'Wherever you go, go with your whole heart.' I told her that was from Confucius. She laughed and said, 'That's fitting, considering the source of your affection.'"

My face reddened, not just because Tucker was telling me I was his boo, but because my race is the first thing French people comment on. It's front and centre for them. It's almost like I'm not even human. First they have to pin my ethnicity. Then they might ask what my name is. Mme. Bérubé is 84 years old, so I'll give her a pass on that, but it's not my favourite thing.

Bastard turned away from Tucker's hand and swung the gun back toward me. "Cute story. Take off your fucking clothes."

"I hear you," I said, trying to sound coy instead of horrified. Tucker was telling me and Bastard that he loved me. That I was his destiny. And Bastard was saying, Fuck me or I'll shoot you.

I had three choices here.

I could move toward the door and, at the last second, bolt. But that would probably buy a bullet for me and trap Tucker in the room with him, still.

I could try and beg off with that shower, but I didn't want him to join me. Time was running out before the cavalry supposedly carried Casey into our dungeon, but I wasn't holding my breath on that score.

Or I could move him toward the bed and see if he'd let Tucker go.

"I'm a little shy," I said.

Bastard grinned, twisting the burqa several times around his fist, so tight that it pulled across my back and made me hold my breath for a second. "It's just us guys here."

Yes. And how was that supposed to be reassuring? But I smiled with as much sweetness as I could dredge out of my soul. "That's kind of the problem. What if we played strip poker? Then it would be more of a game."

Bastard eyed me. His hand relaxed slightly. I smiled back at him as best I could, showing my teeth.

Finally, he said, "We don't have any cards."

"No, but we have music. We could play songs, and if you can't name the song and artist, you have to take off a piece of clothing. You want to get naked anyway, right?"

He released the burqa. I breathed a little easier. He said, "I like the way you think. But no. It'll take too long. I want a quickie before Casey gets here. So take off your fucking clothes, or I'll rip 'em off." He grinned so widely, I knew that he'd like the excuse. "Forget the music. Forget the games. Just show me your ass."

I heard chivalry was dead. But where's the cavalry when you need it?

"Don't do it, Hope," said Tucker.

"Who asked you, Blondie?" said Bastard, but in a lazy way. He was trying to check out my ass, even though I was facing him, in a burqa.

"Hope, it's not worth it. You don't have to go through this."

"I don't want you to die," I said to Tucker, but I was locking eyes with Bastard.

Bastard answered first. "No one has to die. You just have to show me your stuff and get me off. What's so hard about that?"

I swallowed some bile.

"I'd rather die," said Tucker, and something in his tone of voice chilled me.

My body went rigid. It would be just like him to attack Bastard with his bare hands.

Bare hands.

Weapon. We needed a weapon. Preferably several.

Ones that would frighten him more than his gun.

"Yeah? Well, if you don't shut up, Blondie, you'll get your wish. So shut the fuck up."

I said, "Tucker, I'd rather do this than have you die. Trust me on this." I prayed that he'd understand that I was formulating a plan.

Tucker shut up, so maybe he read my mind, but more likely, he was just watching me, waiting for the best instant to attack Bastard like a rabid Rottweiler.

I said, "Why don't we make ourselves comfortable?" I migrated toward the bed and patted it, trying to look alluring and empty-headed. "You're so tall. Like, a foot taller than me. I'd feel better if you lay down."

He pursed his lips, thinking it over.

"I'm shy," I said. Which is true. When in doubt, speak the truth. I've only gotten naked with two guys in my life, plus tangled with Tucker a time or two. It wasn't like I got naked every day for every man.

"Just close your eyes," said Bastard.

I couldn't see how that would help.

I licked my lips, which he couldn't see under the burqa, or maybe he could, because his eyes zoomed in south of my nose. I belatedly remembered that he was lusting after a blow job from me and mentally reminded myself, *No. More. Lip. Movements.*

"It would help if you took off your clothes, too," I said.

Tucker made a choking noise.

Tucker, I've got this, I tried to tell him telepathically.

Bastard snorted. "I ain't falling for that."

Dang. I persisted. "Even just, like, your sock."

"How would that help you?"

I sat on the bed and shrugged, glancing up at him from underneath my eyelashes again. My friend Ginger once told me about a study that guys find you more irresistible when you're smaller than them, and they like the eyelashes thing. To me, it seems somewhat drag queen-y, but if it works, it works. "I'm feeling outnumbered."

"You are outnumbered, baby. Outnumbered and outgunned."

I pouted and dropped to my knees on the floor, lowering my eyes so I could reach for the instruments I'd used on Manouchka and then kicked under the bed. All I needed was one within reach.

I prayed for the scissors.

Bastard waved his gun, but he was more interested in bragging. "I like you on your knees like that, though. If you're good, I'll let you stay right there. In position, you know what I'm saying?"

Yes. You're a dipshit. But what I actually said was, "I'm scared." My hand didn't feel any metal, even though I'd spotted a silver flash out of the corner of my eye. Had the burqa fooled me? Had the instruments tumbled out of reach?

"Don't be, honey. I know what I'm doing. You just need a real man to take you in hand."

"Do you think you could—you know, while I'm getting undressed—" *And dislocating my shoulder, fumbling around on this filthy floor behind my back...*

Bastard loomed forward just as I laid my hand on one of the cool metal instrument handles. I froze, but he was staring into my eyes, for once, so I slid the instrument up the sleeve of my burqa. It would be my secret weapon, like the cyanide capsule that spies kept pouched in their cheeks.

I only wished for better ergonomics. The instrument was so long and thin, my fingers were damp, and the burqa material provided covering but also hampered my dexterity. If the metal clanked down on the floor, Bastard would spot it, pump my brain full of lead, and execute Tucker for good measure.

I was clinging to the instrument with one hand hyperflexed and nestled inside my sleeve, wondering what kind of blood and amniotic fluid was rubbing against the skin of my forearm, while trying to baby-talk a murderer. "Could you, you know..."

"You know what, darling."

I tried to force a blush. I'm always turning red in the most useless of situations, but of course, couldn't dredge up a decent heat now. The burqa would hide it anyway. "I just really want you to get naked, too."

He threw his head back and crowed, "What? You asking me to get naked with you?"

I shrugged and nodded, avoiding his eyes.

"Ask me louder, bitch."

"I—" I glanced at Tucker fast, trying to make sure that he understood, but his brown eyes blazed back at me, mute with fury, which shut me up completely. I shook my head.

Bastard swung around to look at Tucker. "Hey, Blondie, I almost forgot about you. Your girlfriend's begging me to fuck her. How'd you feel about that?"

I shook my head. I never said that. But of course, he heard what he wanted to.

"Well, darling, I'd love to stick my cock in you, but you've got to ask a little louder. What's that you want?"

I shook my head, but he grabbed my hair in his fist and twisted.

Even shielded by the burqa material, my newly-grown hair served as a winch. I gasped. He laughed.

"Get out of that potato sack, open your mouth, and beg me. We'll use that bed later. If you're good enough for a second round. Now I'm going to count to three. One."

So many problems here. I clutched the instrument in my right hand.

"Two."

I grabbed the end of my burqa and ripped it upward. Of course, it got tangled on my shoulders, especially since I only used one hand. That was kind of on purpose, so that I couldn't get naked, and it would look accidental. But it was also dangerous, because now I couldn't see anything except the black cloth enfolding my head.

Like a blindfold.

No, like an executioner's hood.

"Stupid bitch." Bastard chuckled, and then he stepped forward. I knew it was him, because he moved from a foot away to within sniffing distance, and his fingers were none too gentle as he grabbed my breasts. "These aren't half bad, though. Kind of small, but you get what you pay for, right?"

I bleated in distress and rage while his blunt fingers pinched my right nipple. Maybe I should have sounded more interested, but I wasn't that good an actress.

He cackled and grabbed my other breast. "I heard the small ones are more sensitive, though. That right? You feeling this? That good for you, whore?"

I managed to lift the burqa above my head just enough to see him fumble for his pants with his left hand while he hung on to the gun with his right.

And then a blur as something smashed into his knees.

No, not something. Someone. Tucker.

My man, Tucker, tackled the bad guy, slammed into his knees, knocking him to the ground.

The gun blasted.

My ears thundered.

I smelled blood.

One of the guys grunted in pain.

I didn't know what was happening, except that Tucker was in danger. I threw the burqa off my head, not caring if Bastard saw the instrument now.

I had to save my man. That was the important part.

Bastard threw himself on Tucker, pinning him to the ground, and lifted the gun up one more time.

I thrust the forceps at Bastard's eye.

Chapter 42

He flinched, twisting his head to the side, but I dug my left nails into his scalp while I aimed to skewer his eyeball on the forceps.

Eyes are sacred to me. I wear glasses. I've been worried about going blind since I was five years old. But in this case, I was willing to scar. Maim. Kill. Anything I had to do.

If he couldn't see, he couldn't shoot us.

Bastard wrenched his head to the right and then left, breaking my grip. I missed his eyeball. The Kelly forceps bounced off his nose hard enough to fracture it. Blood bloomed out of the wound.

Bastard screeched, but I just reared back, determined to gouge his eye the next time.

Except Tucker promptly rolled him onto the ground, trying to immobilize his gun hand.

Tucker was still trying to protect me.

Bastard hit him with the gun, clocking him on the side of the head and stunning him for a second.

I lunged forward, but before I could stab Bastard, he wrestled Tucker underneath him with a rasp of triumph.

I raised my weapon. I'd spear him through his open mouth before I let him shoot my man.

In that instant, a bang exploded in my dampened ears.

I thought it was his gun until I felt the walls and floor shake, and my peripheral vision registered a hole where the door used to be.

Before I could turn my head toward it, a flash blinded me, like a safety light flooding the entire room.

Even when I closed my eyelids, all I could see was white light.

Bastard howled as a bunch of smoke invaded the room, followed by the sound of people shouting and the thunder and vibration of footsteps surrounding us.

The cavalry had arrived.

But I couldn't be sure they'd immediately lock on to Bastard and prevent him from killing my man.

I willed the light to fade out of my retinas. It seemed to take forever for my eyes to make out even a few shapes through the man-made smog, but with any luck, the smoke would make Bastard wheeze.

Maybe it was an advantage that I'd grown up so near-sighted. I could use my ears to hunt Bastard better than he could find me or Tucker.

Ideally, I'd take out both his eyes. Or at least abrade them so much that he couldn't make us out while he writhed in agony.

I prayed that Tucker would know enough to head for the doorway and escape while the cavalry and I took care of business.

Not only did the smoke cloud the tiny room, it smelled terrible, too, like singed garbage. I held my breath and tried to prick up my ears. My hearing had definitely suffered multiple indignities today, and I couldn't hear half as well as usual, but I still thought I could hear screaming. Or wheezing. Something high-pitched and Bastard-like that I could home in on.

I spread my hands in front of me, feeling my way forward, and suddenly, I nearly stumbled into Bastard. On his knees. Coughing. Eyes closed and protecting his eyeballs, more's the pity.

Uniformed officers closed in on both of us, purposeful shapes through the fog, but not before I re-imagined the forceps like a bayonet and jabbed it straight at Bastard's neck.

I aimed for the carotid triangle, where the carotid artery and internal jugular vein lie relatively close to the surface. We're trained to put IV lines and catheters in there, but now I was using my knowledge to kill.

Except his skin was so thick, and the forceps were long enough that I didn't have enough force. I'd have to use two hands, one to steady the tip while I rammed down perpendicular to the skin. Meanwhile, he shoved me so hard that I slipped backwards on the bloody floor.

Bang. On my ass.

Hard enough to jar my teeth and make me bite my tongue.

About two feet away from Tucker. He was crawling toward me, but his breathing was horrible, frothy and wet-sounding, and I thought, *No. No, no, no. He needs a chest tube, and I can't put one in right now.*

"HELP!" I screamed at the shapes. "I need a chest tube!"

I couldn't take my eyes off Bastard, who was now levelling his gun at me, but in my peripheral vision, I could see the cavalry aiming at him.

This was the most dangerous time, the time when most hostages got killed.

Rescue time.

Tucker was staring at me. I could make out the whites around his pupils. His chest heaved.

I couldn't hear what Tucker was saying, even though his lips moved. I thought the men around us were also yelling.

Bastard pointed his gun at my head. He was so close that the barrel was only a few inches away from my nose. If the cavalry's smoke hadn't been so thick, I could actually have gazed inside my own instrument of death.

An eye for an eye.

It made perfect sense. I'd tried to take out his eye, and now he'd take mine. And my brain, and my heart.

Tucker sprang upward and hung on to Bastard's arm, dragging it down toward the floor. Toward himself.

No.

The gun fired.

Bastard fell onto Tucker. Fresh blood spurted on the floor, mopped up by their bodies, before Bastard heaved himself on his feet and lifted his gun again—

—and the room exploded in gunfire.

Someone tackled me, knocking me off to the side. I still had a good grip on the Kelly forceps so I tried to stab him too, until a hand grabbed my wrist and managed to pin it by my side.

I was screaming the entire time, but this time, I got out, "Tucker!"

I smelled blood.

He didn't answer me.

Chapter 43

When I opened my eyes again, the smoke was starting to clear, and Bastard was an unmoving heap on the floor.

He was dead.

The cavalry had taken off part of his head. As in, the top of his head was missing and his face was pulp. His chest looked like raw meat, too.

Couldn't happen to a nicer guy. Still, I was afraid that he'd rise up like a malignant zombie and start shooting us again.

Three officers surrounded his corpse while two more radioed for help.

I screamed, "Where is Tucker? Where's John Tucker?"

Another officer looked up through the haze and said, "I've got him. He's here."

"Is he alive?"

I started to leap toward Tucker, the too-still shape at that officer's feet.

When I jabbed my hand toward him, I realized that I was still gripping the Kelly forceps.

Which could actually help Tucker. When you're putting in a chest tube, the Kelly forceps is a key instrument. You start with a scalpel to cut the skin, but when you dissect through the layers of muscle, you use the Kelly forceps to enlarge the hole, tunnelling through the chest wall until you pop through to the pleural cavity, where the lungs sit.

If I could clean my hands and get a fresh instrument tray, I could start making the hole for a tube in Tucker's chest.

I didn't need a tube. Maybe I could just use my finger to stent it open, like the boy with his finger in a dike again. The ribs squeeze your fingers, but I didn't care about pain. Just him.

"I'm coming, Tucker!"

The officer beside me said, "Stay down!"

"I'm a doctor!" I snapped at her, which should have been so obvious by now, I might have laughed, except another guy forced my head down to the ground. "Don't look," he said.

That chilled me more than the tile floor against my cheek. "No."

"You're in shock, Dr. Sze. We're getting you out of here one at a time. Dr. Tucker has to go first," said the woman.

"Is he alive? Is he alive, God damn it?"

Both officers hesitated.

"Olivia," I said to the female officer. I had no idea if she was the same person who'd lurked behind the intercom, but I tried to bond with her any way I could. "I've got to know." My voice trembled. I swallowed, even though my mouth was desert-dry.

"He's alive," she said.

I sagged onto the floor with relief, but the way they were talking, they way they were acting...

Don't look.

"He needs help, though. We're moving him out of here. You did your job. Now let us do ours."

"This *is* my job," I said, through my raw throat. My eyes felt like they had silt in them. Whatever they put in the smoke can't be healthy for you, but as long as you survive to complain about it, you're not too badly off. "I'm a doctor. He needs a chest tube. I've got Kelly forceps."

The officers were still talking above me, on their radios.

Olivia took my hand and helped me up and back toward the bed, but used her larger body to block my vision as they carted Tucker out on a stretcher. She said, "Hope. We're going to take care of him."

Then she tried to remove the Kelly forceps from my grasp, and I almost whacked her on the knuckles with them.

I would have, too, except she was too fast. She whipped her hand out of range while the other guy wrestled my arms behind my back and I yelled, "Tucker. I love you! *Don't give up.*"

CHAPTER 44

When it was my turn, they didn't just escort me out of the room. They aimed to run me out of the building.

I squinted at the sudden light of the hallway and balked. "I need him."

They didn't answer, except to yell, "Move, move, move!" They now had me sandwiched between four officers, two of them abreast, one in front and one in back and maybe more, I don't know. It was like a running convoy. I had to keep up. I could hardly see anything except black uniforms.

But when one of them shoved the back staircase door open, I stumbled to another halt.

They were taking me down the stairs.

Tucker must have gone through the elevator, because of the stretcher. They were taking me away from Tucker.

The female officer seized my arm to make sure I kept up.

I planted my hand against the door frame, feeling the cool white wood under my palm.

"Please. Help Tucker. I need him. He's my..." I still couldn't call him my boyfriend. "He saved my life."

"Dr. Sze, we will!" A male officer stared at me with wild green eyes, and suddenly I understood that I was acting illogically, like a patient in the emergency room asking the same questions over and over again. The more time they spent reassuring me and coaxing me out of harm's way, the less time they had to spend on Tucker.

I ran down four flights of stairs, staggering at one point, but with two officers holding my arms, I stayed upright.

They swept me into some unmarked vehicle right by the back door. I don't know car or truck makes, but it was the most tank-like thing I'd seen in my life, let alone in downtown Montreal. The engine grumbled into first gear before I'd fastened my seat belt.

The hind part of my brain was amazed to see the sky again. It was dark outside, and cloudy, pockmarked with streetlights, but I could still see it through the tinted windshield. I was in the centre of the vehicle, flanked on all sides by officers, yet if I twisted around, I could see the sky.

But not Tucker.

"Is he still alive?" I asked.

"As far as we know," said the green-eyed guy.

"Could you please find out?" I said. My throat rasped on the last word, and someone handed me a water bottle.

I stared at it for a second, uncomprehending. Should I be able to drink water when Tucker was fighting for his life?

I felt like making a deal with death. *I won't drink this water. I won't eat. I won't take a shower. I won't do anything if you just save Tucker, okay?*

I reached for my phone. Until today, Tucker annoyed me with his constant texting and messages, and now I'd give anything to have him talk to me again.

My turn to text him, even though he couldn't possibly answer me.

Also, my parents and Kevin must be going nuts. Not to mention Ryan. And now that I was finally free to use my hands however I wanted, I needed my phone.

My fingers fumbled around in my front shirt pocket until I eventually realized that it was empty. At some point, my phone had bounced away from me. My thousand-dollar iPhone. My gift from Ryan. My connection to the world. Gone. Lost.

This is not a metaphor for Tucker. I refuse to believe that.

Still, I would have cried if I could have summoned any tears.

"I need to know if he's alive," I said.

"We're trying to find out," said the female officer. "Just drink your water, Dr. Sze. We'll try and get some food into you too."

"I'm not hungry. I want Tucker." I couldn't focus on anything else. Not the fact that I was being driven away in an unmarked vehicle. Not the fact that Ryan and my family must be rioting behind me, hearing that I was free and they still couldn't see me, couldn't touch me.

I couldn't get to Tucker and they couldn't get to me and I couldn't get to them....It was like a Möbius loop, a benzene ring, an unending cycle of want.

The tank vehicle soldiered down a street I didn't recognize. I can't figure out which way is north at the best of times. Ryan used to orient me when we were walking down the street by pointing at the sun, but it was something I tried to consciously learn, not instinctive.

Who were these people?

Where were they taking me?

True, they'd shot Bastard, which made them the better guys, but still. "Who are you?" I snapped.

Their radio crackled to life with words like *Sûreté* and *police*, but no one answered for a second.

I said, "Are you the police?"

"We work with the police in high-risk situations like this one," said a man with a moderate French accent. He twisted around from the front seat, so I could see his face. He was black, heavy set, with a previously-broken nose, but something about his eyes—and the fact that I wasn't the only melanin-heavy person around—somehow reassured me.

"Did you hear from Tucker?"

"They just brought him to UCH. They're taking care of him."

"He's alive?"

"Yes," said the black officer, holding my eyes. "He's in critical condition, but he's alive. We're praying for him."

That would have reassured Ryan a lot more than me. I've glanced at studies on the power of prayer, but it still falls into the "can't hurt, might help" category for me. I'd rather put a chest tube in him.

"Where was he shot?"

He looked pained. "We don't know the extent of his injuries yet. But when we do, we'll tell you."

They kept saying he was alive. On the other hand, after an unsuccessful code, I know that some doctors won't tell family members over the phone that their loved one didn't make it. They'll just say, "In critical condition." They don't want the family to get into an accident on the way over.

So was Tucker really alive? Or were they just trying to calm me down so I didn't shatter into a billion pieces?

I was starting to shiver. I didn't want to shake. It seemed weak. But I couldn't seem to help it. Not just my hands, but my arms and my legs, all quivering hard enough to jiggle the water inside the bottle I still hadn't opened. Sometimes women shake like this after giving birth.

That's why they call it labour, I heard a nurse's voice echo in my head.

But I hadn't given birth to anything, unless it was helping to kill a murderer.

My teeth chattered.

Something dropped around my shoulders, and I stifled a scream. But when my hands flew up, all I felt was rough wool. One of the officers had tried to wrap a blanket around me.

I patted the blanket. I clenched the water bottle between my trembling thighs, thinking, *Tucker. Ryan. Kevin. Dad. Mom.*

Tucker.

Ryan.

Tucker.

Then I managed to unwrap the blanket and replace it around my shoulders, even though I was still shaking.

What kind of person had I become? I always said I wanted to go into medicine to help people. But here I was, not only helpless, but dragging Tucker into the dragon's den, possibly getting him killed, and then trying to kill people myself.

There's some saying like, when you gaze long enough into an abyss, the abyss also gazes into you.

For the first time, I realized that the more I hunted down murderers, the more I was turning into a monster.

Chapter 45

"We're taking you for a debriefing," said the female officer who might have been Olivia, as the tank laboured its way through the Montreal night. "Don't worry. You're safe."

A debriefing. For some reason, I thought of briefs. Underwear. Bastard, who wanted to strip me down, and Tucker, who stopped him.

Tucker.

"I love him," I said. "I mean, it's complicated, but he's...like, I need him." I knew that I was babbling and over-sharing, things I try to avoid, but I had to unleash this after being confined for so long. "If he dies, I want you to tell me. It's okay if he dies. I mean, not that it's okay, but I can handle it. I'm a doctor." I stopped. I wondered why I kept telling everyone I was a doctor. If they couldn't figure that out by now, they weren't very good police officers, or whatever they were. "I break bad news all the time. We even had a class on it. You're supposed to sit down, or at least lean against a wall, so it looks like you're more permanent. And you have to listen and let them cry. Some people think you shouldn't even offer a tissue when they're crying, because that's too intrusive. We're sitting down now, so you can tell me."

"He's not dead," said the black officer. "They told me they moved him into the operating room. I promise."

I keeled over in my seat and rocked back and forth. Thank God, thank God, thank God. The unopened water bottle tipped out of my lap and thunked to the floor.

I didn't know if I should believe these guys, but I had to believe them until I saw him with my own eyes. "Can you take me to him? I can take a shower before I scrub up for the OR. I promise I won't touch anything."

The black officer shook his head. "Both of you need to be debriefed."

"But can't we be debriefed together?"

They all exchanged a look, and I swear my heart stopped beating for a second before it lurched back into a rhythm, and I knew what they didn't want to say, so I said it for them. "You're afraid that he won't be able to talk. You think he might die."

Jesus, what did the guy do to him? I swear that if Bastard had been in front of me, I would have annihilated him all over again, only single-handed and faster and harder.

I kept rocking back and forth. I'd seen people do this before, when faced with tragedy. Big tragedy. Like bombs exploding, tsunamis carrying away villages, fires ripping through forests. Women rocking their children, as if they thought their bodies moving back and forth fast enough could blindfold them to the heartbreak, the loss, the gnawing bellies, at least for a few minutes.

"I want to kill that bastard," I said. They were the worst people to tell this to, of course. No matter how much the police sympathize with you—and believe me, even more than doctors, police are forced to witness the seamy underbelly of life. If I'm a medical sin eater, the modern-day equivalent of the person who used to eat food off a dead person's belly in order to imbibe the recently-deceased's sins and ensure his or her ascension to heaven, the police are sin *maters*—but they are supposed to uphold the law. Their job is to prevent murder.

Unless it's capital punishment, of course. If the state kills, that's okay.

None of that stopped my mouth. "I want to blow him up. I want to rip out his testicles and feed them to the wolves. Then they'll have a taste for blood and eat the rest of him. Just rip him apart."

There aren't any wolves in Montreal, of course, so one of them said "Huh," a half-laugh, but I wasn't joking.

I was thinking about the Israeli government. You know that Israel was set up after the Holocaust killed so many Jews, the world thought they deserved a homeland? So they carved a piece of land out for them and said, Here you go. Of course, the problem was that Palestinians were already living there, but anyway, the point is, Israel was established by people who had been wronged. And wronged on such a massive scale that they built a homeland out of it.

With revenge. They wanted to kill as many Nazis as possible. An eye for an eye. A life for a life.

Of course, the higher echelons of the Third Reich greased enough palms to escape, often into South America, although Kurt Waldheim became the Chancellor of Austria before anyone thought to ask him what he was doing in the 1940's.

The Israelis didn't spend all their time on extradition and lobbying and education on what a tragedy the Holocaust was. Well, maybe they did, I don't know. But the important part was this: they never lost sight of their goal, which was death for the deserving.

They trained the Mossad, which is like the CIA, only more deadly and precise. Their job was not to overthrow governments and cut down children, no. They worked only to kill. Find and execute escaped Nazis. And they did.

A few escaped. Mengele, for example. Some people would say that the ones who died in prison escaped, too. But I breathed a little easier, thinking that even if they were about to lock me up in a lunatic asylum, I could still orchestrate Bastard's death.

"He's dead, Hope," said the female officer.

"I know." I summoned up an image of his half-exploded head.

I still wanted to kill him.

Part of me knew that I was the one who sounded insane now. Far crazier than Bastard who, in the end, wanted to see his ex and his baby and fuck me on the side.

Lots of guys do that kind of thing, right?

I was the only doctor I knew who got kidnapped and was willing to stab her rapist to death, and go back for seconds if necessary.

I didn't care.

A perfect frame of mind for the debriefing, as the tank rumbled to a halt in front of a brick building.

Oh, they were very civilized about it. They got me the most comfortable chair possible, apologizing for the fact that it was bolted to the floor in order for a TV camera to film the interview, with my permission. They offered to bring me coffee—fresh, from a barista, not the police kind.

"I don't drink coffee," I said, although my eyelids sagged like someone had attached a rare earth magnet on each eyelid. "I just want to see Tucker. Let's do this."

"Water? You need water," said the female officer.

I hesitated. I loved water. I needed water. But Tucker was waiting for me.

"No water. Not until I see Tucker." I sank into the bolted seat.

After that, I didn't remember the interview so much. They wanted to rehash everything. I mean everything. Especially how I got kidnapped in the first place, when he shot Dr. Biedelman.

"How's Stan?" I said, jerking myself upright. I couldn't believe that I'd forgotten about him.

"He's—" The female officer hesitated. "He was moved to University College Hospital."

The English trauma hospital. Same as Tucker. I said, "But he's still alive?"

They exchanged looks.

And I knew what they weren't saying.

"Oh, no. No, no, no," I said, starting to stand up.

"Do you need—should we get a doctor?" one of them said.

"No. I don't want a tranquilizer. Don't you dare inject me." I knew they always did that kind of thing in the movies, but I've never seen it. Of course, I don't hang out in police stations. I was afraid that if they did give me some benzos, I'd fall asleep. And I couldn't do that. I had to get to Tucker. And Ryan. But first, I had to mourn my senior resident, the first victim of the night. "Stan. I'm sorry, Stan. I'm sorry." He was lazy, but he was my friend. He always made me laugh.

He also tried to avoid getting involved in my murder cases, at any cost.

It made me wonder, did he know what was going to happen to him? Was that why he'd refused to help me? Some sort of intuition that, in a few months hence, he'd leave his wife a widow?

I get tired of doing detective work. Really. It weighs on my soul, dragging me down so I feel like I'm drowning in a sea of tar. But before today, I never thought it would cost Stan's life, and possibly Tucker's.

"What about June?" I said. My voice climbed another octave. "Is she okay?"

"She's stable," said the female officer. "She was shot in the abdomen. She's recuperating."

June was alive. I closed my eyes and thought, *Gott sei dank*. That means thank God in German. I got it from Tucker. He was always teaching me little snippets of languages. I don't know why. I don't know why he did half the things he did, but I had to get to him.

"I have to see them. Especially Tucker," I said. I tried to keep my voice calm. They'd never let me out of here if I wasn't calm. "Even if he's dead, I have to see him. He's mine."

That reminded me of what Tucker had told Bastard, and my breath rasped in my throat. *She's mine.*

He'd protected me as long as he could.

He laid down his life for me.

"Please, Dr. Sze," said the officer. "We will take you to him. Just a few more minutes to build your case."

Again, I reminded myself of patients trying to leave the emergency department. We try and reason with them, tell them that we need time to rule out a heart attack. We tell them that we're working in their best interest, that they could die or collapse if they go home. But if they head out the door anyway, they have to sign an AMA form, that they're leaving against medical advice.

"We need you to finish this. For Tucker, and Stan, and June," said the officer, and I understood. They were asking me to delay gratification.

I know all about that. Like, I've been in school for over twenty years. Which means that I will not drink, not go to parties, not stay up late (except for studying!). I will not date the cute boy sitting next to me, because I need to focus on my exams. I will not smoke. I will not pop out babies until I finish my final exams.

I will sit with a madman who is pointing a gun at us, and I will stay in control. Because I have to. Because that is what I do.

But this was the closest I'd come to running out AMA. To saying, *FUUUUUUUUUUUUUUUCK you. I can't be your hero. I can't even save myself! Now let me at my men, and leave me alone!*

But by the time I busted out of the room, they'd drag me right back to this chair. Being cops and all.

So I told them the story. Over and over. And over. And over. And over. Until my throat chafed and my vision blurred, but I kept answering until they finally fell silent.

"Now can I see him?"

They conferred for a while before they lifted their heads and said one word. "Yes."

Chapter 46

Hospitals no longer felt like a safe place to me. They felt like irrational, chaotic buildings that could transform into makeshift prisons at any time.

Through the tank's windows, I spotted patients lolling in the ER waiting room, playing on their phones or leaning on each other to try and sleep. UCH had mounted its Christmas decorations, too: giant, tinseled candy canes battling it out on the wall above patient registration.

I wanted to scream at them, *This could end any second. Don't you know that?*

The tank pulled up right beside the building, lights flashing, engine still running, and I thought, *Good. Announce our presence. Let me through.*

I clambered out of the tank after the female officer, still in a mini pedestrian convoy. We paused at the back door while the black officer punched in the entrance code. Because it was the middle of the night, we had to cut through the University College emergency department. Ambulances flashed their lights around us. It was cold enough in mid-November that my running shoes crunched in the snow and my breath coalesced faintly in the air.

I used to joke with Kevin that I was a dragon when I made "smoke" like that.

I shivered. I still had that scratchy wool blanket around my shoulders, but my jacket, my boots, my backpack, and probably my phone were all back at St. Joe's. I'd fled in the night like a refugee. The officers had offered me a jacket, but just like denying myself food and water, I'd turned down the coat.

They opened the door and waited for me to enter.

I froze.

My heart wanted to head straight for Tucker, but my body refused to cross the threshold.

I glanced over my shoulder, trying to see the sky, trying to suck the November air into my lungs, in case I didn't make it out again this time. The hospital had built some sort of covering over the entrance, to protect people from the snow and rain, but further in the distance, I saw streetlights.

My breath was coming short and fast.

The female officer pressed her hand on my shoulder in silent understanding. She probably saw PTSD all the time. Hell, maybe she had it herself.

"You don't have to go in there. Your family wants to see you," said the green-eyed officer. "Your mother…"

I could just imagine Mom melting down, my dad trying to hold it together, and Kevin wrapping himself around me like a barnacle while Ryan crushed me in his embrace, saying nothing, just smelling like his leather jacket and himself.

I wanted to see them all. I loved them so much.

But one man had thrown down for me, had stood in the lion's mouth with me, and he was the closest to death. I had to see this through.

"I'll go in with you," said the female officer, and I nodded. If her uniform and gun could get me in any quicker than my badge, I was all for it.

"We're all coming with you," said another voice behind me, and I nodded again. The more firepower, the better.

"I love you," I said to Tucker, in my head. It might have been out loud, I don't know. But it was my way of praying, as I stepped onto the rubber mat and stomped the crust of snow off my shoes. Somehow, that bit of normalcy made me feel better, as did the fact that I had to pull off my fogged-up glasses.

Even with my myopic vision, I could tell people were watching us march in. Not just the stretcher patients lined up inside the hallway with paramedics, waiting to be unloaded, as well as the unlucky folks trying to sleep in the corridor, but the staff wearing uniforms with their names embroidered across their hearts.

We probably looked like something out of the Matrix. They stormed in, a mass of black uniforms and crackling radios. Their boots thumped on the floor. Their billy clubs swung with every step. Each of them armed and dangerous.

"It's Hope Sze," said a short, bespectacled brown guy in blue scrubs.

I shoved my own, barely-useable glasses back on. His badge said "Marco" and he'd pasted a Peanuts sticker beside his picture, but I was pretty sure I'd never seen him before in my life.

Marco started a slow clap.

Clap. Clap. Clap.

I stared at his hands, rhythmically striking each other, and gazed up at his unfamiliar face, my eyebrows crocheted in confusion.

A black woman in turquoise scrubs joined in. The secretary whistled. And suddenly everyone in the whole department started to applaud, to laugh, to yell, "Hope, Hope, Hope, Hope, Hope!" and bang on the desks and stamp their feet.

Some of the patients on the stretchers joined in. At least one toothless man who'd barely managed to shave his face shook his bed rails, although I couldn't tell if it was in approval or an escape attempt.

Even a few officers laughed before the black officer made a "turn it down" gesture, and they subsided, still grinning at me.

Tucker would have loved this. I could picture him bowing at them. He'd shout, "*Merci! Gracias! Danke! Obrigato! Xiè xie! Mm goy!* Thank you, and good night!" Milking it. Feasting on it.

He loved the limelight.

Damn it. I was talking about him in the past tense like he was dead. As far as I knew, he wasn't dead. Yet.

I couldn't bring myself to smile at them, but I waved. I guess that's why the Queen likes waving so much: acknowledgement without commitment. Then I kept walking. If they led me to the morgue, I could figure it out.

Instead, they steered me toward a bank of elevators and pressed the button for the tenth floor. We were in the big times now. St. Joe's doesn't even have a tenth floor. And I'm pretty sure the morgue would be in the basement.

So Tucker was still alive. Right?

But as we shuffled our way into the elevator, jockeying for position, I bit my tongue and closed my eyes. I couldn't count on anything. Even if he died, they might not ship him down to the morgue right away. We sometimes keep the deceased in the emerg for a few hours, to allow family to visit, because it's too traumatic for them to go down to the morgue, and the funeral home won't necessarily make a stat pickup in the middle of the night.

So Tucker might be in a room. Even if he was dead.

I watched the white lights of the elevator slowly, slowly mount toward number ten.

Would they hold an ICU bed for him? Would they have kicked him out already, to make room for the next casualty? Or would this be their version of a hero's welcome, that they kept him in his bed for me and let me say goodbye here, instead of surrounded by cold steel and other dead bodies?

At the tenth floor, the door paused before it opened. I sprang toward it, but the officers wanted to check the hall before they beckoned me out.

Finally, our small army stood in front of the locked, frosted glass intensive care doors. The black guy negotiated at the speaker until someone consented to release the automatic doors for us.

My footsteps faltered on the rubber mat outside the ICU.

Don't die, Tucker. God damn it. Don't die. I need you.

And then it was like I could hear Tucker's voice in my head, replying to me. *He who has a 'why' to live will survive almost any 'how.'*

Tucker had read this book by Viktor Frankl. He even brought the book to FMC to show me, but I wasn't that interested in reading about Nazi inhumanity to man. No offence, just that I was already burned out by all the murders, and Tori ended up taking the book home instead. Still, Tucker had said, "You gotta read it next, Hope. It'll help you the next time you run into a murderer. I mean, you've been through hell, but not concentration camps, you know what I mean? And if you've got a reason to live, you'll survive almost any how."

Tucker understood what it meant to have hope. And if he made it, he could have Hope, too, if you know what I mean.

"He's here," said the green-eyed officer, pointing to a room on the right, and I started to run.

I detected a white, bedridden shape through the frosted glass.

"Don't," said the female officer, but I was already leaping onto the mat to make the individual room door fly open. I didn't care that this was the ICU, and all the other patients were asleep, whether real or artificial rest, with multiple lines sprouting out of their limbs and more leading out of orifices. I didn't care that the nurses were quietly writing notes on their patients, with only small, single lights illuminating their work stations.

This was my man. He was mine. And even if he was dead, I'd crawl right into bed with him and beg him to take me with him.

The door yawned open.

Maybe that mound in the bed was Tucker. It could be him, was it him, the hair was squashed and looked too dark, the eyes were closed—

—but the monitor was on and his vitals were flashing: 76, 98%, 22, 107/70.

"Tucker," I said. I wouldn't believe it until I knew for sure it was him. Would they put another body in there, to pose as him, so that I wouldn't go postal and burn down the ICU?

His eyelids flickered. They didn't open, but they moved. I felt dizzy. He was intubated. He couldn't talk with the tube in his throat. But his chest rose and fell steadily. That was a good sign, right?

"Tucker," I said again, and this time, I climbed on the bed.

Things started beeping. His IV, probably. That's one of the first to get kinked. The O2 sat probe gets knocked off pretty easily. And I wouldn't have been surprised if I'd dislodged some of his heart monitor leads.

His face furrowed. His eyebrows and his eyelids, like he was irritated in his artificial sleep.

I didn't care. My heart was starting to beat again, for real. He was alive. Alive. Alive-o.

He opened his eyes.

I opened my mouth.

I'm sure that I smelled absolutely putrid. Like unwashed hair and stale breath and Manouchka's blood and Bastard's remnant stink.

But I kissed him anyway, as best I could, around the tube. Which meant that I kissed him beside the tube. Just a corner of his lips. But enough.

His lips stirred faintly under mine, a twitch barely signaling life, and that would have broken my heart if I hadn't been thinking, *He's alive! He's ALIVE!*

I still didn't know what had happened to him, where he'd been shot, what surgery they'd put him through, but I knew he'd survived this long. He'd made it through the golden hour and come out on the other side. And he was young and healthy.

"I love you, Tucker," I whispered against his lips.

"Love. You." I felt, more than heard, the shape of his words. His breath smelled like an old, dank cave, but I didn't care. He still loved me!

His nurse came in the room, but she didn't say anything. She watched us.

I tried to sit up.

His arms jerked into a hug around me, so I stayed where I was and murmured in his ear, "You're my hero."

He grunted. It sounded like a disagreement, but at this point, I didn't care. I was so happy that he was alive.

"We made it. We're alive," I couldn't help saying out loud.

Tucker's eyes flickered again. His lips shaped one word. I thought he was saying, "You."

"Yes. I'm alive. Thanks to you."

His lips pursed again. I still thought he said, "You."

I figured he was trying to return the compliment, so I nodded and smiled.

His limbs stiffened. He croaked something that still resembled a contradiction.

"You're alive," I said, puzzled.

He turned his head away from me.

My stomach plummeted. Maybe I was confused about what he was saying. The tube was in the way, blocking his larynx, but his body language was...not what I was expecting.

His nurse stepped forward. "He really shouldn't talk so much. And he needs to be alone."

Tucker's arms seized around me again. "He wants me to stay," I said, above the beeping machines. "I'll fix his monitor and his sat."

"We can't have people lying in bed together in the unit," she said.

Why not? It would probably make them heal faster than isolating them. We have kangaroo touch for babies. Why don't we have anything for grown-ups? Maybe I was on to something here! "Touch helps babies," I said.

The corners of her mouth jerked, but she fought back the smile and said, "Five minutes."

I bumped my forehead against Tucker's. He'd already closed his eyes. He must've been feeling pretty raunchy. And in fact, I was feeling a little exhausted myself.

That was the last thing I remembered before the nurse tapped me on the shoulder.

I opened my sleep-crusted eyes. Tucker had drifted back into real or drug-induced sleep, so I peeled his arm off of me, even though his eyebrows flickered and he grunted. I kissed him on the cheek and said, "I'll stick around as much as I can. I love you." Now that I'd started saying it, I couldn't stop.

Just before I stepped out the door, I glanced backward, but there wasn't much to see. His nurse redid his wires and tweaked his blankets over his shoulders with a certain fussiness that broadcasted, *There. Now that's better.*

I still felt a little uneasy, but put it down to Tucker being near death and on drugs. He still loved me. He even said so.

Now I just had to tell Ryan.

Chapter 47

The officers brought me right to my apartment. I mean, up the elevator and everything. They checked every room before giving me the all-clear. The female officer offered to stay, but I was too busy getting buried by my family, who had the key to my place and had been making bone soup, from the smell of it.

"We were waiting for you!" my mother yelled, even as she and my dad hugged me.

"I know," I said.

Kevin stood back for a second before he locked himself around the side of my body. He was so tall now that his face was in my chest, and the top of his head almost reached my shoulder. I looked at him and silently marvelled at how much he seemed to grow between visits. The last year or two, his baby teeth had fallen out. Now he was basically his own little man.

To think how close I came to missing him growing up.

I patted his hair. I love his hair, spiky and springy. Real Chinese hair: if you cut it, it sticks straight up, like mini prongs into your palm. *The way hair should be*, I thought, remembering how I'd stroked Ryan's hair, just before I moved my head in real time and Ryan's eyes and mine locked.

He looked drawn. I'd never seen him like that before. I'd seen him in university after all-nighters, occasionally propped up by Coke or Red Bull. I'd seen him sleepy after a night of marathon sex. But I'd never seen him look like some of his life force had been sucked out.

Out of all the people surrounding the building, my beloveds who'd served by standing and waiting, he was the one who'd best understood that I might die in there.

Kevin was still too young. My dad played everything close to his chest. And my mom…my mom lingered in her own protective bubble, obsessing about recipes and the best way to arrange her junk, and so not too worried.

But Ryan knew. He'd known that I was holed up with Tucker and that he and I might never see each other again.

I swallowed a lump in my throat. I know it sounds funny, but Anne Lamott once wrote that for a true believer, death is just "a major change in address." I guess in the back of my mind, I thought that Ryan's super faith might protect him from despair.

Just looking at him, I knew it hadn't.

But he stared at me, with his liquid, nearly-black eyes, and I mouthed, "I love you, Ry."

The right corner of his mouth shaped a faint smile before he whispered it back to me.

Did I feel bad, telling two different men that I loved them?

A little, since I hadn't explained the full picture to either of them. But I also knew that if a meteor struck me down right now, I'd rather go out with them both knowing how I felt than with my eternal dithering. (Every other woman on the planet probably hated me even more, like I was trying to grab two stuffed animals at the carnival instead of one, but *tant pis*. I wasn't living my life for anyone else for one more second.)

"What was it like in there?" said Kevin, pulling his head back so he could watch my face.

"Scary," I said, without thinking.

"Really? Like, the worst thing that's ever happened to you?"

"Yeah." I'd have to say so. One woman told me, after delivering her baby, that labour wasn't so bad because you could see the end of it, and it served a purpose. But being held hostage was the opposite: no end in sight, and no real purpose. We'd never even found Casey Assim. Speaking of which..."What happened to Casey Assim?"

"She's safe," said Ryan. "She came to St. Joe's to deliver, but as soon as they realized what was going on, they moved her out, to another hospital. She delivered a baby boy."

How strange. Bastard had been right about all those details, and yet so insane. Was she really the fully-dilated woman Stan had intended to deliver?

I was too tired to figure it out now.

I let my family hug me. Ryan moved closer, and I snuck a hand out to hold his. He squeezed so hard that I thought he'd crack my metacarpals, and I didn't care. I wanted him to.

He was mine.

Chapter 48

Later, after I choked down a bit of bone soup, drank enough water to flood Montreal, and savoured an orange, Ryan drew me into the living room and said, "Can you talk about what happened in there?"

"Sure," I said, although my brain stalled. I should tell him about Bastard, but he also needed to know about Tucker. "I guess I'll stick to the most important bits."

He nodded. "Always a good plan."

I smiled a little. "Okay. Um. So." I twisted my hands. He reached over and patted one of them, and I turned my palm up to catch hold of him, so our arms ended up getting tangled up together. His skin was warm against mine. I smiled.

I told him about Bastard. The more I talked, the more distant it felt, like I was telling a story about someone else. I hung up the story mid-sentence. "I know you want to talk about that, but I wanted to tell you that while I was in there, I had...thoughts."

Ryan swivelled to stare at me.

"Yeah. I know it doesn't sound too crazy. I mean, we're always thinking, right? So that we 'are'?" Now his eyebrows drew together, so I explained, "'I think, therefore I am.' Never mind. Okay. So. The important thing is, I was thinking about us, and I realized, I love you. I want to tell you that. It was horrible, being locked in there, knowing that you didn't know I love you."

He half-laughed, half-coughed. "I knew it."

"You did? But—"

"Hope. I know you. I know you love me. You were just confused. And that's okay. I shouldn't have—I should never have let you go."

I stopped to absorb that. How did he end up blaming himself? Or trusting that he'd win me in the end? Ryan had known that I was torn between him and Tucker, but he'd figured I'd eventually recover my senses and realize how much I already loved him?

On the other hand, the dude was all about faith. So I guess it's not that big a stretch to go from trusting some big kahuna in the sky to figuring out that your hemi-girlfriend will come around eventually. In fact, any atheist would figure that between me and God, I'm Ryan's better bet, being corporeal and all.

"You don't have to worry about it, and you don't have to talk about it. I just love you," said Ryan.

I blinked. I found it both refreshing and completely weird that he'd applied his all-encompassing love to me. On one hand, it made me feel safe. Tucker was always negging me—you know, kind of bugging me, provoking me, making me pay attention to him. Ryan was more relaxing to hang around. He did his own thing, he trusted me, and he was happy for himself.

On the other hand, I did like Tucker's brand of stupid bravery, like throwing himself into a hostage situation with me.

Le sigh.

I took a deep breath. "I do have to talk about it, though. Or at least about how I chose you and Tucker."

He smiled. "You mean chose me over him."

"No. I mean—" My heart thudded. I didn't want to do this. I could let Ryan think he'd won. Tucker was in the hospital, broken—I didn't want to think of him that way, but I did. Something was very wrong with one of my men. My sunny, 'Weebles wobble but they don't fall down' man—"I realized that I can't choose. So I pick both of you."

"What?" said Ryan.

"Yeah."

Ryan's cheeks turned a dull red under his brown skin. I realized that I rarely saw him blush, except when he'd just had an orgasm. He doesn't get too flustered outside the bedroom. I remembered him, his hair jagged with sweat, his eyes slitted, gasping for breath, and thought, will I ever see that again? Did I just flush that down the toilet, and I don't even know if Tucker a) wants me anymore, and b) will survive?

Ryan turned away from me for a second. He said, with his back to me, "You fucked him in there?"

"What? No!" He must not have heard about Bastard attacking me. I'd fill him in on that later. I already had my hands full with this damage control. "How would we have done that? We had a lunatic with a gun in there!"

His shoulders set. "You kissed him?"

I hesitated, but I said, "Yes. And if you'd been in there, I would have kissed you, too."

"Hope. This goes against everything I believe in."

"I know that, Ryan!" It was my biggest fear come to life, that I'd hesitated between these two perfect men and would ultimately end up with no one. But I had to tell the truth, damn it. Having a gun pressed to my head, the inability to go to the bathroom without witnesses, the fact that Tucker had almost died, and that part of his soul seemed to have withered...all that made me realize that I had to tell the truth. That was all I was good for.

Even if it cost me my men. Even if it left me broken and alone.

That was what I did.

"I'm not on board with this," said Ryan, with his back to me. I could see he was trying not to swear, not to yell, to keep it cool, not to traumatize me after all I'd been through. He was trying to keep it together, even though I'd just about killed him too.

"I know that," I said softly. "It goes against you, and Christianity, and Western norms. And this is the dumbest thing I've ever done, because Tucker doesn't want it, either. I've probably lost both of you. But I realized in there, I can't choose. I need you because you're like the other half of me. You're my dream guy. Smart and sexy and loyal. It's like, I couldn't make you up as an avatar in a video game because it would be too unreal."

Ryan likes video games. His shoulders relaxed a little, even though he said, "That's what avatars are for."

I didn't say the other part, which was that Tucker challenged me, drop-shipped me into uncomfortable situations (I realize I shouldn't point fingers at this, but there it is). I never knew what he'd do or say next. And I wanted to know it. He was like a drug, and Ryan was like my honeymoon, if that makes any sense.

I thought I could choose. I thought I could throw myself head-first at Ryan, because he was my first, last, and always.

But I guess all this stupid detective stuff changed me, too. I wanted to know the unknowable.

If I stayed with Ryan, I'd turn into Bluebeard's wife, yearning to sneak inside the forbidden room. No matter how big a castle he built for me, I'd always wonder if I could take a tiny peek in that chamber.

If I stayed with Tucker, we'd probably have a good ride before we killed each other.

Neither was a perfect mix.

I walked up to Ryan very slowly. He didn't move away, which gave me the courage to pause beside him.

Ryan didn't look at me. He said, "I don't want that."

"I know you don't, and I'm sorry." I said, "Anyway, it may be too late for me and Tucker. He's..."

"Dead?" said Ryan, not in a nice voice, and realized how much I'd hurt him all over again.

"Screwed up," I said. "And maybe he'll die. I don't know. But at this rate, a murderer will knock me off first."

Ryan looked down at me. "Please don't die, Hope."

"I'll try not to," I said. And I knew it was an underhanded trick, reminding him that I'd almost kicked it. But life is short. Razor short. Especially if you tango with killers every day, the way that I do.

So I only felt a little guilty when I rose up on my toes and kissed Ryan, and after a split second pause, he kissed me back.

His lips parted. His mouth tasted almost sweet, which meant that I probably tasted like an ashtray, but he didn't stop. He wrapped his arms around me, and it felt like a present, like a benediction. And I thought, *Never give this up. Don't walk away from this. You'd have to be crazy.*

But the rest of me was still curled up in Tucker's bed, in intensive care, with my hand on his chest, feeling his heart beat.

THE END

Acknowledgements

"Feeling gratitude and not expressing it is like wrapping a present and not giving it."—William Arthur Ward

This novel was inspired by the 1991 hostage-taking at the Alta View Hospital in Salt Lake City. When I heard a woman gave birth at gunpoint, I knew I had to write about it. Journalist Robert C. Yeager's article, "Born a Hostage," helped enormously, along with Ben Lopez's book, *Negotiator: My Life at the Heart of the Hostage Trade.*

Dr. Séverine Laplante fine-tuned the obstetric details and fixed my French. I sequentially picked the trauma brains of Dr. Paul Irwin, Dr. Yen Dang, Dr. Rob Chen, and Dr. Jacinthe Lampron.

The following people generously attempted to educate me about firearms and security: Ontario Provincial Police Physician Andrew Reed, OPP officer Jeremy Falle, GL of the Cornwall Gun Club, and Jacques Leclair of Leclair Corporate Security.

Dr. Greg Smith stayed up until 3:30 a.m. to read the first draft of *Stockholm Syndrome.* Author Richard Quarry provided incisive feedback. Louise Sproule performed copy editing magic. Advance readers included Dawn Kiddell, June Kendall, Kathryn Brunet, Becky MacKay, and the Alexandria Library. All errors are my own.

I'm grateful that *New York Times* bestselling author David Farland told me, "I'm hooked. I could see it as a movie. I'd like to see you go big." My colleagues at Dave's professional writing workshop offered intelligent criticism while Dave's niece, Marie Seager, took care of my son Max and therefore made it possible for me to attend the conference in the first place.

I offer my everlasting love to Matt, Max and Anastasia.

And thank you to you, the reader. Thank you for reading. Thank you for reviewing *Stockholm Syndrome* and telling your friends about it. As author Ben Okri pointed out, reading is a creative act. We couldn't do it without you.

Reader Question

Why is this book called Stockholm Syndrome?

Author reply: I wanted to play with the idea of psychological dominance and submission in a hostage situation. I knew Hope would never lust after an oppressor, but I wondered if the reverse could happen. However, none of the four adults in the room turned out to love each other except Tucker and Hope.

About the Author

Melissa Yi is an emergency physician trained in the crumbling corridors of Montreal. She was nominated for the Derringer Award for the best short mystery fiction.

For a preview of the next Hope Sze novel, ***Human Remains***, join Melissa's kamikaSze mailing list at **www.melissayuaninnes.com**.

"Only those who will risk going too far can possibly find out how far one can go."—T.S. Eliot

Made in the USA
Middletown, DE
06 April 2016